HIS BITTERSWEET REGRET

CHRISTINE MICHELLE

2025 Paperback Edition
ISBN: 979-8-89706-001-6

This is for all the readers out there who want the longer story, the dirty details of a relationship on the brink before things get better. This is for the people who don't want to skip the angst of heartbreak before the characters find their happy ending. It's a little bit women's fiction, a little bit romance, and a whole world of real.

What it is not, is overly steamy. There will only be a few small portions where things get a little spicy. If that's what you're looking for, this won't be the book for you.

This book is for everyone who wants to experience a little life, heartache, and love.

💜

Author's Note

Specific note about **His Bittersweet Regret**:
There isn't any cheating in this story (by main characters), but that doesn't mean seeing your significant other with another person (during a breakup) isn't just as tough. So, if that type of thing bothers you, then this story might not be the right one for you!

About the Book

Opal Morgan *was always meant to be mine. And she was, right up until I let everyone else inside my head and threw her away. Six months after our last goodbye, I was on another lackluster date, regretting my life choices, when I finally saw her again. She took my breath away for more than just one reason, the biggest being the well-rounded baby bump she couldn't hide behind her bulky sweatshirt.*

Marshall Kennedy *was my one true love. There had never once been a doubt in my mind, even as everyone around us tried to tell me that a love like ours could never last. Then, one day out of the blue, he told me it was over and just like that, he walked out of my life. I had to tell him my news via text and all I got back was that it didn't make a difference. Goodbye meant goodbye. So, why was he surprised when he finally saw me again? Maybe it was just wishful thinking on my part, or bittersweet regret on his, either way, he was back and now I was the one second guessing everything.*

Chapter 1

OPAL

"WHEN ARE YOU GUYS GOING TO GROW UP AND TRY NEW PEOPLE on for size?"

"Excuse me?" I turned to see the smirks on Marsh's brothers' faces as Cassy Andros asked the awful question. I pretended not to know what she meant, but it was stupid to do so. Marsh and Opal, together since they were fifteen years old, had always been the running joke amongst most of our friends and family. We had been one another's firsts. Well, not first kisses, but everything else. It had been me and Marshall Kennedy against the world since we started dating in our sophomore year of high school, and nothing had changed since. We were now both going on twenty-three years old and still together. Even though we were still happy together, everyone around us still tried to tear us apart. I often wondered if it was just jealousy because we had found our other halves so soon without having to go through all the crap everyone else seemed to. Who knew?

"Oh, come on, isn't it time you two took a break and explored new people?" I didn't miss the way Cassy's eyes wandered hungrily over Marsh's body. He kept himself in good shape, even though he would never be mistaken for a gym rat. Sure, he ran and worked out, just not to excess. His hair was trimmed short, with the top portion of his light brown locks hanging down his forehead while the rest was tapered down from a buzz cut to a close shave by the time you got to his nape. The hair he lacked on top of his head was made up for by the full, well-maintained beard and mustache, a few shades darker than what grew on his head.

I loved his beard. I remembered when he couldn't grow one at all and just had sparse little sprigs of hair everywhere as he tried. It always brought a grin to my face when I thought of it, and that was one of the things that made us special. We had history together. We grew together as the people we were now, and that meant we had a closer bond than most of the couples we knew.

"Why in the world would he need to do that? Just so you can have a turn on the only Kennedy brother you haven't managed to sink onto?" Granted, it was a bitchy thing to say, but it was the absolute truth. Cassy had been with Bastion, Brixton, and Jimmy. I doubted she had been with Ryker, since he was still only seventeen, but I honestly wouldn't put it past her. That meant the only brother who wasn't disturbingly close to the age of consent was Marshall.

Cassy laughed at me. "Oh honey! If I wanted your little boytoy, I would take him from you. You guys think you have this crazy bond, but..." She pointed her finger to the left, where Marsh was laughing at something a cute little blond was saying. She looked like a pixie, but one that had her law degree and fought crime for a living. Cassy tittered as my eyes lingered on the scene she pointed out.

"Good for him," I heard Brixton mutter. I turned to face him, more because I didn't want Cassy to see the moisture building in my eyes, than anything else.

"What have I ever done to you?" I asked. At least the flush

on his cheeks showed that he was a little embarrassed, but that didn't stop him from speaking his mind again.

"Listen, Opal, it's nothing against you. I just don't want to see my brother plodding along miserably five years from now, with two toddlers underfoot, wondering why he never bothered to live his life to the fullest while he was able to."

"I don't understand why you guys hate me so much," I whispered. There was no mistaking the fact that the Kennedy boys didn't want me with their brother. The twins had tried, numerous times, to break us up while we were in college. That started because instead of going to their father's Alma Mater as the rest of the boys had, Marsh had gone to a local state university with me. The whole family had been disappointed in his decision.

I don't know why they were. The rest of the boys – except Ryker who was still in high school – all carried six figure student loan debt. Marsh didn't owe a dime thanks to scholarships, cheaper tuition, and being able to live at home, and then our apartment, rather than dorms.

I watched Marsh, who was still chatting with the pixie girl, until he finally glanced over and remembered that I was there. He immediately left her side and came to mine.

"What's wrong?"

"Nothing. I'm not feeling well. I'm going to head home, but you should stay."

"I'm not staying if you're leaving."

"Marsh, please, stay. Your brothers already hate me. They think I trapped you into a life with me somehow and that you're not living it up to the fullest."

"This again?" Marsh asked with a roll of his eyes. When I said nothing, he glanced back down to see the hot tears that threatened to fall. "Opal."

My name was a whisper on his lips as he leaned in and

kissed the top of my head. I was dainty compared to Marsh. In fact, the blonde pixie was probably an inch taller than me. While other people might have described me in the same light that I had done for her, I never saw it when I looked in the mirror. I was girl-next-door pretty with my black hair, short, tanned legs, and slender body. My boobs were a B-cup on a good day and my eyes were just as dark as my hair. There was nothing spectacular about me.

The crazy thing was, knowing all that, I knew there didn't have to be anything spectacular because Marsh loved me for the whole package – inside and out. It gave me the confidence to know I never had a thing to worry about. At least, I never had before tonight. I recognized that look in his eyes when he'd been talking to the pixie. It was interest. Cassy – though I'd never admit it to her – had been right.

"You know I don't mind coming back home with you."

"I know, but honestly, you should stay and have a good time. I'm feeling a little queasy and don't want to ruin anything for you."

"If you're feeling queasy, I should be there to help you."

"Yeah?" I asked with a little tease in my tone. "How are you going to help me to not be queasy?"

His brows pulled together as he thought, then he grinned down at me. "I'll be your snuggle pillow. That always makes you feel better." I couldn't hide the smile that his answer elicited from me. He wasn't wrong about that. I patted his chest with my hand in appreciation.

"Stay, please. It'll give me a chance to get a little rest before you get home." I glanced over toward Brix, who was scowling at me. "Besides, Brixton was looking forward to you being here tonight. Please, don't let your brothers down on my account."

"Fine, but I won't stay long, just long enough to appease them." I sincerely hoped that wasn't true, because I was beginning to think the only thing that would appease Brixton Kennedy was if I fell off the face of the earth and his brother nailed at least three of the single women at the party before going home.

Chapter 2

MARSH

"Where did your ball and chain go?" Brix asked me when I made my way back over to him after walking Opal out.

"What the hell is your problem with my girlfriend?"

"Aww, come on little brother, you know we don't have a problem with Opal."

"Really? Could have fooled me. She left here feeling unwell."

"What's her tummy ache got to do with me?"

"Maybe nothing, but the tears in her eyes definitely seemed to be a problem that maybe you caused."

Brix threw his hand up as if to wave away my words. "I can't help that your little high school crush is sensitive. It wasn't even me that made her that way."

"Yeah? Then who?"

Brixton laughed as our brother – his twin – Bastion stood there watching us banter back and forth. "Well, little brother, she was being schooled by Miss Cassy Andros about that longing look you were throwing to Tandra."

"Who the hell is Tandra?" I asked, seriously not having a clue. "And why would Opal ever be ruffled by anything Cassy had to say? She knows what her agenda is and that it will never happen in this lifetime."

"Tandra was the cute, blonde fairy-like girl you were just hanging out with while your soon-to-be-wife stood over here with Cassy in her ear, pointing out that longing look on your face."

I got ready to deny it, but Bastion stopped me. "Don't bother denying it. We all saw how interested you were, man. Opal included." He tacked on the last bit as I glanced back toward the door. My stomach clenched as I thought about Opal leaving after thinking that I might be interested in someone else.

Why had she done that? As much as I wanted to deny it, what they were saying was true. I might not have known the girl's name, but she had been fascinating in a way other women hadn't been for me in a long time. I rubbed my hand across the center of my chest, trying to ease the discomfort there.

Did she think I wanted to stay for the other woman – for Tandra? I hoped not.

"Hey man! Been looking for you." My best friend, Cramer – who I'd called Crayfish since we were in grade school – called out while slapping my back.

"Been standing right here for a while."

"Yeah, I know. I was going to talk to you earlier, but saw that you were finally interested in someone other than Opal and wanted to leave you to it." That aching pang hit my chest again – dead center. Did everyone in the whole party notice? "Don't get your nuts all bunched, man. Don't think anyone else realized."

"Wrong!" Bastion called out before he walked away to go grab another drink. Brixton sniggered and followed in his twin's wake.

"Damn, the twins caught you too, huh?"

"Worse," I admitted while allowing my head to hang

heavily on my shoulders. "Apparently, Cassy had to go run her mouth to Opal again and she managed to point it out."

"Damn, what did your woman have to say?"

"Not much. She said she wasn't feeling well and left. That was before I knew that Cassy pointed out that I was talking to Tandra and ran her mouth about it."

Cramer laughed, and not for the first time, I kind of wanted to punch the asshole in the face. "Seriously? She didn't even want to force you home or stick around to make sure you didn't follow through?"

That question might have been what was gnawing at my chest. She simply left and didn't seem worried about leaving me behind either.

"What if she's the one getting sick of you, and this is her way of setting you up to take the fall?" Cramer surmised. "Oh shit! Seriously! Imagine if she was the one to leave your ass in the dust after all these years. Maybe she finally saw the writing on the wall and figured it was time."

I punched the bastard that time. "What the fuck man? I asked you before to stop talking about Opal like that. Why is everyone so against the two of us being happy together?"

"We're not, dude. We've all told you before, we think you just need to take a break from her to go fishing for a while. There are tons of other women in this vast sea. The fact that you noticed one tonight speaks volumes. You two settled down early, it's not natural."

"My parents met in high school. They're still together."

"Remember that time we overheard them yelling out in the garage about your dad's secretary?" Cramer asked, eyebrow cocked up in a questioning gesture. My heart sank. We had overheard that argument a few years ago. My parents were still together, but their marriage had been on rocky ground for a while there, and if I were being honest, it still wasn't back to normal.

"I just want what's best for you. I know it would kill you if you ever stepped out on Opal while you were together. Look at your dad, man. He's been miserable ever since we heard them fighting, maybe even before that. He's had to scrape and claw to keep your mom and I don't think he even stuck his dick in the secretary, it was more like a sexless relationship where he carried his marital problems to her and she thanked him for it with hugs and the comfort he wasn't getting at home."

Unfortunately, I heard more than just that one argument between my parents over the past couple years, and Cramer wasn't wrong. Just because it happened with my parents, after nearly thirty years of marriage, didn't mean shit, right? That didn't mean it would happen with Opal and me.

"I was planning on going to get her a ring this weekend."

"What? No! No fucking way. Brix, Bas! Get over here, quick!" Cramer shouted. I wanted to fucking punch him again.

"What's up?" Bastion asked as they both sauntered over.

"This idiot wants to get a ring for Opal this weekend and make it official and shit."

"Aw, man, and here I thought we were finally getting through to you!" Brixton lamented before sipping on his beer again.

"Dude, you don't even know if you're having good sex," Bas taunted.

"I get off just fine, thank you."

"My point exactly. You think that just because you get off, that the sex with Opal is good. You two fumble-fucked your way through losing your virginities to one another and it's probably just been trial and error – if that – ever since. You know what variety is, brother? It's the spice of life. There are things other people teach us that we didn't even know we needed to learn, and that can't happen if the only woman you're ever with is Opal."

Oddly enough, that was the one point my brothers had

made that I couldn't argue with. There were times when the sex was just a way to scratch an itch. There wasn't really anything exciting about it. It wasn't always like that, but it had been a lot lately.

There was also the issue of the intense buzzing energy I felt when I'd talked to Tandra earlier in the evening. I hadn't felt that kind of energy since I first asked Opal out and we started dating at fifteen. It was a crazy mix of excitement and anticipation. I stared at my best friend and brothers, wondering if maybe I should have stopped being hard-headed when I was in college and listened to them.

I knew I'd missed a few experiences by living at home and going to a local state college as opposed to what they had all lived through. Granted, I was also more financially stable already because I wasn't bogged down by major student loans the way they all were. Truthfully, I think the tradeoff was better on my end in that respect, but it didn't stop me from wondering what I'd missed out on. Who I had missed out on. What would those experiences have been like had I not been hooked on Opal all this time?

I loved her. There was no denying that. Still, there was a part of me, especially recently, that wondered if maybe there was something more out there. That voice in the back of my mind always nagged that I was missing out, like everyone kept telling me I was. Even my father had given a few subtle hints that maybe I needed to truly be on my own for a bit to see what life was like without Opal before settling down with her. He told me he didn't honestly see me with anyone else, but that he also didn't want to see me struggle with regrets and what ifs the way he had from time-to-time through the years.

"Looks like he's finally giving things some serious thought, fellas." Brixton was a dick, but he also wasn't wrong.

"Think about all that sex you could be having. Right now, Tandra could be sucking you off in the bathroom, or you could be fucking her on the counter. If not her, maybe you could make Cass's dreams come true and let her have the final Kennedy brother."

"What about Ryker? Wouldn't he be the final one?"

"He would have been if he hadn't fucked her last weekend when his girl broke up with him," Bastion informed me.

"Jesus, are you serious? He's not even eighteen yet."

"So what? Our baby brother was plenty willing."

The scowl I sent my brother's way only made him laugh. "Come on, Marsh, let's go find that little blond you were so hot for. You've never been with anyone else. Maybe, it's time for a real change of scenery to realize that you've been missing out on quite a bit of life while playing happy couples with the first girl you dated."

My stomach tossed and turned with nerves as I allowed my brothers to guide me back over to the girl who I had been so infatuated with earlier. Guilt tickled somewhere in the back of my mind, but I quickly doused it in another beer. I wasn't doing anything wrong. I was talking to another girl, but that was it. For some reason, the argument that my parents had, played out in my memory, and reminded me that my father hadn't physically done anything wrong with another woman either. My mom had still felt completely betrayed by the actions he took.

The minute Tandra smiled up at me, I forgot all about the troubles my parents had and how they related to what I was doing. I forgot all about my girlfriend, and the fact she had gone home not feeling well. I definitely forgot that I told her I wouldn't be much longer before I joined her at home. Instead, I let myself go and enjoyed talking to a woman who intrigued me and offered a heightened level of excitement I hadn't felt in a really long time.

Chapter 3

OPAL

"WHAT ARE YOU GOING TO DO IF YOU ARE PREGNANT?" I whispered to Bethany, my best friend since seventh grade, and the only person who didn't seem to have an issue with the fact that I'd found my soulmate at fifteen. She thought it was romantic that we had stuck together this long and still seemed happier than ever together.

"No clue," Bethany mumbled. "What are you doing?" She asked as I grabbed one of the ten pregnancy tests she had purchased from the pharmacy earlier.

I shrugged my shoulders. "Figured I'd take one with you. Bestie solidarity!"

Bethany laughed and then hugged me as we each held a test in our hands. "Thanks, O. I needed that laugh."

"You probably needed the laugh more than you needed all ten of these tests. Why so many?"

It was her turn to shrug. "I didn't know if one worked better than the others. Why don't you go first?"

I laughed at her. "I'm not even the one who thinks she's pregnant, but fine, chicken. I'll go first."

I took the test to the bathroom and peed on the stick. As I

left the bathroom, I let her know that I'd left mine on the back of the toilet so that it was out of the way and wouldn't get mixed up with the three she took in with her, since she needed more counter space.

It took Bethany a few minutes to come back out, which made me nervous for her. "Everything okay in there?" I asked.

When my bestie opened the door, I realized that none of her boxes were even opened yet. "Um, Opal," She started to say.

"What? They all have pretty simple directions. You basically pee on the end of each stick and then set it down to wait three-to-five minutes for them to process."

"Opal!" Bethany startled me with the urgency in her tone. "Look," She pointed to the back of the toilet, where my test sat. I moved toward the toilet, thinking maybe some pee had been dribbling off the test, and grossed her out or something.

That wasn't what startled my friend though. As I glanced down, I realized why she was so concerned. My test, the one I only took to make her feel better, was positive.

"This can't be," I whispered after picking the test up to examine it, as if that would make the results different.

"I'm so sorry I made you take a test with me," she apologized. I shook my head to dismiss her apology.

"It's not like the outcome would change. I just wouldn't have known for a while longer. Hurry up and take yours," I pushed her back into the bathroom while taking my own positive test with me. Briefly, I wondered if maybe I should take another one, just to verify, but then the ache in my overly tender breasts reminded me that I still hadn't had a period this month, even though it was…

I glanced at my phone and the period tracker I had there. "More than two weeks overdue," I mumbled to myself. How had I not realized sooner? There was work, and all the worries on my mind lately about everyone trying to sabotage my relationship with Marsh, even though I thought he was headed in a completely different direction. I had honestly expected him to take the next step toward becoming more serious, not less. Ugh! I had to stop thinking about his stupid brothers.

When Bethany finally came back out of the bathroom, it was with three pregnancy test sticks and a guilty look on her face.

"Not you too?" I asked, feeling sympathetic, because she was not in a committed relationship the way I was. Marsh and I weren't necessarily ready to have kids yet, but we were financially stable together, and in a healthy relationship.

"No, I'm not. I just feel bad that..."

"Stop!" I told her in no uncertain terms. "It's fine. You did me a favor because now I know and can start planning on getting to the doctor. There are vitamins I need to take, I think. Obviously, I need to buy a book about pregnancy or something," I rambled. My best friend stood there staring at me, and my brain spewed the first thing to come to mind in my nervousness.

"Beth, what would you have done if you were pregnant? Do you know who the father might have been?"

"Wow! That's kind of an asshole thing to ask," She snapped at me.

"Sorry, it's just that you've gone out with several guys, and I'm worried about you. If you thought you were pregnant, then are you being careful? I don't want to see you end up with a baby to take care of on your own, let alone whatever diseases might be possible."

"I know, I'm sorry I snapped at you. Honestly, I'm just angry with myself because I don't know. And God help me, I wouldn't even know how to get in contact with two of the guys because they were just random Tinder hookups." She moved to hug me, and once again, I had to stop her.

"Can you throw your pee sticks away and wash your hands before we hug it out?" I asked.

Both of us laughed as she did just that. I'd already placed my test into a plastic Ziplock bag, so that I could show it to Marsh when he got home. We hadn't really talked much since the party a few nights ago because of our work schedules. He also had to go help his family with a few things that had been keeping him busy and away from the apartment.

"What are you going to do?" Bethany asked.

"Bring my baby up with two loving parents. I think Marsh is hunting for an engagement ring. He's been a little cagey lately, and I bet anything he's worried about getting something I won't like." I laughed lightly at the thought. "Honestly, I'll love anything he brings to me because I'll know it was from the heart."

"Aww, you two are so damn sweet." I grinned at her. "I wish I could find what you have with Marsh." A worried look consumed her then, and I poked her in the side to get her to spill. We didn't keep secrets.

"What's wrong?"

"Please, don't take this the wrong way because I know you hear it far too often. I'm not saying it like the others do, but what if something happens between you and Marsh? What if the others truly get into his head about how he needs to split up with you and go fuck every available woman in the country before deciding to settle down?"

I laughed at the thought. "That would never happen, Beth. You know Marsh."

"Sure, but what if?"

"Then, at least I'll still be able to tell my child, or children, that they were brought into this world because their mom and dad loved one another. I don't want them to think they were an accident from a night of sloppy sex with a stranger who never deserved my time." I gave my bestie a knowing look.

"I know. I know. Trust me, I learned a lesson this month."

"There's no judgment here, but Beth, if you really want something like what Marsh and I have, you won't find it on a hookup app or by hopping into bed with a man before you even know his name."

"You're right." She agreed as her teeth sunk into her bottom lip and sad eyes moved to meet my own. "I always thought it would be Brix," she admitted. I had known about Beth's crush on Marsh's brother since we were in middle school, but the asshole had never given my best friend the time of day.

Brix being blind to my friend's crush wasn't what made him an asshole. He couldn't be held at fault for not being attracted to my best friend. It meant his taste in women was questionable, but didn't make him the jackass that he was. He did that part all on his own in so many other ways.

"He's a jerk of the highest order, Beth. It's time to forget that crush and move on. Lord knows, he isn't waiting around for anyone."

"I know that too," She lamented. There had been many nights when we would all go out and she'd have to watch him leave with a different woman each time. I understood her heartache, even as I was glad I never had to suffer through it the way she did. What I would never understand is what she saw in Brixton Kennedy. He really was a class-A jerk.

"Are you going to tell Marsh tonight?" She finally asked me.

"No, I'm going to get an appointment with my doctor, so I can verify I'm really pregnant before I tell him. Hopefully, I'll get one of those sonogram pictures of the black and white blob that everyone is always going on about. Then, I can put it in a little card and hand it to him or something." I contemplated all the ways I might surprise my man with the news of our growing family. As I planned how to spring the news on him, I grew more and more excited about the prospect of seeing his face when he found out.

"I wish I could be there to see his face," Beth told me, as if reading my mind.

"It's going to suck having to keep the news to myself for a few days while waiting for an official confirmation. Please, don't tell anyone."

"My lips are sealed."

A WEEK WENT by since I took that test with Bethany, and the day of my doctor's appointment had finally arrived. Marsh knew I had an appointment and would be late getting home. If the doctor confirmed my pregnancy, I'd have the test plus a sonogram photo – I hoped – to take to him to help me deliver the news. My nerves were a little frayed thinking about it because Marsh had been a bit distant lately.

I wondered if the funny looks he'd been giving me were because we were so in-tune with one another and he already knew, but was waiting on me to tell him. Then again, it could have been because he was still trying to figure out if the ring he was thinking about getting would be the one I wanted.

Our plan had been to finish college, get a year in with both of us employed in our chosen fields, and then take that plunge when we were secure and well on our way to being able to save for our own house instead of renting the apartment we were in. We had six months left on our lease, and just enough between the two of us for a small down payment on a starter home.

Neither of us wanted a huge wedding that would dip into our savings, so we were just going to do something small with our closest friends and family in attendance, but even that might set us back a tiny bit.

Chapter 4

MARSH

"Are you sure about this, Marshall?" Our landlord, Gary, asked me. He was a nice, retired man who acted as sort of a grandfather to Opal and me since we moved into the apartment building. My gut clenched again. The nerves about confronting Opal left a sick feeling in my stomach as I handed the money to him.

"I'm sure. I already moved all my things out today."

Gary's head shook back and forth twice before he bowed it in what I could only assume was disappointment. "Opal is going to be devastated. Did she even have a clue you were going to do this?"

I swallowed thickly, trying to ease the growing ache in my chest. He wasn't wrong. She would be broken. I was about to break the love of my damn life and for what? To go fuck some strange pussy? To see what the bachelor life was like that my brothers and best friend kept bragging about? I wasn't sure if those experiences would be worth what I was about to do.

"I hope you know what you're doing, boy. Some mistakes we make can't be taken back. Have you really considered the ramifications? What if you realize Opal is the only woman for you, but while you're gone she discovers a new man? He might not be right for her, but she might stick with him stubbornly because he's the one that is there for her after you leave her high and dry."

"That's not fair, Gary. I'm not leaving her high and dry. I just paid for her rent for the next six months."

"Yeah? Where'd the money come from, son?"

"I was saving it for her engagement ring," I mumbled.

He chuckled, but I didn't hear an ounce of humor in the sound. "Her engagement ring, huh? Bet she's expecting that's why you've been acting a bit of a fool lately. Poor girl probably thinks you're gonna get down on bended knee any day now. Boy, you seriously need to rethink this. I've seen you two together. Never in my life seen two people so damn in love. Why are you doing this? Every man gets cold feet at some point, but what you're doing… What you're about to do to that girl, son I don't think you realize that there might not be any coming back from it."

"I know what I'm doing, Gary. I have thought about it."

He scoffed at me. "Think your brothers have been in your head so much you ain't actually doing the thinking. This is them telling you the grass is greener. It ain't greener, son. It's messier, and you do this, that mess will follow you no matter what happens. Broken hearts never get put back together the same way."

"What's that supposed to mean?"

"It means, even if she's still waiting for you, when you finally pull your head out of your ass, she won't be the same sweet girl you know. She'll be different, broken, and that change will be on your shoulders."

Gary turned away from me then, and went back into his own apartment. He owned the whole building, but kept the entire first floor to himself, besides the entryway that led to the stairs that went up to the second and third-floor apartments.

My head hung low on my shoulders as I climbed the steps up to the apartment I'd shared with Opal for the past year and a half. When I opened the door, it was like walking into a stranger's house. There was nothing left of me inside. I moved to the couch, the one that faced the front door, and waited for Opal to come home. She had a doctor appointment after work today. I figured she was just going in for a regular checkup, but felt like a bit of dick because I hadn't even asked her what she was going there for.

It didn't matter anyway. I guess, from now on, it wouldn't be my business to know. My stomach lurched again, queasiness rolled through me, burning my insides with the acid that rumbled around in there. My brother's voices taunted my mind, reminding me, once again, that I was doing the right thing. Opal and I had to know, once and for all, that we were meant to be. There was no other way to know that without giving ourselves time apart to discover it.

Gary's question came to mind to taunt me as I waited. What if Opal found someone else? I shook that idea off immediately. She would hate this idea. She would never agree to a break like this. There was a time, before college, when she might have. That time had long passed. It was why I'd cleared the house of all my belongings before she could get home. She was going to need a clean break, but I didn't worry about her going out with other men. She would still be there when the six months were up. I knew it in my heart.

Forty-five grueling minutes later, keys jingled outside the door, indicating that Opal was finally home. When she came walking through the door, it was with a giant smile on her beautiful face. She radiated beauty in a way she hadn't in a while. She had always been gorgeous to me, but there was something extra about her as I took in that smile and everything else about her. Opal's hair seemed shinier and her skin was glowing with a fresh radiance that made her smile feel brighter. Maybe she had gone to a beauty salon while she was out? That was probably it.

I noticed the gift bag in her hand, and winced, worried that she might have picked up a surprise for me on the day I was about to leave her.

"Oh, good! You're here. I have a surprise for you!" She all but squealed in her giddy excitement.

"Opal, you need to come sit down and…" I saw it then. When it dawned on her that the apartment was not as she'd left it this morning.

"W-what's going on?" Her voice trembled as she asked the question.

"Please, come sit down for a minute." I indicated the chair, instead of the empty space beside me on the couch. There was no way I could handle her being near enough to touch.

She did as I asked, but the glowing color on her skin that I'd just been admiring seemed to dim under the trepidation in her voice as she asked again. "What's going on, Marsh? Where's…" she glanced around, trying to take inventory of what was missing.

"Opal, I'm leaving. I moved my stuff out already," I blurted. "I thought it would be better this way. I just saw Gary and paid the rent for the next six months, so you don't have to worry about the rest of the lease."

"You what?" She asked as a tear ran down her cheek. I tried to ignore it, even though everything in me wanted to pull my woman into my arms and hold her, comfort her, until…

Until what?

I didn't fucking know anymore. I was leaving her. There wouldn't be anyone to comfort her once I left. I felt like a complete tool for the first time that day as I realized the impact this little talk was about to have.

"I'm leaving. I think we need some time apart to just be single, to explore life outside of our relationship."

A sob broke free from her, parting her lips with the anguished sound that nearly broke me as I sat there watching.

"Why, Marsh?"

"Neither of us has ever been with anyone else. Don't you think that's weird?" I asked.

"No. I always thought we were lucky," She insisted. "We found each other and never had to deal with the baggage and rotten exes the way most of our friends and family have."

I swallowed thickly again when the emotion clogged my throat. She had a point, and a fucking good one. Gary said something very similar to me earlier that day, but it hadn't clicked fully during that earlier conversation. Still, my brothers were right. It was weird, and this separation had to happen. If for no other reason, my brothers would never truly accept Opal as a member of the family if they thought she was the one thing holding me back from experiencing all life had to offer.

"I love you, Opal. You'll see that this is the right thing to do, and in six months, if we decide we're still right for each other, we'll know beyond a doubt." I stood then, because if I stayed much longer, she might convince me to change my mind.

I got almost to the door when her voice made me turn back to see her standing there holding the gift bag limply in her fingers. "I had a surprise for you," She all but whispered. The words were like a symphony of misery, difficult to make out around the tears she shed.

"You should just keep it. I don't deserve any surprise you might have for me." Then I left our apartment – her apartment now - and didn't look back. I couldn't. It was all too much and I hated my brothers, my best friend, and most of all myself as I walked to my truck while Gary sat on the front stoop, watching in judgment, and shaking his head at me as I went.

Chapter 5

OPAL

"DID THAT JUST HAPPEN?" I ASKED THE EMPTY APARTMENT. Then I glanced around, and it truly was devoid of anything that made it 'ours'. The space felt cold and unloved, or maybe that was just me and my pitiful little heart. I had been waiting for him to get me the perfect ring, and instead he had been busy planning his getaway.

The gift bag in my hand suddenly felt like it weighed far more than its contents. Inside, had been a sonogram picture of our little blob, the pregnancy test (in the Ziplock bag still), and a love letter from me, telling him how he was going to become an amazing father, and I couldn't wait to see how he cherished my growing belly, and eventually our little one, because I just knew that each of those moments would make me fall in love with him all over again.

Those moments would no longer come to fruition. He wanted six months on his own to see if he could find something - someone - better than me. The sniffles that followed those thoughts were outrageous, as were the tears. My heart ached with a physical pain I didn't know was possible.

I didn't know what to do. The bag hung onto my fingers for

a moment longer, before it slipped off and landed with a small thud on the hardwood floor in front of the chair.

The hardwood floor...

Marshall had taken the rug that he had picked out, the one that made our apartment seem a bit tacky, since the blue and gold design didn't quite go with the green chair and tan sofa we had picked up secondhand.

I sat there staring at the bag at my feet, on the naked floor, for what must have been hours. The sun had gone down at some point and bathed the room in the soft glow of a full moon. I stood and moved to the bathroom, only because nature called and I couldn't ignore it any longer. When I was done, and moved to the sink to wash my hands, there was a vacant spot on the counter where all of his toiletries had been just that morning.

Fresh tears sprang free from my eyes as I moved to our bedroom to see that all of his clothes were missing, along with the sheets he had picked out that had been on the bed when I left. The last sheets I bought were too girly for him, so he'd gone and picked out a more neutral pair. They were missing from the bed they'd been on only hours ago. His scent was lacking from the room too, having dissipated as anything he'd touched had been removed. There was nothing left.

It was only then that I realized the other things that were missing. Our pictures, a timeline of our love and relationship displayed in frames throughout our apartment, were all gone. Marsh had taken our memories with him when he left. That was probably the most devastating blow of all – besides him walking out the door earlier. Not only had he removed himself from my life, but he had stolen my memories too.

I didn't even make it to the empty, naked bed. I crashed down on the carpeted floor in front of it instead. Of course, he'd left that rug. I had chosen it. I lay there, dying inside, crying for the loss of my love and the life I thought we were starting together. Sure, we'd started our lives together at fifteen, but we were supposed to be starting our family together tonight.

Sobbing eventually gave way to physical pain, as my chest, head, and face ached with the effort. My eyes closed when they became too swollen and irritated to keep open a moment longer, and before long, the sweet oblivion of sleep pulled me into her embrace and held me tight until morning light started pouring into the room and a pounding sound indicated that someone was knocking on the door.

I ignored whoever it was, hoping that they would just go away. Much to my chagrin, I heard a key turn in the lock instead. That could only mean it was one of two people. Either Marsh had come to his senses – which I highly doubted – or my best friend was here for some reason. She never used her key – unless I accidentally forgot mine while out with her.

"Opal?" She called out in a pitying voice, and that was all it took for me to know that word had spread about my relationship's demise while my heart had been physically breaking open in my chest. I rubbed my hand across the spot where the ache had not dissipated.

"Opal?" Bethany cried out when she saw me on the floor. "Oh my God! Are you okay?" I turned slightly and when she got a look at my face, my best friend started crying too. "Oh, Opal!" She came to me, wrapped her arms around my body, and just held on tight as I continued to grieve.

Eventually, she coaxed me into sitting up and drinking some water. "You have more than just you to think of now," She reminded me gently. That reminder only made me feel worse. I was going to be a single mom and I was already screwing things up for my baby.

"How did you know?"

"I went to the movies last night with Chad Baker," She told me. "Ryker and his friends were there. I overheard him complaining that his brothers were all out on the town getting Marsh drunk because he dumped his girlfriend."

"Great, so between the high school grapevine, and whoever saw the Kennedy brothers out celebrating the end of my relationship last night, everyone will know."

"It wasn't bound to stay a secret long."

"Why did you wait until morning?" I asked.

"What?"

"Why did you wait to come here?"

She sighed and rubbed her hands through my hair soothingly. "I thought about how I would feel, and figured I'd give you the night to just cry about it. No offense, but I wouldn't have wanted you there, at first, if it happened to me."

"No, I get it. You were right."

"He took everything, huh?"

I nodded. "Cleaned any hint of himself out of the apartment while I was gone to the doctor to find out I was for sure pregnant with his baby."

"Did you tell him?"

I shook my head. "I had a gift bag with things in it and told him I had a surprise to give him."

"Let me guess, he wanted to give you his news first?"

"Pretty much, and then he just left. He told me it was over. Said he already took all his stuff, and generously paid up the rent for the next six months, and then he left."

"Just like that?"

"Yup."

"No explanation?"

"None needed. His brothers finally got to him. Everyone finally got to him. He thinks that if he doesn't find someone better in six months, that I'll still be waiting for him."

"He said that?"

"He implied it, when he said we needed to give ourselves six months to see if this is really what we wanted."

"Oh, Opal, I don't even know what to say about that. Do you think he would have said that if he knew about the baby?"

"No, but then I guess, thanks to everyone always talking shit to him, that he would have eventually resented me, and maybe the baby too, if we were the reason he stayed after finally getting the courage to do what everyone else always wanted him to do."

"Are you going to tell him?"

"Why?" It was an honest question as I turned my full attention to my best friend. Her midnight black hair was almost a match to mine, if not for the texture difference. Her skin was about five shades darker than my summer tanned, olive complexion. Our eyes were both brown, nearly the same shade. She had a model's figure, tall and lean with a jawline most people would die for and eyelashes so thick and long, people always asked where they could buy them.

I had always been slightly envious of her beauty, even as she was envious of my relationship. *"If you weren't the most beautiful of us, you wouldn't have been able to snag Marshal Kennedy and keep him bound to you all these years,"* Is what she used to always tell me. I guess she was wrong. My beauty faded for him. Something had faded between us without my knowing it. Why else would he leave me?

"You're going to be parents. Both of you made that baby. He deserves to know."

I sighed.

"I know. I'll text him."

"You can't just text the man that he's going to be a father."

"Well, Beth, I would have told him in person. I had the whole gift bag and love letter about what an amazing man he is, how he was going to be the best father to our baby, and how much watching that process was going to make me fall in love with him over and over again. The problem is, he left before I

27

could give it to him. He didn't want anything else from me. So, now he gets a text."

"Point made."

"Well, what would you do?"

"Honestly, my first inclination would be to tell him immediately, so he doesn't miss out on anything. Then again, you just made a good point. After the way he left you without even talking to you about it and preparing you first, I would forget to tell him for those 'six months'. He wanted to go find something better out there, he can wait to find out about the family he left behind while he does it."

"Why?"

"Because if you tell him before then, you'll always wonder if the only reason he came back was for the baby. You already worried about whether or not he'd resent you both. I imagine that might happen in this situation. He'll feel trapped."

"Maybe, but if I wait that long to tell him, he'll be angry because I didn't tell him sooner."

Bethany laughed. "Good. Serves the asshole right. Let him be mad, girl. He's the one that walked out on you. It's not like you weren't planning on telling him yesterday when he so callously left you."

"I guess. I'm still going to send him a text though. Even though what you're saying makes sense, I think he deserves to know sooner rather than later, in case he wants to be there for doctor appointments and stuff."

My shoulders slumped as I thought about how torturous it was going to be if he was there and then left me to go back to whichever flavor of the week he was sticking his dick in.

"What if he gets some other woman pregnant? What if he falls in love with someone else and I have to share my child with the woman he chose over me?" I asked my best friend.

Her eyes swam with tears the same way mine did. This was going to be awful, no matter how it played out. I took my phone out, ready to get this over with before I posed any more 'what if' questions for myself.

> Opal: Yesterday, before you dropped your news on me and left, I had something to tell you. It was important. The gift bag would have said it all for me, but since you didn't want to take it with you, this is all you get from me now: I'm pregnant.

It took ten minutes for him to respond after the message showed it was read.

> Marsh: It doesn't matter. Goodbye meant goodbye. Don't bother me again.

I sucked in a painful breath as I handed my phone to Bethany. "Who in the hell does he think he is?" She started messing with my phone then.

"Please, don't message him back," I begged.

"Oh, you bet your ass I'm not! He's blocked now!" She handed me my phone back, so I could see that his number was indeed blocked. "Let that be a lesson to him. You told that cruel fucker that you were having his baby and he told you goodbye and to leave him alone. So, that's exactly what you're going to do."

It was at that point, that the waterworks started all over again. Never, in my wildest dreams, would I have thought Marsh would respond that way when I told him we made a baby together. Then again, I never thought he'd leave me so coldly and without even talking to me about it first.

As my best friend held me together for the second time that day, I wondered if I should tell Marsh's family – his parents specifically – that they were going to be grandparents. Then, I figured that was his news to break to them. I had my own family to tell.

That announcement wouldn't amount to much. They had moved to the west coast during my sophomore year in college and hadn't looked back. Sure, my mom and dad called and texted periodically, but they were off living their retirement dream. It's not like they would drop everything to come hold my hand through this. As the thought crossed my mind, it left just as quickly. I would wait to tell them.

"Beth?"

"Yeah, sweetie?"

"Please, don't tell anyone I'm pregnant. I just can't handle anyone else knowing right now."

"My lips are sealed."

"Thank you."

"Never thank me for having your back. It's what good friends do. Now, what about my momma? I think she should know because she would want to be there for you since your family's out in Oregon now."

The non-committal humming noise I made was met with a bout of tickles. "You know my momma won't tell a soul, especially once she hears what happened."

"I know. Can we wait a few days to tell Momma Vi?"

"Of course. This is your party and we'll do it your way."

"This party sucks."

"It won't suck forever, sweetie. One day soon, you're going to hold that sweet little baby in your arms and it will be like cuddling the best thing in the world. The best thing you've ever created."

"I'll be doing it alone."

"Says who? You'll have me and my momma by your side."

"That's not what I meant, and you know it."

"It won't be what you always envisioned, no. We'll make the best of it, I promise."

Chapter 6

MARSH

"FUCK MAN! STOP THE MOPING, ALREADY. IF WE KNEW YOU were going to be like this, we never would have convinced you to leave her."

"You didn't see her that day, Brix. She was shattered. Absolutely fucking shattered."

"Who cares?"

"I fucking do!" I shouted at my brother. "I fucking care. Something you assholes have never gotten through your skulls. I might think we need to explore other avenues, but I never stopped loving Opal. I just don't want to end up like Mom and Dad one day."

"Dude, you're a fucking idiot," Ryker said as he strolled by us to get a soda out of the fridge.

"What the hell is that supposed to mean, Ry?"

"It means what I said. Opal is the best person in the world. If I was old enough, I'd step in and marry her, since you don't want her anymore." He then gave me a look that dared me to argue. When I didn't take the bait, he smirked and shrugged his shoulders like he didn't have a care in the world. "She won't be available by the time I turn eighteen, so I guess it doesn't matter what I would do."

"What do you mean?"

"Did you forget that your girlfriend – sorry, ex-girlfriend – is hot as fuck? She's so tiny and," he made a lewd gesture like he was squishing his dirty little paws into her ass or her tits, or whatever. "So damn fuckable. Plus, she can sing and play that guitar like no one's business. Her latest song on her channel is something else." His playfully, taunting demeanor changed then. His face drooped before his eyes met mine. "Do yourself a favor and don't listen to it. She cut me to pieces with that song and I wasn't the dumb fuck who left her."

Ryker grabbed his drink and headed back out of the room before he turned around and looked me in the eyes again. "Have you told Mom what an asshole you were to Opal yet?" He didn't wait around for the answer, then again, he didn't need to. The bombs my seventeen-year-old little brother dropped, landed exactly where they were meant to, right in my fucking heart.

"Don't listen to the littlest Kennedy. He still doesn't know what's good for him," Brixton cut in, but I could see a bit of doubt slip into his gaze as he avoided looking at me. Then they cut to my phone again, something he had been doing more and more the past week or so.

"Have you tried to reach out to her, since you left?"

"You know I have. She isn't answering and none of my texts have been delivered."

Brix winced. "Do you think she blocked you?"

"Why would she block me?"

"I don't know? You cleaned all your shit from your apartment and left her after a brief conversation telling her it was over," He reiterated.

"I didn't tell her it was over. I told her we would see how we both felt after a break in six months."

Bastion winced that time. "Man, Marsh, everyone knows a 'break' is the relationship equivalent of the kiss of death."

"No, it's not. It's just a fucking break."

"Maybe, baby brother knows more than you do. This is why we kept telling you that you needed to get out and experience other stuff, man. You don't even know what a 'break' really means."

"And just what the fuck do you think it means?" I asked, getting irate with my brothers all over again.

"It means that you're out there looking for something better, and if you don't come back, you found it. If you do come back, then you didn't find anything that sparked your interest long enough, so you might as well settle for what you had before."

My eyes were probably as round as my mom's tea saucers at that point. "Please, tell me that's not what everyone thinks a 'break' means?!"

Bastion bounced his shoulders once. "That's pretty much the definition."

"Son of a bitch," I hissed under my breath. No wonder she wasn't talking to me. I'd really fucked up.

"You still going out with Tandra tonight?" Brix asked.

I nodded my head. "That was the whole point in doing this," I shot back at him. No part of me felt up to going out with anyone. Tandra was someone I wished I had met *after* my break with Opal. Maybe a few months after, to give me some time to heal. As it was, every time I thought about going out with her, my nerves got the best of me. Not because I was excited at the prospect of a date with her anymore, but because I dreaded it.

Once I went out with Tandra, it would make things real and final. Opal would no longer be the last woman I took on a date, kissed, or hung out with. She would be a memory in the realest sense. I wasn't sure what the hell I was doing anymore because part of me ached at the thought of replacing those memories, of having someone else come in and taint them.

The awful feeling inside my heart was all my own doing. I'd made the decision to do this, so that I wouldn't one day end up like my parents. They had been thirty years into a marriage when my father wondered if they had missed out on something more, and their marriage had been strained every since.

"He looks fucking miserable. You should tell him," Bas whispered to his twin. I glared at them, not even caring what they were talking about anymore. Before any of them could tell me anything – which probably meant they had news about Opal – I stood and went to go get ready for my first date after leaving the love of my life behind.

"WHEN CASSY TOLD me you had been dating the same girl since high school, I thought she was joking." Tandra laughed as she admitted that to me.

"What's so funny about that?"

"I don't know. I guess it's just weird to talk to a guy who has only ever been with one woman." Her nonchalant attitude about having sex with multiple partners wasn't exactly a turn on for me. Part of what I loved about Opal was that she had always only been mine and she deserved to have the same from me.

"There's nothing wrong with being true to the person you're with," I told her.

"No, but most people our age have gotten around a bit and know a few extra things as a result."

"How many people have you been with?"

Her eyes rolled up for a minute, as if she was deep in thought and looking for the answer somewhere in her brain.

The fact that it was taking so damn long for her to come up with that number was concerning. She was only twenty-three years old.

"Um, I think seventeen."

I choked on the beer that I'd just sipped. "You've been with seventeen people sexually?" I asked, a bit shocked by the sheer volume. If she started having sex at fifteen, like I did, that would mean she had been with at least two people and then some per year since. She narrowed her eyes at me.

"Don't judge."

"Have you ever had a committed relationship?"

"Not really," She replied quickly. "What's the point? I'm young and look great. Might as well enjoy everything life has to offer, right?"

"Uh-huh. And what about when you're home and feeling lonely? Wouldn't it be better to have someone there to hold you at night when you're having a bad day and need to know that someone has your back, no matter what?"

She threw her napkin down. "If it was so great, why did you break up with your girlfriend?" Before I could answer, something vicious flashed in her eyes. "For that matter, I wonder who is holding your ex while she cries about the fact that you left her high and dry when she was apparently expecting you to propose any day."

"What the hell are you talking about?"

She laughed. "You really are clueless, aren't you? Cassy said your girl was expecting you to buy her a ring and propose because it was 'time' according to some grand plan you both had."

No. Fuck. The plan.

I'd forgotten all about it because everyone was always in my fucking ear about all the shit I was missing out on by being with Opal.

"Ah, it's starting to click, huh? You left your girl right about the time she thought you were getting engaged. I wonder who held her all night and had her back while she cried over your sorry, judgmental ass?" She shook her head and stood up.

"Cassy was wrong. I don't know why she's waiting around to get a chance to jump on your dick. I don't think you're worth the ride after all. You want to know why I'm just out having fun and enjoying myself?" She leaned in close over the table, flashing her cleavage as she did, but even though it was there in my face, I couldn't look away from the emotion displayed in her eyes.

"I never wanted to be the sad, lonely girl crying in my bed after the love of my life dumped me and left me there like yesterday's garbage. I watched my mom go through it four times before she finally gave up and became a shell of the person she once was. There are only so many times, and so many ways, a person can be broken before they end up completely destroyed and I won't allow that to happen to me."

"Seems to me maybe it already has," I mumbled as she left me sitting there to pick up the bill for the dinner that neither one of us managed to eat.

So far, I hadn't been missing out on anything by being with Opal. Maybe, I'd missed the chance to get a few sexually transmitted diseases if everyone else's sexual numbers were anything like Tandra's or my brothers'.

"What am I doing?" I asked myself again before I threw down enough money to cover the bill and tip and then left the restaurant. For a moment, I almost broke down and drove to the apartment I used to share with Opal. The thought of her crying, alone in our old bed, hit me right in the heart and left a scar there that I didn't think would ever heal.

I pulled my phone out and texted her again.

Marsh: I'm sorry if I hurt you. That was never my intention.

As with the last texts I'd sent, it didn't appear to go through.

Chapter 7

OPAL

"It's been three months," Bethany whined.

"And do you know what hasn't changed in those three months?" I asked sarcastically.

"Your attitude?" She asked with just as much sarcasm.

"Ha! No. The fact that I'm pregnant, Beth."

"So what? No one else knows that yet."

"You don't think it would be dishonest to go on a date with a man and not tell him I'm pregnant?"

"Honestly, if you did, it probably wouldn't be a deal breaker for most guys."

I glowered at her, unsure what the hell she meant by that. "Why the hell wouldn't it be?"

"If you're already pregnant, they can't get you in that state." She shrugged as if it was a given.

"Ew! I am so not having sex with anyone else while carrying Marsh's baby," I informed her.

"Marsh doesn't care about that baby, or you, otherwise you would have heard from him by now. You are almost five months along. When are you going to stop carrying that torch for him?"

"Beth, that's not fair. I'm angry with him, believe me. There's a part of me that never wants to see that man again after what he did to me. How he left me – us." I patted my belly as I said that. "Then there's the part of me who never stopped loving him. Missing him. I can't help that. It's like he died."

"Only he didn't. And you know what else? None of his family has bothered to even check on you to make sure you are okay, or they might have noticed that you're expecting his kid. You claimed that his parents liked you and never pressured him the way his brothers and that toad of a best friend did, but where are they?"

Okay, that hurt. I had expected at least a phone call from Marsh's mom, telling me how sorry she was that things didn't work out. When my parents moved away three years ago, she stepped up and became my surrogate mom. I wouldn't tell Bethany this, but I had been crushed when the first couple of weeks went by and no one reached out to me. After a month, I was despondent. After two months, I wondered what in the hell was wrong with me. Why was I so damned unlovable? Why was it so easy for everyone to simply walk away and leave me behind?

Marsh was the one who left me without so much as a conversation after seven years together, yet everyone rallied around him like he was made of gold and they were waiting to chip a piece off.

"Can we not talk about this? I don't want to date. I am not ready and there's no way you can convince me to be ready for that before I have this baby. It's just not possible. Please, you and Momma Vi are the only people I have to lean on, unless I want to move across the country with my parents. If I do that, my child will never know their father's family."

She scoffed. "Your baby probably won't know them anyway, judging by how little – as in none at all – contact they've had with you." She eyed me again for a moment. "Are you sure Marsh was the one who got the text about you being pregnant?"

"Of course, he was."

"I never thought I'd see the day where that man could ignore the fact that he had a baby on the way, especially one that was growing in *your* belly." Her eyes dropped to my stomach, which was hidden behind another baggy sweater.

"Stop staring," I whisper-hissed.

"Sorry," She whisper-yelled back at me. "You know, you don't have a whole lot longer before baggy clothing isn't going to cut it. I'm pretty sure people are already speculating about your condition."

"Let them speculate," I grumbled. Just as we walked past Dave's Pizzeria, a group of teenage boys came barreling out of the place and nearly knocked me over.

"Oh, shit! Sorry!" One of them hurried to say as his hands wrapped around my arm and waist to steady me. As soon as I had my feet solidly under me again, I looked up into the bright blue eyes of Marsh's youngest brother, Ryker. His fingers were splayed around my waist, the one that used to be tiny, but now bulged out in front.

He slowly slid his hand down, as if he was about to remove it, but then he moved it around to the front of my stomach. I watched as his eyes grew wider with the movement, when he realized I hadn't just eaten my feelings over the past few months.

"Does he know?" He asked quietly.

"I told him."

"What did he say?"

"He said 'Goodbye'." I told Ryker as I slung his hand off my belly. "I'd appreciate it if you wouldn't go blabbing my business to anyone else. It's humiliating enough that your brother left me the way he did, considering everyone has given me their input on how wise a decision it was on his part. I'd rather not have to hear the town's thoughts on what a fantastic decision it was for him to abandon our child too."

I swiped angrily at the tear that fell free without permission. Just as Ryker pulled me in for a hug. When I tried to push away, he held tighter. "Trust me, keep hugging me," I heard him say.

Just about the same time, I heard my best friend's strong intake of breath before she came up, and made it a group hug, putting me in the middle of her and the boy I once thought would be my brother-in-law one day.

"He's somewhere close by, isn't he?" I whispered into Ry's ear.

"Please, don't ask questions. You won't like the answers, Opal."

That meant Marsh wasn't just close by, but that he was with someone else. I didn't think it was possible for my heart to break any more than it already had, but I was wrong. Before long, Ryker wasn't just hugging me, he was holding me up as I sobbed into his shirt. Poor kid would be soaked by the time we were able to move.

"They're gone," Bethany said as she released her embrace while drawing comforting circles on my back with her fingers instead. Ryker did not let go of me.

"I'm so sorry that my brother turned out to be an asshole like the rest of them. He was always the one I looked up to, like my hero and shit," He murmured against my ear. "I can't even talk to him anymore because I can't stand the thought of him leaving you behind. You've been in my life since I was nine years old, Opal. You were always meant to be my sister."

"Oh, Ry," I whimpered against his shoulder, not knowing what else to say.

"I hate him."

"He's your brother."

"No, he's an asshole."

"He's still your brother, Ry."

"Can I come see you sometime? What about doctor visits? You don't have anyone. Can I go with you?"

"Excuse me, young sir, but she has me," Bethany argued with no small amount of sass.

"You're her friend. She needs a man by her side sometimes," Ry expressed. The funny thing was, he might have still only been a boy, but like his brothers before him, he had grown into something resembling a man early on. There was nothing scrawny or boyish about him until you realized he still had so much to learn about life.

"I'm not sure that would be a good idea, Ry."

"Why not? I'm the baby's uncle," he reminded me. "Family should be there for you both." I was trying to think of an excuse for why he couldn't come to my appointments when Bethany poked me in the side to get my attention.

"What would it hurt? I can't go to your next appointment, anyway. Besides, they're doing the ultrasound since you had to miss it before. Maybe it would be a good lesson in birth control for the kid," She teased.

"Fine," I relented and gave Ryker the information for my next appointment. "But please, I don't want anyone to know just yet…"

His eyebrow quirked up at me. "You know you can't hide that much longer, right?"

I nodded. "I know. For as long as possible, I want my baby to be something I can be happy about and not some nasty gossip for everyone's entertainment."

"I promise, I won't say a word. Can't wait to find out more about the little…" he paused a moment. "Is it a boy or a girl?"

"I was supposed to find out at my last appointment, but the ultrasound machine was down and I couldn't go to the appointment at the other place because of who works there, so… I guess, maybe I get to find out at that appointment on Thursday."

"No way! I get to be there to see it too?" His voice rose an octave in his excitement and I had to quickly put my hand over his mouth to stop him from accidentally spilling the beans.

"Shh."

"Sorry," He whispered, making me roll my eyes.

Ryker was the sibling who looked the most like Marsh. His hair was the same color, though he wore it long, almost down to his shoulders. There was no facial hair, though I saw signs of stubble where he had been shaving already. I ached at the familiarity, but was so glad for the differences between he and his brother.

"Opal?"

"Yeah, Ry?"

"I don't understand why he did it, but it was the dumbest thing he's ever done."

I shrugged my shoulders. "I'm guessing he was with someone when you and Beth tried to hide me from him or the other way around. So, it seems like he's happy with his decision."

"He's not, though. That's the thing. My brother isn't happy anymore. Marsh never smiles and he's just going through the motions."

"No offense, Ryker, but what do you want me to say here? He left me, not the other way around. Whatever misery you think he's suffering, it's of his own making."

"I know that. I just thought maybe you should know too."

"It doesn't really matter since he's not in my life anymore. He chose that."

"I know." He offered me a sad smile before he turned to look for his friends who were waiting for him further down the road. "I better get going." He shifted his attention to Bethany and something passed silently between the two of them. OInce he got the answer he was looking for, he nodded and took off to catch up to his peers.

"He's a good kid," Beth commented.

"Let's hope he stays that way, because it's the same thing everyone used to say about his brother."

"They still do," Bethany snidely added. "That man can roll in shit, and this town acts like he doesn't stink from it."

"I think we should just go back to the apartment," I muttered before turning around to head back the way we'd come.

"That's probably for the best."

Chapter 8

MARSH

"What were you doing in town today?"

"None of your business," My smartass little brother answered back. There was a time when we were a lot closer and he practically worshiped the ground I walked on. That time passed the minute I broke up with Opal. Ryker didn't understand, and he took it all out on me.

"Ry, come on man, when are you going to stop giving me so much attitude?"

"Never, if you don't pull your head out of your ass and realize what a complete fucknut you're being."

"Watch your mouth, kid."

"How about you get to lecture me about shit when you own up to your own responsibilities and become an adult?" My brother threw the words at me like they were weapons.

"Last I checked, I worked, paid my own bills, and made my own decisions without mommy and daddy supporting me."

"Last I checked, mom and dad at least knew how to support their own. But you know what? You don't know shit about that, do you?" He yelled at me, then turned around and walked away. I spun to see the twins standing there, looking shell-shocked.

"What the fuck was that about?"

"Who knows," Brix finally mumbled as he pulled out of whatever weird vibe he had going on.

"Kid has a point," Bastion told Brix.

"Shut it. You and I both know it was just a ploy."

"I don't think so, man. I've heard things," He retorted quietly.

"Whatever, Bas. You're with me or against me, at this point."

"Yeah. Brix, you made that perfectly clear, but your plan doesn't seem to be panning out. The asshole is miserable. Never seen him look this unhappy before in his whole life. Is that really what you wanted for him?"

"How about you two take your fucking argument some-where else, especially if it's about me? I don't want to hear shit you have to say right now."

"Did another date bomb?" Brix asked with a knowing smirk. I didn't bother to answer him, but then again, it wasn't really necessary. "Get the fuck over her already, and maybe you'll get somewhere on these dates you keep having. Have you even had your cock sucked by one of them? Touched a new pussy at all? Licked one? Fucked one?" He asked and then turned away from me, but not before I saw the disgust on his face. "Never gonna be happy until you dive in there, and actu-ally go all the way, Marsh."

He had a bit of a point. My cock was tired as hell of the games my hand played with it. I would be hard as a rock when I woke up from another dream about Opal, but gnawing guilt over beating off to the woman who I threw away wouldn't allow me to go much further than touching myself. I never made it to climax, and being unable to get off was starting to affect my moods in a major way.

Opal and I always had a healthy sex life. We were together seven damn years, and never went more than two days without getting one another off in some way or watching as we mutually masturbated. Opal was a fucking dream in bed. She had zero hesitation when we were together. If I suggested we try something new, she was all for it. Sometimes, it was Opal who brought up some new thing to try in bed, or out of it. She wasn't afraid to be adventurous with our sex life.

I missed it. Missed her. Every message I'd sent went unanswered. Her phone went straight to voicemail until it didn't. She no longer wanted to hear from me, and I couldn't blame her. Ryker was right. The way I left her – I had been a coward. It had been the wrong way to handle things. What was done couldn't be undone, though. So, I kept trying to make shit work because if it didn't work out – this dating other people thing – then what was the fucking point in throwing away the woman of my dreams?

There didn't seem to be a point. The experiences my older, twin brothers, kept insisting that I needed to have before settling down were shitty. They weren't worth giving up my woman for. Not by a long fucking shot. I'd asked around, since my brothers were no help, to see if Opal had started dating or not. I thought, maybe if she didn't date anyone, I'd be able to go back to her in six months and patch things up between us. It was honestly what I always thought would happen anyway.

We would both go live, explore, maybe learn some new things, but eventually find our way back to one another. The only flaw in that logic was something my baby brother had pointed out to me months ago.

"That might have been all fine and dandy, if you had talked to her about it ahead of time and she actually agreed to that bullshit you're spewing. You didn't have that talk. Instead, you emptied your apartment out while she was gone, and then you just told her you were done and walked away without giving her a chance to say anything. If you think she'll wait

around or come back to you after that — you're a bigger idiot than you made yourself out to be."

His words burned into my soul because I knew, somewhere deep down inside, that he was absolutely right. My youngest brother was turning out to be the wisest of us all.

Chapter 9

OPAL

"SEE THIS HERE?" DOCTOR BURNS ASKED AS HE POINTED TO the center of my baby's splayed legs. Before he could get anything else out, Ryker hooted out loud, like the little lunatic he was.

"It's a boy!" He yelped. "You're having my nephew!"

I couldn't help the grin that spread across my face, since Ryker's exuberance was contagious. "A boy," I all but hummed.

"Are you excited?"

"I've been excited since I found out I was pregnant. It didn't matter to me what gender the baby was," I explained honestly. I'd pictured both a little boy, who looked like his father, and a baby girl, who looked like me. If I were to be truthful, I had been hoping more for the little girl but only because I thought it would be easier on my heart and as a single mother.

"Don't worry, Opal, I'll make sure he has all the male bonding time he needs."

That declaration from Ryker made me break down sobbing in front of the only one of my baby's uncles who liked me, the doctor, and the nurse who had to be in the room with all of us for some stupid reason or other. The pity in her eyes compounded my hormonal problem.

"Oh shit! Please, don't cry, Opal. Whatever I said, I'm sorry."

"Don't be sorry about what you said, son." Dr. Burns interjected. "She's pregnant. You just triggered those hormones because she appreciated the thought." Doc patted my thigh and our eyes met. He knew better. That wasn't why I was crying, but he was trying to help me save face. We already had a discussion, in the beginning, about the baby's father not wanting to be in his life. *His*. Jesus. I was having a baby boy and his father wanted no part of him. Of us.

My heart squeezed so tightly in my chest, I was surprised when it didn't burst.

"Everything is on track for your June delivery, Opal. He's growing healthy and strong in there. I am a little concerned about your weight gain. He's doing great, but if you don't start putting on more weight, we're going to have to do something about that. You're eating for two. Momma needs her share of the nutrients too. Don't forget it."

"I promise, I won't. I've just been incredibly..." My words trailed off because I didn't know how to fill in the blank myself. Busy? Sad? Angry? Confused? Frustrated? Take your pick or all of the above would do as well.

"I'll make sure she at least gets a good dinner tonight," Ryker offered.

"Good man. Will you be at the next appointment too?"

Ryker looked at me with a twinkle of excitement in his eyes. "It won't be like this appointment. You won't get to see the baby again."

He shrugged his shoulders. "Will we be able to hear the heartbeat?" He asked. Both the doctor and I nodded. "Then I don't want to miss it."

"Aw, you are such a sweet boy," the nurse cooed.

Ryker narrowed his eyes at her in displeasure. The doctor had just called him a good man, and she downgraded him to boy level again. Typical seventeen-year-old that he was, took it as an insult.

"All right folks, we're finished up here. I'll see you again in four weeks. Monica will get you set up with an appointment up front."

"Monica?" I asked, not liking the sound of that. I knew both of the women who worked up front and that was not either of their names.

"Monica James. You probably went to school with her at some point. She just started here a couple weeks ago."

"I don't like having her know my business," I admitted to the doctor.

"She's a professional and bound by HIPAA laws like everyone else who works here, Opal. I wouldn't hire someone who would take liberties with my patients' information."

That's what he thought. Monica James had the biggest mouth in the south. There was no way half the town wouldn't know that I was knocked up, how far along I was, the gender of the baby, and when my next appointment was, by the time I walked out the door with the appointment card in hand.

Chapter 10

MARSH

"Are you expecting a baby with anyone?" Monica asked me as we sat down to dinner. She was my thirteenth date since I left Opal.

I still hadn't had sex with any of the women I'd taken out, and none of the dates had led to a second. My last, with Gabby Morrisey, a nurse who worked at the hospital, had at least ended in a heavy petting and make out session. About the time our clothes started to come off, she brought up Opal, and that effectively shut everything down.

"Why on Earth would you ask me something like that?"

She shrugged her shoulders at me, but her eyes never left mine, as if she was waiting for me to lie to her.

"I have never gotten anyone pregnant," I told her. It was the truth. I hadn't had sex with anyone since Opal, so it would be impossible. We were almost at the sixth month mark since I'd left her, and I thought maybe I'd have sex with at least someone else by now, but it just never seemed right.

"Oh. Well, now I understand then."

"Understand what?" I asked, feeling a bit peeved.

"Well, I just thought…" She stopped mid-sentence and

pointed out the window of the restaurant, where we had come to catch an early dinner before heading out to see a movie. Then, the plan was to go back to her place for some possible long-awaited action. "I thought that was yours, and I wasn't ready to be someone's stepmom, is all."

"What was mine?" I turned in the direction she had pointed and saw my brother, Ryker, grinning down at a short brunette with a juicy ass. That was all I could see of her. Jesus, the kid had similar tastes to my own. A few years ago, that might have been me standing there with Opal.

"Well, obviously that's my brother and some chick he's been…" the girl with him turned so that she no longer had her back to me. When her profile came into view, I was shocked as shit to see that it was Opal. What was even crazier than seeing her on the street sharing a moment with my youngest brother, was the fact that she accidentally pulled her sweatshirt tight against her frame as she reached into her pocket for something. That was not the same figure Opal had when I left her, not by a long shot.

I stood and stared, unable to make my feet move. Unfortunately, the glass wasn't as tinted as I thought, because my brother caught sight of me and grabbed hold of Opal's arm to pull her away. He glanced from me to the woman who had been sitting across from me on my date with an accusatory eye, and then pulled harder on Opal's arm.

Curiosity won out, and she turned to see what he was trying to pull her away from. The minute she saw me, her eyes widened and her left hand moved to her protruding belly as if she was protecting what was there. From me. Then those beautiful, warm chocolate-dipped eyes of hers swept over toward my date. I couldn't decipher the look that crossed Opal's face then. Mostly, because she turned quickly and finally allowed my traitorous little brother to tug her away.

"I'm sorry, Monica. We're going to have to cut this short."

"You didn't know, did you?"

I shook my head and turned to go, but before I could leave, she pulled me back. "I'm not supposed to tell you this because of privacy laws, but her file said the father knew and didn't want anything to do with the baby."

That shocked me to my core, and I had to sit down to take a load off before gravity took my slackened legs out from under me in a different way. Opal was pregnant by someone else? She looked pretty far along. Had she wasted no time crawling into bed with someone after I left her? I couldn't see her doing something like that. Hell, I hadn't been able to make it happen because she was always there, haunting my every move.

It didn't help that I'd been playing her damned video of that song over and over when I was alone in bed at night. Every time the video ended, there was a moment where she swiped the tears from her face that was like a kick to the balls for me. The song was about me leaving her. I knew that. Any fucking moron who knew who she was had to know that. The sheer amount of pain she put into those lyrics, into the music, it tormented me day and night.

Now, I had to wonder if she was really as tormented as she seemed. How could she be pregnant with someone else's kid? There was no way I could ever get over that. I loved Opal. Fuck, I was stupid to ever break up with her in the first place, but there was no way I could go back to her and raise someone else's baby. No fucking way.

Chapter 11

OPAL

"Sorry, Opal. I don't think he noticed anything except the fact that I was with you," Ryker tried to appease me. That wasn't why I was upset though. My ex, my baby's father, was on a date with the woman in charge of making my obstetrical appointments. I felt sick. Literally, sick to my stomach, and by the time we got a few feet away, I had to stop and throw up in the bushes outside of Whitlock's Watering Hole.

"Sorry, Opal. Shit! What can I do?" Ryker asked in a panicky voice, clearly brought on by my vomiting and tears.

I held up a finger, the universal sign for him to hush and wait. Once I was done, I swiped my mouth with the back of my hand and glanced over my shoulder. I figured maybe Marsh would have come chasing after us, but he hadn't. I wasn't sure what was worse, thinking that he would, and being disappointed, or knowing that he refused to leave his date behind to check on his pregnant ex-girlfriend one fucking time.

I was the woman he once claimed to love. The one he said would always have his heart. Marshall Kennedy was a goddamned liar. If he could abandon not only me, but his baby too, then he was never the man I thought I spent seven years of my life being in love with. It was almost eight now, but I refused to count any of the time after he'd walked out our door for greener pastures.

"I need to go home. I think it's time I take my parents up on going to stay with them."

"No! Please," Ryker begged. "Please, don't take my nephew away." That just made me cry harder. The baby's father should be begging me not to take his son away from him, not ignoring me for the staff at my doctor's office. The same staff who knew good and well that Marsh was listed as the father and that he said he didn't want anything to do with our baby. How a woman could know that a man abandoned his pregnant girlfriend and baby, and still want to date him, was beyond me.

"Ry, I can't do this. I can't raise a baby alone and I definitely can't handle seeing him out on a date with the woman who sets up my baby doctor appointments."

Ryker glared back in the general direction of the restaurant. "I knew that bitch looked familiar. I'm having a talk with Dr. Burns. She had to tell him something to make him not come down here and check on you."

The poor kid was so adamant that his brother wasn't a piece of crap human. I once believed in Marsh with that same unwavering naivety too. Look where it got me. Pregnant. Alone. Miserable. And all the while, he was out living his best life.

"I think I need to go, for my sanity, Ry."

"Yeah? How sane are you going to feel with your hippy-dippy parents who left you too? They moved clear across the country and never looked back. When's the last time they visited?"

"That's a little cruel," I told him as we continued walking, despite his words making me take a stumbling step. It was cruel, but true. My parents hadn't been back once to visit me since leaving for the shores of Oregon. They always invited me to come there, but they refused to come back here – even to see their daughter.

"You have me. Bethany and her mom are here and they're like family to you. They've been there all this time. What will they say if you up and leave them?"

"You're an asshole to lay all that guilt at my feet right now, you know?"

"I'll do what it takes to keep you and my nephew here," he tossed back immediately.

"Even if it means making me completely miserable?"

"I'm sorry about that part. Maybe I can convince Marsh to leave and you won't have to see him anymore. Problem solved."

"You'd essentially throw your brother out of town for me?" I asked, slightly amused, even as the topic itself was heart-breaking beyond measure.

"Yeah, Opal. Neither of you did anything wrong. There was never anything you did to deserve the way he's treating you both. All you ever did was love my brother. I used to go to sleep and dream about finding someone like you. There aren't any Opals in school with me though. Marsh doesn't even know how lucky he was and he threw that luck away."

The teary-eyed image I got of Ryker made it almost feel like the younger Marsh – the one I'd fallen in love with – was standing beside me again. I had to shake off that feeling because that man no longer existed. He was also more of a man when he was younger than he was as an adult. I hoped Ryker didn't ever change in the same ways.

"Have you told my mom yet?"

I shook my head. "I thought that should be Marsh's responsibility, but considering he doesn't want anything to do with us, I guess she was never told."

"Would you do me a favor and tell her? She needs to know that she's going to be a grandmother. It'll be one more person on your side in all this. You might not have Marsh there, but I swear to you, Opal, you'll have a family for your son."

"Ryker, one day, some girl is going to be incredibly lucky to have you as her boyfriend."

He smiled at me. "Thanks, O."

"Not you too!" I groaned.

"What? That's what Bethany calls you sometimes."

"Yeah, but her calling me that is an inside joke."

"So, tell me the joke, and then it'll be okay."

I blushed furiously in response because there was no way I could tell Marsh's baby brother, who wasn't even out of high school yet, that my best friend started calling me that after walking in on me mid-orgasm. She hadn't been able to get my full name out. Just "O", and oh, how appropriate that had been.

"I see," Ryker offered as he sniggered. "I'll just have to ask Beth myself."

I groaned again. "Please, never do that. It was traumatic for all of us."

"Will you think about staying, or at least give me plenty of warning before you leave?"

"Of course, I will. No matter what, I could never be so cruel as to leave without telling people in advance." We both knew I was referring to the way his brother hadn't given me the same courtesy.

"It probably isn't healthy or wise to travel that far at this point anyway," Ryker carried on, making his case. When we got to the apartment building, Mr. Pendleton, or Gary, as he asked to be called, was sitting on the stoop.

"That boy still hasn't come to his senses?" He asked. My only answer was the same shake of my head I always gave him. The man glanced at my ever-growing belly and then back up to me. "If you need anything, I'm just downstairs. Never be afraid to ask. Raised three of my own. They're all gone now. A person should never lose their children first, but those were the cards I was dealt. They might be gone, but that doesn't mean I don't remember what it was like to raise them."

"Thank you," I whispered to him before looking at Ryker. "I think you were right about telling your mom."

"If you want to go now, I'll go with you."

"That's a wise choice, Ms. Opal," Gary said as he stood and stretched. "Be seeing you later."

He left, and Ryker and I got into his car. I hated that I didn't have a vehicle of my own. It was something that Marsh must have conveniently forgotten when he left me high and dry. I had no transportation. Before I was pregnant, it was nothing for me to walk to work, since it was a little less than a mile up the road. He'd always been there to drive me, if it was raining though. Not to mention, we had always taken his truck on grocery store runs. Now, I could only buy what I could carry and bring back without completely wearing myself out. Unless I was too worn out and asked Bethany to help me out with a ride.

"Would you be more comfortable taking your car, so you can have a quick getaway if needed?"

I shook my head. "I don't have a car."

Ryker had just turned the car on and his hand dropped from where he'd turned the key as his head swiveled around. The shock on his face turned quickly to something akin to horror as he realized I wasn't joking. "How in the hell have you been getting around?"

I tapped the sides of my legs, as if I'd been wearing boots. "These boots were made for walkin'."

"Holy shit! I'm really going to kill my brother now. You've been walking to and from work all this time? The doctor's office?" He asked. I nodded my head, knowing he was going to lose his shit. "That's two miles from your house. That's a four mile round trip, Opal!"

"I am well aware."

"You can't keep doing that!"

"Well, I can't exactly afford a car right now. Marsh paid the rent up until now, but I have to take over the whole thing starting next month, plus get all the baby's supplies, and I'm paying all those copays for the doctor visits. There's nothing left over for a car."

"What about the savings you have for the house?"

"It was in Marsh's account, not mine."

"He took all your money?"

I shrugged. "He probably didn't even think about it. Unless he's spent it all on his dates."

"Opal, this isn't right. He should have given you your half of the money back. Hell, he should be the one helping to pay for the doctor visits and all the baby stuff. This isn't right. It shouldn't all be on you."

"It wasn't supposed to all be on me. When I went to the doctor the first time, I took the test, the sonogram photo, and a cute little onesie that said, 'I love the best daddy ever' and put them all in a bag to give to him."

"I don't understand how he could have seen that, and not cared. That's not the brother I know."

"Ryker, he never saw it. That was the day that I got home to find all his things gone. He barely told me he was leaving me before he was up and out the door and when I tried to give him the bag, he told me he didn't deserve anything I had to give him and left."

"So, you never actually told him?"

"I texted him after that and he told me 'Goodbye meant goodbye' and not to bother him again."

Ryker gave me an odd look and then his face turned red with anger. "That also doesn't sound like something Marsh would say," He muttered while continuing to drive us to his house.

"Well, I never thought Marsh would secretly clear the apartment out and leave me without even talking to me about anything either, but I guess that means neither of us knew him as well as we thought."

Ryker's leg bounced up and down on the other side of the car so hard that the car would have bounced with his movements had we been sitting still.

It didn't take long to get to the house where my ex-boyfriend's parents lived, which was kind of a shame because my stomach was in knots. The baby must have felt my anxiety because he started moving around and kicking the crap out of me. Maybe my son was telling me to stop being a coward and go face the music so he could one day meet his grandparents, even if his dad didn't want anything to do with him.

I sat there long enough that Ryker had come around to my side of the car and opened the door for me. "Come on, Opal. You know my mom loves you. She'll be angry that she didn't know about the baby before now, but that anger won't be directed at you."

Unfortunately for me, the first people we saw when we entered the house were not Ryker's parents. The twins were seated on the sofa – a reminder that it was the weekend, still early enough that Ryker had probably just missed family dinner, and unfortunately that meant the twins were there too.

Ryker put his arm around my waist to guide me through to the kitchen, but Brixton's snide comment stopped us both in our tracks.

"Couldn't have one brother, so you decide to go for the underaged one and pretend to fall in love with him too? Maybe we should call you Cass?"

I turned, but Ryker's hand had a firm grip on my hip, which made my shirt pull tight. Bastion sucked in a harsh breath at the sight it created.

"I fucking told you she wasn't lying!" It was an accusation

thrown at his twin, who looked just as stricken by my condition.

"I thought it was just a desperate ploy to get him to come back," Brixton said.

"What in the world is going on out here?" Kathy, the boys' mother, asked before another sharp intake of breath let us know she'd seen my belly too. "Lord in heaven!" Marsh's mother looked between me and her youngest son, her eyes narrowing just a bit in accusation.

"Wipe that look off your face right now," Ryker growled at his mother. "That's not my baby, but I do seem to be the only Kennedy who has stepped up to be there for Opal. So the rest of you can fuck off with your judgments and your games."

"Boy, you better watch your mouth," Mr. Kennedy stated coolly to his son as he walked into the room before taking careful observation of everything, including my burgeoning belly.

"Think maybe we all need to sit down and figure some things out. One of you assholes call Marsh."

"Please, don't." I begged.

"No offense, sweetheart, but I think you've kept this news to yourself long enough. My son deserves to know he's going to be a father."

"He already knows!" I yelled at the man I once thought would be my father-in-law.

He took a step back as if I'd physically assaulted him.

"What the hell do you mean, 'he already knows'?"

"Just what I said."

"She was going to tell him in a really cool way the day she came home to him leaving her," Ryker cut in. "When he refused to even talk to her beyond telling her he was done, she sent him a text." Ryker sent a scathing glare toward the twins then. "After today, I have a funny feeling that text might have been intercepted because the response Opal got back didn't sound like Marsh at all."

"Let me see it," Mr. Kennedy demanded. I opened my phone, pulled up the text messages, and handed it over. He turned his head toward the twins. "What in the hell have the two of you done? We knew you were pushing him to go experience things, but this is beyond the fucking pale."

"I thought she was just bullshitting him to get him to come back," Brixton admitted and immediately my legs could no longer hold my weight. Thankfully, Ryker still had a good hold around my waist.

"Ryker, son, what on earth is your place in all this?" His father asked, ignoring Brix.

"I accidentally ran into Opal coming out of a pizza shop a little over a month ago. When I realized she was pregnant, we talked, and I begged her to let me go to her doctor appointments. She needed someone there and Bethany can't go to all of them. I got to see my nephew on that ultrasound thing. It was wild." The previously angry boy beamed with his elation over the fact that he got to witness his nephew moving around inside me.

"Why didn't you tell us?" His mother asked in a hurt tone.

"Opal asked me not to," He admitted.

"And why the hell not?" She shot at me angrily.

"Whoa! If you're going to be mean to her, then we'll leave right now," Ryker stepped up. It only made his mother angrier, but his father beamed with pride.

"Son, while I appreciate your protectiveness over your brother's girlfriend-"

"I'm not."

"What?" Mr. Kennedy asked.

"I'm not his brother's girlfriend. In fact, he's out on a date, right now, with the woman who schedules my doctor appointments. So, if you think he doesn't know about the baby, just because your other sons are complete assholes, then you're wrong because Monica James can't keep a secret to save her life – or her job."

"Okay, let's all sit down and talk through this," Mr. Kennedy tried to be the voice of reason again. "Kath, I think you need to take a breath and calm down. From what I'm hearing, Opal has been through it, and at the hands of our family. If I were the girl, I wouldn't have told any of us either." His eyes drifted to his twin sons and the sheer outrage and disappointment in that look had both of them cowering on the couch, despite the fact that they were both full-grown men at twenty-six years old.

"Now, how about you walk us through everything from start to finish, Opal, so we know exactly what we're all dealing with here."

So, I explained that the pregnancy hadn't been a huge worry, when I found out, because I'd been expecting a proposal from their son. Nothing that came after me learning I was pregnant was left out. Instead, I laid the entire awful series of events out for my ex-boyfriend's family. What I didn't realize, at the time, was that Bastion was filming me the whole time.

When I was done, Mrs. Kennedy got up and came to sit beside me on the couch, on the opposite side from where her youngest son sat, offering me comfort as I spilled my heart out. She threw her arms around me in a hug so tight, I couldn't breathe.

"I'm so sorry for what my boys have done to you, Opal. I don't know how you could ever forgive them. Any of them, besides Ryker. I swear to you that Ed and I didn't know any of this was going on. We thought things had just run the course, and when you never called or…" she stopped and waved those words away. "No, that's an excuse. I know your parents aren't around, and I'm just as guilty for not checking on you myself. I didn't think you'd want to see me since my son left you."

What could I really say to that? She was both right and wrong. Everyone sat quietly for a minute before Ryker spoke up.

"We have bigger problems, that Opal didn't add to her story," He informed everyone. Damn it, this kid.

"What kind of problems? Is everything okay with the baby?"

"He's fine," I said at the same time Ryker said, "No."

"Well, which is it?" His father asked.

"The baby has no way to get home from the hospital when he's born, for starters."

I sighed. "That's not true."

"Yeah?" He asked. "So, you get a ride that day, then what? You can barely carry groceries home now. What about next month when you're even bigger and shouldn't be walking that far? What about when you have an infant to carry too and you're exhausted from being up all night? Are you going to be able to walk to the grocery store and get everything you need, plus all the things he needs, and get them back to your apartment?"

"Why in the hell are you walking to the grocery store?" Brixton asked, sounding irate for the first time since... Hell, since my ex-boyfriend was still refusing to break up with me like he wanted.

"Because I don't have a car."

"Or money to get one because Marsh took off with all their joint savings they had set aside to buy a house with," Ryker tattled.

"My son did what?" Kathy all but yelled in my ear.

"Please, tell me you're exaggerating, Ry," Mr. Kennedy said.

"Nope. Opal here seems to think that he didn't realize he took the money with him, but how could he not? Half of it was hers. She's been struggling without a car. Walking in the rain to work while pregnant, walking to and from the grocery store too. And you should ask her how she gets to her doctor appointments that are two miles away from the apartment."

"Opal! Why didn't you tell us?"

I turned to look at Kathy then, my anger bubbling up to the surface, or maybe it was my pride raging inside me. "Why would I? It was your son who left me because your other sons convinced him that screwing every other woman in town was going to be better than being in a relationship with me. It was your sons who thought my pregnancy was a damn joke. The only boy you raised right was Ryker, and no offense, but I thought that about Marsh at one point too, so give it time and he's liable to be influenced by the others as well."

Kathy looked away from me as she sobbed. "Now, Opal, I understand you're hurt, and some members of my family have done you wrong, but there's no need to take it out on the ones who haven't."

"Haven't you?" I asked as I stood from the couch. "Haven't you all? Not a single one of you checked up on me. Ryker wouldn't have either if he hadn't run into me that day. No one cared, and now you think that I should have trusted any of you with my circumstances, or expect that you might help to make them better, when it was this family that made them so bad to begin with?"

No one had an argument for that. I turned to Ryker then. "I'd leave on my own, but as you pointed out, it's a bit far for me to walk. Please, take me home."

Mr. Kennedy stood. "You stay son. I'll take Opal home."

"I'd rather you didn't."

"And why is that?"

"Because this is all your fault."

"Excuse me?" He bellowed, completely taken aback.

"You're the reason that their taunts and jabs at Marsh

worked." I explained while pointing an accusatory finger toward the twins.

"Don't, Opal." Brixton pleaded.

"No, son. I'd love to know why Opal thinks I'm at fault here."

"Your children overheard you and Kathy arguing about your secretary and how you thought you were falling in love with her. They overheard your conversations and fights about how you and Kathy got together too young and never experienced anything else. Why do you think the twins were pushing Marsh so hard? Why do you think he finally listened to them? Marsh didn't want to become you, and regret being with me, in twenty or thirty years."

Kathy's sobs grew louder as Mr. Kennedy plopped back down into the chair he'd been sitting in moments ago. He buried his face in his hands and to everyone's surprise, started to cry. For the first time all night, Bastion put his phone down. It was then that I realized the bastard had been filming us. I'd had enough.

I took my phone out and called Bethany's mom to come get me. Beth had picked up a shift at the hospital and wouldn't be able to do it, but I knew her mom had off. I left the Kennedy family to pick up the pieces of their own drama, while once again contemplating whether moving to live with my parents would be the best option. No one followed me outside the house. Nor did anyone come to see if I managed to get off safely. They were most likely too wrapped up in themselves to worry about little old me. Never mind the fact that their drama had not only bled into my life, but absolutely ruined it.

Chapter 12

MARSH

"ARE YOU READY TO GET OUT OF HERE?" I ASKED, KNOWING full well that we hadn't even eaten yet.

"Sure. Do you want to just go back to my place and talk?" Monica asked. With a nod of my head, I agreed to that.

What the hell was I doing, keeping myself from really being with other women all this time, when my ex-girlfriend had apparently moved on to someone else right away? Sure, I'd dated, even made out with someone, but the thought of Opal had always stopped me from being able to go that final step toward being truly intimate with another woman.

She had not had that same problem.

How could she have moved on so quickly? And to a man who wouldn't even stand up and take responsibility for his actions?

"Let's go," I offered my hand to Monica. The beautiful blonde looked nothing like Opal, and for that, I was thankful. She was tall, slender, had more curves than I'd ever really been attracted to before. Truthfully, when I'd set out on this date, I'd done so to prove to myself – once again – that no one could measure up to my former girlfriend. We were at the end of our six months apart, and I wanted it to be over, in the dullest way possible, which was why I'd accepted the invitation of a date with Monica. I knew nothing would ever go too far with her because I wasn't all that attracted to her.

All things considered, I was going to give it my all and finally fuck another woman. Didn't matter that it was Monica. I needed to get all the pent-up emotions out of me. I needed to fuck Opal out of my head and my heart because apparently, she'd already done the same. Maybe that was the real reason she blocked my number all those months ago. She had already replaced me, or thought she had. Then, when she fell pregnant, she knew there would be no going back anyway.

Those were the thoughts that plagued my mind the entire drive back to Monica's place, which ended up being across the street from where Opal lived. I hadn't realized before, that she lived that close to our old apartment because I'd picked Monica up from her parent's house, where she'd been visiting when I'd agreed to our impromptu date.

Once we managed to get up to her apartment, everything went from zero to sixty in seconds. One minute we were standing there, just inside her door staring at one another, the next, clothes were flying in every direction.

Monica tried to kiss me, but I turned so that her lips hit my cheek instead. I might have been about to take my shit out on her physically, but I didn't want her mouth anywhere near my own. Even though I'd kissed and made out with other women, I just couldn't stomach the thought of kissing Monica. Not when images of faceless men doing the same to Opal taunted me.

Instead, I stripped Monica naked, and allowed her to fist my cock until it was hard and ready while we stood there next to her front door. Then, I turned so she was pinned to the door, hoisted her up with more effort than it ever took to do the same with Opal, and wasted no more time thinking. Instead, I sank deep into a woman who was not the love of my life, and with every stroke of my cock in that unfamiliar pussy, I grew sicker and sicker to my stomach. Still, I stuck it out and continued to pound into her until she climaxed, or faked it. Then, I pulled out, still hard as a steel beam, and dropped her to her feet.

"Bedroom?" She asked in a sultry voice with half-lidded eyes that were full of promise for what we'd do once we got there. That freshly fucked look on her would have compelled any other man to do just that. The urge to go and satisfy her again, until finally getting myself off, just wasn't there. For me, my stomach turned once more and all I could think of was my gorgeous ex-girlfriend who lived across the street – where I left her – and the words of warning our landlord shot at me the day I paid her rent up in full.

He warned me that if I took the path my brothers pushed me down, that Opal might not be there when I finally pulled my head out of my ass. I never, in a million years, thought there was any truth to that. For whatever reason, in my stupid, fucked up head, I thought she'd just sit around waiting for me.

I bent to pick up my jeans and managed to get one foot into the leg before Monica's hand shot out to stop me. "What are you doing?"

"I can't do this."

"What do you mean, you can't do this? We just did it. And now you're just going to get dressed and leave?"

"Monica, do you really want a man in your bed who can't stop thinking about his ex?"

"She's pregnant!" She yelled at me.

"And nothing about that stops me from still being in love with her."

She scoffed at that and ended the sound in a laugh. "That's rich of you. If this is how you show that you're in love with a woman, I'm glad we aren't going any further. Poor Opal. Finish getting dressed and get out of my apartment."

There was no need to say anything else, and truthfully, she wasn't wrong. I'd fucked up. I'd known during that first date with Tandra that I'd fucked up, and yet I stuck to the stupid idea that I needed six months of trying this out to know for sure. I stupidly stuck to what my brothers kept muttering in my ear, that if I didn't try, I'd end up just like Dad. It didn't matter that I knew it was wrong the whole time, I continued to walk the wrong fucking path, and now I'd pay for it for the rest of my life, knowing that the only woman I'd ever loved was having another man's baby.

By the time I got dressed, and was leaving Monica's place, an older model blue Buick station wagon was pulled up at the curb on the other side of the street. I stood there and watched as Opal got out of the car, swiping at the tears on her face. The door behind me opened up and Monica came out with only a robe on her otherwise naked body.

"You forgot your boxers," she snipped at me while holding them outstretched in my direction. I glanced down at the incriminating evidence of what I'd just done, and then back to where Opal's devastated features displayed her misery like a piece of art. Her shoulders shook as she turned and made her way inside our old apartment. Her apartment.

"Damn," Monica hissed behind me. "She's probably going to get me fired now."

I turned on her then. "What the hell do you mean?"

"I told you, I saw her records. She goes to the doctor I work for."

"Yeah, you mentioned something. You forgot to say who was listed as the father who didn't give a damn."

Her eyes widened in surprise. "You're serious?" She asked. I nodded and Monica looked as though she might laugh at me or possibly kill me where I stood.

"What happened to you?" She asked instead of answering my question.

"What the hell is that supposed to mean?"

"Me, and every other woman in our age range, have always been jealous of that girl. She had you, the perfect Kennedy brother. The one who stayed faithful, who loved his girlfriend so much we could all feel it. What happened to you?"

"Nothing happened. I grew up and realized there was more to life than being strapped down with the same woman forever." It was a callous statement and one I didn't mean. That was Brixton talking in my head again. And my anger over Opal having been with another man.

"I never thought I'd see the day you left Opal, but I just figured things weren't working out. But to hear you admit that you walked away from your own baby too, that's too much. Do me a favor and don't come around here anymore." She got ready to shut the door on the apartment lobby before she turned back to me. "Oh, and if for some reason I end up like Opal, I won't be keeping the baby, since I already know you'd just abandon it too."

"What the fuck?"

I didn't get an answer to the question as she shut the door and ignored my outburst. It was only then that I realized I never used any protection with her. I hadn't come – at all, let alone inside her – but I also wasn't stupid. A little pre-cum was sometimes enough to knock a woman up. Jesus, what had I been thinking? I was angry at the world, but mostly at myself, and hadn't been thinking at all. That lack of forethought stared me in the face when I turned back around.

The blue Buick was still sitting there, double parked in the road. A dark-skinned woman watched me with hate in her eyes. It took a moment to place her as Bethany's mother. "Boy when you screw the pooch – you really go for broke."

Small things broke through the haze of my confusion in

increments as I stood there staring at Beth's mom. The one that stuck out the most, was that Monica had accused me of possibly abandoning her baby, too. As if I'd done something like that before.

"Putting it together yet?" Beth's mom asked.

My eyes drifted up to the third-floor apartment, where I knew Opal was probably losing her shit. Where a pregnant Opal was so distraught, she had been wiping tears from her face moments ago, shoulders shaking as Monica delivered my boxers to me, while in a robe herself, which could only mean that I'd been naked with her moments ago.

"I never took you for a piece of garbage like my ex-husband, but I suppose my judgment never got any better. Why don't you do everyone a favor and stay as far away from this apartment and this street as possible from here on out. That was beyond cruel. You made that poor girl witness your tryst with another woman while she's been struggling, alone, and pregnant with your child."

"My child?" I asked, even though I'd just deduced that was what Monica had been trying to allude to.

"Yes, boy. Don't play dumb with me. I know she texted you about it after you were in such a rush to leave her that you wouldn't listen to her break the news to you."

"Break the news to me?" I pondered out loud. "The surprise she had," I mumbled as I thought back to the day I left Opal in the apartment I'd just cleaned out. She had a gift bag with her. I thought the surprise was just something she bought for me.

"No. No fucking way! She wasn't coming to tell me she was pregnant the day I left," I said out loud, not even remembering that Beth's mom was there watching as I talked to myself.

"That's exactly what I'm saying, and if you didn't get that text, you might want to think about who could have received it and sent her that nasty message back."

"What nasty message?" I asked. Anger brewed in the back of my mind, as I thought of my brothers and maybe even Tandra, possibly being responsible for me missing out on that news. I'd left my phone on the table while I went to the restroom before our big blowout.

"Maybe you should figure that out." And with that, the angry momma bear took off, leaving me standing there holding my underwear on the side of the street and staring up at my old apartment. My old life. The one where apparently, I'd be snuggled up right now with my very pregnant woman – probably my wife by now – if only I hadn't been stupid enough to listen to the bad advice of my best friend and brothers.

"Remember what I said to you that day?" A man's voice called out to me. I looked around and didn't see anyone until a screen popped out of the first floor window of the apartment building my Opal resided in. "Right here, kid."

"Gary," I acknowledged.

"Remember what I said to you that day?"

"Yeah, I remember," I mumbled back.

"How's it feel to have my words bite you in the ass?"

Okay, so Gary was no longer a fan of mine. He could join the growing list of people who were pissed beyond belief. I took a step to cross the street, but Gary shook his head.

"You leave that girl alone. I'm sure it was hard enough for her to see what she just did. Girl's been walking these streets back and forth to work, to the grocery store carrying all those bags, living a miserable, difficult, lonely existence while you've been slumming it with the likes of that Monica James across the street." Gary shook his head at me in disappointment as he spoke. "She's had about all the hurt she can handle today. Go home, boy. If I see you attempt to enter my property, I'm calling the cops."

That stopped me in my tracks. "You'd call the cops on me for going to try to straighten things out with Opal?"

Gary laughed at me then. "I'd call the cops when you're trying to trespass and make that girl more upset than she already is. You don't have a hope in hell of straightening shit out with her after what you've done, boy. I warned you. You didn't listen. Why is it that the young never listen when wisdom is spoken?"

The last was asked while he looked to the sky for answers. Not sure if he received a reply, but he did shut his window, and effectively closed the conversation so I couldn't beg my way into the building.

I wasn't stupid. Gary meant what he said. Those words were no idle threat. So, instead of tempting fate, and local law enforcement, I got in my car and headed out to my parents' house. I needed a round of their special brand of wisdom to fix what I had royally fucked up.

I NEVER COULD HAVE IMAGINED that a full-on world war had blown up at my family's house while I'd been out on that stupid fucking date, and yet, the minute I walked through the door all I could hear was my father and mother yelling and snippets of my brothers trying to get a word in but failing.

"What is going on today? I feel like everything is going to hell every which way I turn."

"Imagine that, since you're at the center of everything," Ryker accused snidely.

"Why were you with Opal earlier?"

"Because someone had to be," My little brother yelled at me.

"Monica just informed me that the baby Opal is carrying is mine," I said, talking to Ryker. "Is that true?"

"Why didn't you ask Opal that question?"

"Because Monica lives across the street from Opal, and she was just getting home as I left Monica's place."

"Oh God! Tell me she didn't see you," Ryker moaned, as if the thought of Opal seeing me there with Monica hurt him. I nodded my head, unable to voice exactly how bad the situation had been. "Mom, I understand you want everyone here for this, but I have to go."

"Go to her, honey. Make sure she's okay."

"Wait a fucking minute!" I yelled. "Where the hell do you get off going to comfort my girlfriend?"

"She's not your fucking girlfriend, asshole. And after her seeing you not only on a date with another woman, but leaving her home, I'm guessing she never will be again. She is, however, the mother of my nephew, and I've been the one going to her doctor appointments with her, so fuck you, Marsh!"

"You've been going to her appointments? When were you going to tell me that I was having a baby?"

"She already told you! As I recall, you didn't fucking care." Ryker didn't wait around, but I also didn't miss the accusatory glare he threw at our brothers, who were sitting there on the couch looking equal parts guilty and chastised.

"Tell me you didn't do what I think you did."

"I thought she was lying to get you to come back and talk to her," Brixton murmured so low I almost missed it.

"Opal sent me a text, informing me she was pregnant, and you sent what back?"

"It wasn't good, son." It was my father who admitted that.

"How would you know?" I asked incredulously because there was no fucking way my father was in on this Opal sabotage with my brothers.

"Opal was here just a bit ago. She told us the whole story from finding out about the pregnancy to you leaving, and she showed me the text exchange on her phone."

"Text exchange," the words slurred in the hazy red anger that clouded my eyes and judgment. "What did you say to her?"

"Just told her it didn't matter that goodbye meant goodbye. I figured if she was telling the truth, she would have argued the point."

"She thought I told her that her pregnancy didn't matter, after I left her. Why the hell would she try to argue with me?" I screamed at my brother. "You stupid, soul-sucking, son of a bitch!" I launched myself across the room at Brixton and started pummeling him, while wishing I could do the same to myself. I let my brother's bullshit ruin my fucking life. Worse, I let him talk me into ruining Opal's.

"I've missed out on her entire pregnancy because of you! She could be my wife right now!"

"That was your decision!" He yelled as he started fighting back.

Before long, strong arms locked around my waist and yanked me off my brother, but I turned to find the other one, who was just as responsible. My anger shifted gears and my fists found his face too. Somewhere in the background, I think I heard my mother scream for us to stop, but the buzzing of pain, adrenaline, and something ugly wouldn't allow reason past my only thought. That was to destroy the twins the same way I'd allowed them to wreak havoc on my life.

"You knew too. There's nothing the two of you don't discuss."

"I told him she wouldn't lie about something like that," Bastion attempted to excuse his part in the matter.

"And at what point did you come tell me any of it? If you thought she was telling the truth, why didn't you come to me? That's my fucking kid! That's your damn niece or nephew!"

"Nephew," he whimpered.

"What?" It wasn't the first time that word had been said

since I made my way home. It was just the first time I really understood its meaning.

"Nephew, according to Ry. He was there for the sonogram when she found out."

"He was there?" I whispered the question. My little brother was there to find out that I was having a son when I didn't even know he was a possibility. *How had my life become such a huge puddle of shit? And when did my family start lying and keeping so many fucking secrets from one another? We used to be happy. We used to love one another. What the fuck happened to us?*

"That's what I'd like to know," My mother agreed with the thoughts I hadn't realized I'd been speaking out loud. I think that took the wind out of all of our sails.

Dad had left the room and came back with a few ice packs, which he tossed to my brothers and me. "Opal said something to me earlier," my dad mentioned. The sorrow in his voice was damn near devastating. "She laid this whole mess on my shoulders, and at first, I thought she'd lost her mind, or was blaming me for making the lot of you. Then, she explained that you all had overheard some things that were never meant for your ears."

My stomach did somersaults in my body, making bile rise up my throat just enough to be uncomfortable, but not enough to make me physically sick – yet.

"Boys, sit down," Dad demanded. "You need to hear some truths about life that apparently, I should have taught you all long ago." He glared at the twins, "Especially you two."

We all sat and used the ice packs where necessary as my father started to explain himself. "Human beings make mistakes. Sometimes, and it doesn't matter how much you love a person, you will wonder – especially during tough times – if there is something better for you out there. Once in a while, someone will come along to catch your interest in a way you haven't felt in a long damn time." He sighed and raised apologetic eyes to my mother.

"Your mom and I were having one of those tough times. She thought I was working too much, kept nagging about taking a vacation, and I agreed. When the time came to take it, I wasn't able to because of contractual obligations at work. Granted, it was me who screwed up the scheduling for those obligations in the first place.

"She put pressure on me to just go anyway, and I refused like the idiot that I was back then. I thought I knew better than she did and said some hurtful things to your mom, which caused her to start ignoring me. That is where the danger lies in any relationship. It's not when you screw up or forget to make time. It comes when you stop communicating at all.

"Because of everything that was going on, and my secretary working those long hours with me, I confided in the wrong person. I talked to her, instead of my wife, about my marital issues. The problem with doing so was that she had her own agenda."

"She was in love with your father," Mom interjected, not allowing him to sugarcoat things for us.

Dad sighed. "It's true. She had fallen in love with me somehow during all those long hours working on projects with me. The feeling was not mutual. I need all of you to understand that. She was more of a sounding board for me. But the advice that came back from her was skewed in a way I didn't see at the time, because she wanted me for herself, and her advice was meant to make that happen."

"Your father was an idiot because he's always been blind to how attractive he is to the opposite sex. It's something I've always been prideful of because it meant that he only saw me that way. I never realized it could be the beginning of the end for us because he didn't see what was happening – not the real extent of it - until it was almost too late." Mom and Dad both looked at one another for a long moment before she continued the story there.

"I couldn't take the space between us any longer, so I packed this big ol' lunch up to take to the office as a peace offering." Mom sniffled and her shoulders hunched in on themselves before she spoke again, so softly that we all had to lean forward to catch what she said.

"When I got there, your father, and the witch, were kneeling on the floor facing one another. Papers were scattered all around them on the floor. I guess some files had fallen, and the witch was apologizing while giggling and touching Ed's chest. He leaned in and pushed her hair out of her face. They were just about to kiss, when I made some kind of noise that caught their attention."

"Would you have kissed her?" Bastion asked our father.

The guilty look on his face was answer enough. "It was a moment of weakness that probably would have happened had your mom not shown up. Would it have gone further than that? I don't think so. I'd like to say a definitive 'no', but that's the part of me talking who has perspective at his back. Instead, I was lucky enough to receive a wake-up call before anything else progressed. It made me realize that there was no world in which I'd want to live without your mother by my side."

"But," Mom threw in, "it also meant we were arguing about it a lot. We thought we hid that from all of you, and apparently, we didn't do a good enough job. Everything that happened between your father and me proved we forgot to appreciate one another. We forgot that making things work is something you can't just do effortlessly and without spending time together talking and doing other things."

My dad looked directly at me then. "Son, the biggest mistake you ever made was deciding to leave Opal and not including her in the conversation."

I started to argue, but he held his hand up to stop me. "You didn't give her a chance to have her say. Even if you thought it was truly what you both needed, to have that time apart, then you should have talked to her about it. You made the same mistake I did. You talked to your brothers instead of the person who mattered. The way you went about things was the most disrespectful thing you could have possibly done. You blind-sided that poor girl, and at the worst possible time too. You couldn't have known she was pregnant, but did you at one time love her?"

"I still love her."

"You have a funny way of showing it," My mom inter-jected. "Why on earth would you ever want time away from Opal? You two were always so happy together. Or was that just an act?"

"It wasn't an act. We were happy, but sometimes things felt like there wasn't anything exciting anymore. It was just... I don't know... Status quo."

My father laughed. "One day, Son, you're going to be thankful for those status quo moments where you can just be content with what you have. Think about what you've put yourself and Opal through over the past few months. Which would you rather have? The exciting dating life you've been living, or status quo with the love of your life?"

There was no denying what my answer would be as I hung my head in shame. I knew, beyond a shadow of a doubt, that my father was right. As I had been miserable alone and on the many dates I attempted. Now, I had the baggage of having slept with another woman to carry around with me too. Not only did I have that baggage, but Opal knew as well. She had the image of another woman bringing me my underwear while she was standing on the curb crying over me, over what I threw away, over the family we would probably never be.

"How did I let everything spiral so far out of control."

"I can answer that," My dad said in a tone that meant business. "First off, that best friend of yours has wanted your girl for as long as you've had her. Why the hell you'd let his jealous ass influence your decisions, where she was concerned, was beyond me."

"He's never liked Opal," I argued.

"No, Son. He's always liked Opal, far too much. He's never liked the fact that she picked you and not him."

I stared at my father for a few minutes and then turned to my brothers, who both nodded in agreement. "You guys agreed with Crayfish," I argued.

"For different reasons. I thought you'd be happier without her. Seriously, Bro, I only saw the fact that she was holding you back from experiencing things that you used to talk about doing when we were younger."

"Like what?" I asked.

"You always wanted to follow in Dad's footsteps and go to his school."

"I decided not to go there because I didn't want to start my life out in debt," I argued. "Turns out, it was a wise decision considering you still need a roommate to get by and can't even afford the new truck you keep drooling over because of it."

"Yeah, well, it wasn't just that. What about all the adventures you wanted to go on? There was even the cross-country road trip we all talked about, but it had been your idea."

"That was mine and Opal's honeymoon plan," I admitted. "We were going to go explore the country together in one of those rental RVs. The smaller ones are perfect for us, and don't cost as much as going to a resort for the same amount of time."

Bastion punched his twin in the shoulder when I admitted my dreams hadn't changed all that much, just the timeframe and who I was going to experience those things with.

"I'm sorry, man. I thought you were giving it all up for her."

"So? What if I was?" I scraped my hands down my face and then winced at the sting when I met the swollen portion of my cheek where my brother had clocked me good at least once. "Why couldn't you have let me do my own thing? I'm not like either one of you. I never even slept with any of those girls I went on dates with because I couldn't stop thinking about Opal."

"Then why were you at Monica's place?"

I blew out a breath. "Momentary insanity that I will never be able to forget, and not in a good way. When I saw Ry outside the café with Opal, I thought she was pregnant with another man's baby."

"You're an idiot!" My mother huffed in exasperation.

"Yeah, we've established that. I figured if she had been pregnant with my baby, she would have contacted me about it, though." I turned narrowed eyes on my brothers then. "If I had known she had contacted me, I never would have slept with Monica. I'd have never dated any other women, and I would have gone directly back to Opal from the very beginning."

Both twins looked chastised, but it really wasn't enough. It had been entirely my fault that I left Opal. I was the dumbass that listened to their bullshit and let it erode away at the feelings I had for my girlfriend. But the fact that they hid her pregnancy from me, that was unforgivable. And it was the one thing that probably cost me any chance at ever reconciling with the love of my life.

Bastion stood and came to hand me his phone. "I think you should watch this before you do anything else."

"What's this?"

"I wanted to make sure you got the full story from the other side of things earlier, so I recorded everything Opal had to say."

I didn't know whether to be thankful or angry with him for

recording what was basically her confession. It was her version of events since I'd left her, or maybe even before that. I got ready to hit play, when my father's large hand moved to stop me. There was moisture gathered in his eyes as he glanced down at the screen.

"You're going to want to watch that in private, Son."

My mom's accompanying sniffle confirmed what he was saying, so I took my brother's phone and walked into the den, where the curtains were still pulled shut so that my father didn't have to deal with a glare on the television when he watched college ball earlier.

I knew the heartache that I experienced while listening to Opal tell her story couldn't even compare to what she'd been through, what I'd put her through, and I'd never felt so worthless in all my life.

"How in the hell am I supposed to make up for all that?" I asked the quiet room when I got to the end of the video.

"Going forward, you need to do your best to be the man she used to know. You're also going to have to follow her lead, and go at her pace this time." I glanced up to see my dad leaning against the entryway to the room. "You told her that you were taking a break for six months before. She didn't get a say in that, Son. It's up to her now, how long it takes to forgive you."

"Do you think she can ever forgive me?" I stopped him from answering, so that I could explain what Opal saw after leaving their house earlier that day. My father's head hung in shame, as if he had been the one to offer her that final slight and disrespect.

"Do you want honesty or hope?"

Well, that said it all, didn't it? "Honesty. I think we've all had enough lies and miscommunications."

"You would be the luckiest bastard alive, if that girl ever gave you a second chance. If, for some reason, you hit that particular lottery, you better hold on and never stop working to prove yourself." Well, that didn't sound too bad. "But, Son, she was talking about leaving and moving to Oregon with her parents earlier, so you may never get that chance."

"What?"

"You heard it on that recording," He reminded me.

"Yeah, but Ryker talked her out of it."

"He did, and then she saw proof of you with another woman. One who held your underwear in her hands, and pretty much painted the picture for her of what the two of you had been up to – after you saw her pregnant and standing on the street in front of the café and didn't run to check on her. You damned yourself today, boy. Good and fuckin' proper too. Wouldn't surprise me a bit if that girl was home packing a bag as we speak, and let me be clear on this, I wouldn't blame her one bit. After the hurt our family has laid at her feet, I'd probably do the same if I was in her shoes."

"She's carrying your grandchild," I growled at him.

"Yep. And since our family wronged her, I guess we'll have to suck up the expense to go see that baby when it gets here." My father tapped the wall and then turned his back on me. There was no denying who his loyalty belonged to. Truthfully, I was thankful that someone was in Opal's corner, because from what I heard on that video, she had only had Beth and her mom all this time, until my little brother – of all people – stepped up to be the best fucking uncle a seventeen-year-old kid could be. He'd done better than I had.

My dad poked his head around the corner, anger still present in his gaze when it landed on me. "And boy, you better give that girl her damn savings back. I can't believe you walked away from her and took all that money with you."

The tips of my ears immediately burned with shame at his reprimand. "I swear, I didn't even think about it at the time."

"Didn't think much about leaving her with no transportation when you took all the money either, did you? You just thought about yourself, every step of the way. You want honesty, Marshall? You don't deserve her because you're self-ish." He didn't wait for my answer, and honestly, he didn't need one. There was no possible way to make me feel any lower than I already did.

It did, however, give me the idea for a plan that just might put me in Opal's good graces once again. More importantly, it would give her some security and a safe place to bring our son home to when the time came. Not that the apartment we had shared wasn't safe, but traversing three flights of stairs with a baby and other things would be a challenge for her that she didn't need.

Chapter 13

OPAL

"Opal, honey, you know we'd love to have you here, but there's just nowhere to put you and a baby. We only have the one bedroom. Things are more expensive out here, so your father and I had to downsize the housing situation."

"I understand," I told my mother. It wasn't just lip service. Going to stay with them, until I could get on my feet, was a long shot at best.

"When is the baby due?"

"A little less than two months to go now," I confirmed, because knowing my mom, she wasn't asking for exact dates. They wouldn't matter to her. My parents weren't bad people. They'd been good to me when I was younger. They just weren't of the opinion that kids remained your responsibility once they hit that magic age of eighteen. They still cared – just not enough. Not like Marsh's family always cared about their adult children.

"I see. Well, I'm not sure if we'll be able to make it out there. Maybe, by Christmas, you'll be in a position to fly out with the baby so we can meet her."

"Him," I corrected.

"Right. I forgot, you already found out it was a boy."

"It's your only grandchild, Mom. How could you forget?"

"Oh, stop. You know how I am," She excused away her behavior. "I'll tell your dad that you called. Love you. Take care of yourself, sweetheart."

"Yep, you too," I returned, but it was to the dial tone because Mom had already hung up the phone. I sat there, listening to the tone because I was just too tired to move. The doorbell ringing startled me out of my stupor. For some stupid reason, my heart kicked into fifth gear, thinking that it would be Marsh coming to explain that what I thought I saw wasn't real. I knew it was, and yet, my stupid heart wouldn't give up hope that my relationship with him wasn't well and truly over.

I opened the door to find a Kennedy standing there, even though it wasn't the one my heart pined for. "What are you doing here, Ryker?"

"I thought you might need me," He suggested.

"He told you that I saw him coming out of Monica's place, and that she kindly came down in her robe, to give him his underwear that he left behind?"

"That motherfucker!" Ryker fumed.

"Oh, I guess not, then," I mumbled as I stepped back so Marsh's brother could get into the apartment.

"Opal?" Ryker asked as he stepped inside.

"Yeah?"

"Why are there boxes everywhere?"

"I can't afford to stay here after this month," I admitted yet another defeat. It was something I didn't bother telling my mother because it would have made no difference.

"What? I thought Marsh paid the rent up?"

"He did. He paid it six months out, which was the rest of our lease. I can afford it without a roommate, but no one wants to room with a newborn. I've interviewed a few people, or tried to, and the minute they see I'm pregnant, they say this isn't the living situation they're looking for. I can't blame them." I shrugged my shoulders. "When Marsh was here, we split the bills. Without the help, I can't keep this place."

"What are you going to do?"

"I was hoping to go move to Oregon," I admitted.

"You said you wouldn't," he argued.

"I don't have a lot of choices, Ry."

"You can stay at our house. I'm sure Mom would tell you the same thing."

I laughed. "Yeah, because I really want to sit through family dinners while your brother brings his dates around and ignores our son," I growled.

"Opal, I need you to hear me out here. I honestly don't think he knew about the baby until today."

"Okay? He found out, and his response was to go fuck the bitch across the street from my apartment."

Ryker shook with his anger. "Pretty sure he did that because he thought you were carrying someone else's baby."

"Whose baby could it be? Did I make it myself?"

We both plopped down on the couch. Well, he plopped, and I did a half backbend-awkward-waddle sit. "That looked wildly uncomfortable," He commented.

"It was. Thanks for noticing." I tossed back at him. "I'm so tired, Ry." The admission was beyond my lips before I could pull it back. He scooted closer and wrapped his arm around me until my head rested on his sturdy shoulder.

"I know you are, Opal, and for what it's worth, I'm sorry that you've had to deal with all this while growing my nephew."

"I just don't understand what I did to deserve any of this," I said as I rubbed my hands over my burgeoning belly. "There was never a moment, not once since I met your brother that I wished for something different. We were supposed to be happy. We were supposed to be getting married. There was no concern on my part when I saw that positive pregnancy test, because I just knew that we had a stable relationship to bring him into."

Ryker didn't seem to know what to say, so he just continued to hold me as I whined. Only, I stopped whining because what more was there to say?

"I was wrong about everything. Your brother didn't love me."

"I don't think that's true at all," He attempted to argue.

"If you loved someone, would you treat them the way Marsh treated me?" I asked and looked up into Ry's too serious face to see the answer there, even though he didn't give a verbal answer. He would not. This was not what you did to someone you loved. You didn't leave them in the hopes of finding someone better, or with the promise to come back if you didn't find it.

"The thing with our dad really messed him up."

"So, that gave him the right to take it out on me?"

"No. I'm not saying that or arguing in his favor. Honestly, I'm just trying to understand the same way you are. This might sound shitty in one respect, but I honestly don't think he thought about 'you' in this equation at all."

"Well, that certainly makes me feel better."

"I don't mean it the way you took it. I just meant that he was thinking of himself, that he had to know for sure before settling down. I'm sure he thought you would want that answer too."

"I wanted that answer in an entirely different way, Ry."

"What do you mean?"

"For me, I had zero doubts that we were meant to be together. The only thing I was waiting on was for your brother to decide whether he felt the same. If so, he would have chosen me, no matter what his friend and brothers tried to put into his head. Then, I would have known he felt the same way I did, and never doubted our being together."

"You've never been attracted to anyone else besides my brother?" He asked with a hint of disbelief in his voice.

"Of course, I've been attracted to other people, but no way in hell would I have ever acted on that."

"Why not?"

"Because I loved your brother. In my mind, there was no way I could ever find better than what I already had. Even during the times when we fought, or just seemed to bore one another, I still knew that no one could ever compare to him."

"Damn. You are girlfriend goals, Opal."

"Too bad your brother didn't think so," I lamented.

"He's a fucking idiot."

"Well, that's something we can both agree on."

"You're sure you won't move away?"

"I have to move, but Oregon is no longer on the table."

"Sorry your parents are weird."

I chuckled. "That's an understatement, but thanks."

"Do you have somewhere in mind?"

I shrugged. There was a place I had in mind, and it was affordable, but it was in the worst part of town and would nearly triple my walking commute to work. "I'm pretty sure that I found something that's workable."

"How are you going to move all your stuff?"

"That's the suckiest part. I have to dip into what little savings I have to get someone to move it for me."

"Or I could borrow my dad's truck and get some of my friends to help."

As much as I wanted to take Ryker up on that offer, I didn't want him to see where I was moving to. He would throw a fit, and being seventeen and still living at home with his parents, he wouldn't understand the choices I had to make.

"That's a nice offer, but I already scheduled a moving company."

"That was dumb. Can you cancel?"

I shook my head. It was the first lie I ever told Ryker, but a necessary one to keep my pride intact. "I'll lose the deposit if I cancel this late. They're coming tomorrow." I knew there was a cancelation policy because I'd been hoping to go stay with my parents, but had a contingency plan set up, since I didn't think they'd take the baby and me in.

If only Marsh had waited just two more days to have his little tryst with Monica, then I would have never had to see the proof of what they'd done with my own two eyes. I sighed at the thought and Ryker hugged me a little tighter.

"Things will get better soon, Sis."

I managed a sad chuckle in response. "I'll never be your sister now, Ry." The admission wounded me, but I tried not to cry on one of the three people who had been there for me lately.

"You're always going to be the mother of my favorite nephew, so I'm still going to call you that."

"I wish you were my real brother," I told him.

"Well, that would make your situation a bit weird, don't you think?" He teased while patting my belly.

"You're gross! I take it back."

"No take backs. We're siblings now. My double-nephew agrees with me," he tacked on as my son gave a mighty kick to his uncle's hand.

"Please, do not ever call him your double-nephew again, and definitely don't try explaining that to people."

"Aw, come on, Sis," he continued teasing to lighten the mood. "What's the matter with telling people that my sister got together with my brother and made my double-nephew?"

I reached over and gave Ryker a titty twister that had him howling. He glared at me playfully.

"Dammit, Opal, that hurt," He yelped as he lifted his shirt to look at his abused nipple. The boy was going to make some lucky girl a fine boyfriend one day. Hopefully, he would learn from his brother's mistakes and not listen to the rest of the idiot siblings he had. Then, maybe he wouldn't screw his life up or someone else's.

"I better be getting back soon before they send out the calvary." He walked over to the door. "Are you sure I can't help with this?"

"I'm positive. Why don't you stop worrying about me for a day? Go hang out with your friends tomorrow, before you have to be back at school again Monday."

"Because they're not as important as making sure you're taken care of."

"Ry, I appreciate it, but it's not your job to take care of me."

"It's Marsh's, but he isn't doing his job, so I'm stepping in."

I offered a weak smile to him, because it truly was noble that he was trying to pick up his big brother's slack. "Ry, go be a kid for a day, so I don't have to feel bad about you being around so much. Please? It would make me feel better."

"Fine, but once you get settled, I expect to get your address, so I can come check on you and squirt."

"Okay, once I'm settled," I agreed. That one wasn't a lie. He just didn't need to know how long it would take me to get settled into my new, much smaller, one-bedroom apartment.

After he left, I grabbed my beat up old acoustic guitar from the corner and sat down with it. I turned my phone on and logged into my channel, determined to sing an upbeat song for the first time in months. Only I sat there and stared at the camera for a few minutes before I said, "Sometimes, life just plain sucks. This is for everyone else who is stuck in a rut, right along with me."

I started strumming a slowed down, softer version of The Downfall of Us All by A Day to Remember. It didn't quite encompass what I was feeling, but I could identify with the 'life being turned upside down' part. Plus, Marsh had been right. He was happier without me. It was my turn to accept that I'd been wrong about us, and learn to be happy without him too.

Chapter 14

MARSH

"What do you mean, she doesn't live here anymore? I just saw her here two days ago."

Gary was getting on my last nerve with his gatekeeper bullshit. I understood he was looking out for my girl, but dammit, I was trying to fix things.

"I meant what I said. She told me she couldn't afford the place on her own and that she had to get something else. I tried to work something out with her," He sighed. "But with all the added doctor bills, and things she needs for the baby, money's just too tight for her to hang onto this place. Damn shame too because I don't know too many other rentals available for much cheaper. Not for the space she needs for the baby and her."

"I paid the rent up when I left," I reminded him, unable to conceptualize her not being able to afford zero dollars.

"Son, you paid for six months. That six months was up two days ago."

"Son of a bitch," I muttered to myself. Hadn't I just been thinking that the six months were nearly up and that I could go get my girl back? That was before she saw proof that I'd been with another woman though.

Fuck! Fuck! Fuck!

"Hey handsome, finally come to your senses?" Monica called out from across the street. I ignored her and continued staring Gary down.

"Ah, ghosting another girl you got involved with, huh?"

"I never ghosted Opal. She blocked me on the phone."

"Did you forget where she lived?" Before I could answer his stupid question, he shook his head. "Nah, couldn't have, because here you are. Six months too late to do anything about the mess you made."

"Gary, if you know where she is, I need to know. She's carrying my baby."

"Nice of you to finally acknowledge that after she's been struggling with everything on her own all this time."

"I just found out two fucking days ago!" I shouted at him. That must have been a shock because his jaw actually dropped so far I thought it might hit the stoop he was perched on.

"You're seriously trying to tell me, that in a town this small, when your little brother has been a nuisance around here for months, that you had no clue Opal was with child?"

"My little brother stopped talking to me when I left Opal," I admitted. "And yes, that's exactly what I'm telling you."

"She didn't leave a forwarding address," Gary informed me. "The moving company she used is that one with the green and yellow trucks."

"Home to Home?" I asked.

His shoulders bounced in answer. "Maybe that's the one. They probably can't tell you anything either, but might be worth a try. You could always ask that little brother of yours. I'm sure he knows. He seems to be thick as thieves with Opal these days. That's a good boy looking out for his nephew's momma when no one else will."

"Son of a bitch," I muttered as I walked away from Gary's venomous truths. He knew how to hit a man right where it hurt.

I tried the moving company. They wouldn't tell me a fucking thing. In fact, the owner threatened to dig a hole out back and put me in it if I tried to bother him for client information again, especially that specific client. I could say one thing for Opal, she earned people's loyalty wherever she went. It wasn't lost on me that I hadn't given her the same loyalty that total strangers were capable of.

"What are you doing here?" My little brother asked as he came into Mom and Dad's house after school let out.

"Came here to talk to you."

"Wasted trip then, if you ask me."

There was that loyalty again. Not that Opal didn't deserve every bit of it, but damn if it wasn't making things impossible for me.

"Did you know Opal moved?"

"I know she didn't have a damn choice but to do so," He threw back at me with an air of accusation.

"I understand that, but I need to know where she is. She blocked my phone months ago, and I need to get in touch with her."

"Why now? You suddenly tired of fresh pussy?"

"It wasn't like that?"

"No? So that wasn't Monica delivering your underwear to you on the street, right in front of Opal, then?"

"That was a one-time encounter."

"You mean a one-night stand?" My brother corrected before rolling his eyes at me. "Funny, because you know how many one-time 'encounters' Opal had since you've been gone?" Ryker asked while using finger quotes when he repeated my wording. When I didn't answer, my brother continued to dig the knife in just a little deeper and twist it.

"None. Because she's not an asshole. And of the two of you, only she would have been in the right to go off and do just that. Who knows, maybe she would have if she hadn't also found out that she was carrying your baby."

"There's no need to keep trying to hurt me, Ry. You couldn't possibly hurt me anymore than I've hurt myself."

"Yeah, I could. I could hurt you the same way you did Opal, because I promise you this, asshole, she's been hurt far more and for far longer, and in more ways than even I know to count."

"It's not that big a deal, really." I heard the voice of the woman we were arguing about and turned to see her walk through the door with my mother.

"It is a big deal that you are seven months pregnant and walking through that neighborhood. If I hadn't seen you, who knows what could have happened."

"What neighborhood?" I asked, wanting to know why my pregnant ex-girlfriend was walking anywhere that my mother claimed might get her hurt.

"Brambleton Manner," my mother huffed.

"What in the hell were you doing walking over there?" I asked. Brambleton Manner was notorious for the criminal element who lived, hung out, and carried on their illegal business there. My mother was right, it wasn't a place the mother of my child should have been walking through, even if it had been a shortcut.

Opal ignored my question and continued to only focus on my mother. "Listen, I need to get back. Can you please just take me?" She looked about two seconds from breaking down and crying as her hands shook almost as hard as her voice did.

"Nope. You're staying for dinner. End of. That's my grand-child you're carrying. I'm going to make sure you eat well tonight."

Opal huffed in frustration as big, fat tears tracked down her cheeks. "This is kidnapping!" She yelled at my mother, who only chuckled at her.

"Call it what you will, but you aren't leaving here until you eat."

Opal bent, or tried to bend, to massage her calf muscle until she realized she couldn't reach it comfortably. Then she moved to take a step and her leg nearly went out from under her. I moved at the same time Ryker did, and we ended up running into one another instead of helping Opal. Thankfully, my father had come up just in time to catch her before she went down.

"Whoa there, girl." He leaned in, picked her up and carried her to the couch. "Let's see what we're working with?" He checked out her leg. "That's a pretty big knot in the muscle, but what on earth is going on with your feet?"

We all glanced down to see Opal's far too worn shoes and the blood that trickled out the back of one where a blister appeared to have been rubbed raw enough to pop.

"Kath, grab the first aid kit," My dad ordered. "How the hell much walking have you been doing?"

"My new apartment is further away from work. It's just a bit of an adjustment is all," Opal whispered to him, but we all heard and immediately went on alert.

"How far?" My father asked again in a tone that did not invite argument.

"A few miles," she sniffed.

"Miles? As in more than one?" My father asked, only to be answered by a shrug from Opal's shoulders.

"I was almost home when Kathy kidnapped me."

"Good thing she did too," My father grumbled. Dad's eyes came up to meet mine and I swear, if he could have killed me where I stood with that glare, he would have. This was all on me. No matter what else had happened, I put Opal in a position where she was walking several fucking miles to and from work each day at seven months pregnant.

"Does your doctor know that you're walking so far every day?" My mother asked as she handed Dad the first aid kit.

"It's a newer development," Opal admitted.

"It ends today," My mother demanded.

Opal laughed and that sound set everyone on edge.

"How's that going to end, Kathy?" Opal asked. My mom was visibly flustered by the seething anger that spewed forth with the words she spoke. "How exactly am I going to avoid the walk? Maybe I should just spend all the money I have saved for a crib on cab fare every day?"

"Well, there are other…"

"Or maybe I should go hungry instead. Oh, I know, I could stop paying the $4,000 that I still owe the doctor for the delivery fees and just have my baby in the bathtub or something. Isn't that how people do home births now? You people are so used to making good money that you don't know what it's like to struggle. I've been doing just fine, and keeping my baby healthy, this whole time. You don't get to step in at the end and judge me for what I have to do to survive!"

"No one is judging you, darlin'. We're simply worried about you," My dad tried to tell her in a calm, even tone.

"Yeah, because I happen to be carrying your grand baby. You didn't give two shits whether I was dead or alive before you found out," She tossed back at him and jerked her leg away before he could clean up the wound on her foot. My parents were stunned still and silent as Opal got up.

"I'm leaving. Thanks for making me have to spend some of my hard-earned savings to get back to my apartment when I was only a few feet away earlier. I really appreciate the exact opposite of help. And I'd really appreciate you all leaving me the hell alone from here on out. Every time one of you comes into my life, it gets worse. I can't take anything worse happening. I've reached my damn limit, so just stop!"

Opal limped out of the house and down the driveway to wait on the taxi she called, and we all stood in the living room of my family's home, absolutely shell-shocked. The sweetest girl in the world had just turned into a wounded animal, lashing out at people for trying to help her and that was all my damn fault.

"I was just trying to help her," Mom whimpered as Dad pulled her into his arms.

"Kathy, I hate to say it, but I think too much damage has been done to that girl. We're going to have to wait and see if maybe she comes around after the baby is here."

"But…" Mom hesitated, trying to get her argument together. "She can't keep going like that. She's walking miles to and from places every day, Ed."

My dad turned on me then. "Did you ever give her money back?"

"I haven't been able to find her."

"Well, you have a damned good place to start now. You might want to get on it, so that girl isn't killing herself and our grandchild just to keep a roof over their heads."

I nodded in his direction.

"And Son?"

"Yeah?"

"Don't come back to this house until you get that mess you made straightened out. I mean it. I can't even stand to look at you right now. You aren't the man that I thought you were. Letting your woman live like that when she's carrying your baby while you're out carrying on with some stupid idea in your head that you need to date other people."

"Ed," my mom tried to coax him into settling down.

"We raised a bunch of assholes, Kath. First the twins, now this shit with Marsh."

That was the last thing I heard as I closed the door of my family home, knowing that my dad wasn't wrong. "Wait!" I heard behind me and turned to see my brother standing there.

"Are you going after her?" I nodded. "I need to come too."

I was going to argue, but honestly, he was probably the only one who could get through her door once we got there. That was, if we didn't take so long that we couldn't follow the damn taxi that just picked Opal up.

"Let's go then."

Chapter 15

OPAL

THE CAB PULLED UP TO MY SHABBY APARTMENT IN A SECTION OF town that was known to be the lowest of the low, the worst of the worst. This was where the criminals supposedly lived. That's what people told themselves so that they felt better about the fact that this was in fact where people who had no other options lived. The downtrodden and weary lived here. Sometimes, those same downtrodden people might turn to a life of crime to help put themselves in a better situation.

That last bit was something I told myself often, so that things wouldn't seem so scary when I had to walk home later than usual, like I had earlier that day. Unfortunately for me, Kathy Kennedy had been driving by and saw me. It was almost laughable that she thought she was rescuing me from walking through the neighborhood, when I lived here.

"This you?" The cabbie asked.

"It is, thank you for coming so quickly," I told him as I passed him a twenty-dollar bill. "Keep the change," I offered, knowing I just gave him seven extra dollars that I didn't really need to part with right then. Thanks to being pregnant, and needing to take some time off of work, I had to pay four months ahead on my rent when I got the place, just to be sure that I would be covered for any emergencies that might pop up and give me enough time to start working and earning a paycheck again.

It was true, I made plenty of money, and could even afford a place in a slightly better neighborhood. The problem was, I couldn't afford to pay ahead for emergencies in those places. What savings I had managed to put away, thanks to not having to pay rent for the past six months, had quickly dwindled down with doctor bills, baby items that needed to be purchased, and a few clothes that would fit my ever-expanding waistline. Not that I splurged on those. I had exactly three pairs of pants and two shorts that I shifted between along with a few different tops, now that hiding behind a sweatshirt was no longer an option. It was either quit wearing them or suffer a heat stroke, so I was glad to be over hiding my condition.

I just needed to get past people's need to talk. More to the point, let them talk themselves out of being interested in my life before I gave them a little something else to gossip about.

I unlocked my door and hobbled my way inside. My feet were killing me, and my leg cramp felt like what I assumed labor would be like. It was nearly unbearable. I grabbed a banana off the counter and started eating it without thought as I made my way to the couch that dwarfed the current living room it resided in.

I had left my bed behind, knowing that the new apartment only had one tiny bedroom that would be just big enough to fit the crib, changing table, and a little rocking chair in it. The couch had become my bed, as evidenced by the sheets and blankets still thrown over it. What was the point in making it look like a couch again anyway? It wasn't like I'd have any guests beyond Bethany.

My already dark mood plummeted even further as I pulled my shoes off my aching feet. It didn't occur to me to get my own first aid kit before I sat down and got comfortable. I stared longingly at the bathroom, as if thinking hard enough would make the damn thing come to me. Unfortunately, my mind powers did not work to teleport objects to me. Too bad. That could have come in handy one day.

Just as I finally talked myself into getting up, there was a knock on my door.

"What now?" I asked the universe. "Maybe this time it can be one of those sweepstakes things that I don't enter, and I could be the winner. That'd be great." It didn't escape my notice that talking to myself had become a regular thing of late, but it took place of the banter that used to occur between Marsh and me.

I didn't even bother looking to see who was outside. Instead, I threw caution to the wind, tossed the door open, and allowed the doorjamb to prop me up before I even realized who was standing there.

"Opal?" Ryker said my name so gently that I thought he might cry. "Why didn't you tell me this was where you were moving to?"

"Ryker, go home, please. I'm tired, sore, and I just want to bandage up my feet, eat something more than a banana, and go to bed."

He didn't listen. Not that I thought he would. Instead, he pushed his way past me, but not before he leaned his head back out and looked down the open-air hallway. "It's 1272," He yelled, much to my dismay.

Then he pushed past me again and stood dead center of my living room-slash-kitchen combo and frowned at the couch with my bedding still on it. I didn't see what he did after that because another body pushed its way through my door. I was more familiar with him, and he wasn't exactly welcome in my home or my life for that matter.

"What the absolute fuck, Opal?" Marsh asked as he made his way inside and closed the door behind himself.

"I really don't have the energy for this visit. I'd appreciate it if you'd both leave."

"Where is your bed?"

"What bed?" I asked Ryker.

"Exactly. You just told me you were going to see to your wounded feet, eat, and go to bed. I don't see a damn bed anywhere."

"Why the hell not? I left a perfectly good bed behind with you at the apartment."

"It wouldn't fit, and honestly, I didn't want the reminders of you in my new place. The other furniture had to come because I didn't have anything else, but I was glad to leave the bed behind."

"Do you hate me that much?"

"Yes," I answered him before turning to face Ryker, who still stood there and glared at me.

"Opal, you better not be sleeping on this couch."

"Where the hell else do you expect me to sleep, Ry?" I was so damned tired and frustrated. "I didn't invite you here," I whined to both men while wishing they would just go away.

"You can't stay here," Marsh demanded.

"I can. I have. I've already paid up for four months in case of emergencies with the pregnancy or baby. This is my home now, for better or worse."

"Opal, I know you can do better than this place."

"No, you don't, Marshall. You don't know anything about me anymore. You know absolutely nothing. Now, I really want you to leave."

I pointed to the door, or tried to, but my body was just too exhausted to have much follow through on the gesture. Standing sucked. My feet hurt. My back hurt. And I just wanted to close my eyes for a solid week.

Unfortunately, bad dreams awaited me on the other side of my closed lids. Sometimes, they were simple flashbacks to Marsh leaving me. Others were worries about the baby and what might happen during childbirth. Then, there were the dreams about Marsh with someone else, laughing at me walking our child to school because, for some reason, I still don't have a car in the future.

Speaking of which, that was the other reason I chose to live in this apartment complex. I needed a car. The walking, and damage done to my body and my soul as a result, were too much for me. It was getting hotter too. Beth had been gone to some nursing seminar while all the drama unfolded this week, but she was due back tomorrow and promised to take me car shopping the minute she got back.

Tomorrow, I would splurge on a cab to and from work. There was no getting around that with my feet in the condition they were in. It took me a minute to tune back in to the fact that Marsh had been speaking while I was lost to my thoughts.

"... want to leave that kind of cash sitting around here, or hear that you're walking to the bank with it."

"What?" I asked as I worked my way out of my exhausted daze. "What are you talking about me walking around with cash for?"

"Told you she wasn't paying attention to your dumbass. She's tired. Why don't you just leave?" Ryker taunted his brother.

"Because this is important." Marsh snapped his fingers in my face, and I stepped back away from him immediately.

"Rude!"

"Listen then! I'm trying to find out what you want me to do about your half of the savings account we had? I didn't even realize that I had all that money because it was supposed to be for us to buy a house. That wasn't happening, so it wasn't on my mind."

As if I needed another punch to the gut? He had to go and remind me that we were never going to buy a house together after all.

"As far as I'm concerned, you used it to pay the rent in your absence."

"Nope. Both of our names were on that lease, which meant that I was responsible for half of the rent anyway until the lease was up."

"Whatever, Marsh. I'm exhausted. There's nothing left in my tank. I really need to get some sleep which means you need to go."

"Where are you sleeping?"

I pointed to the couch with the bedding still on it.

"You can't sleep there," he told me.

"For once, we agree," Ry chimed in.

"Well, it's all I have and I'd like to get to it." I moved, slowly and painfully to the door, unable to hide the wince and grunt of pain that gave it away as I moved.

"Come on, you're coming back to my place for the night until we can figure something else out."

"I'm not going back to your place and sleeping in the filthy bed where you've fucked other women," I snarled at him so viciously that even I was a little frightened of myself.

"I never slept with any women there."

"Yeah right," I huffed.

"There's no way in hell I would bring anyone back to the twin's place, even if I did sleep with any of the women I went out on dates with."

"First of all, I would never be inclined to step a toe into a place where your twin brothers live. Ever. Not even if it would save my own life to do so," I informed him. In my eyes, they were to blame the most because of the years of harping on their brother to leave me. "Second, I don't believe you are seriously sitting here trying to make out like you never slept with your dates when I saw first-hand that you absolutely did. Unless you are going to try to tell me you and Monica were just working on laundry day together, but it was totally plutonic?"

"Monica was the only woman I slept with while we were apart."

"We're still apart," I threw in, but he ignored me and kept going.

"And I only did that when I thought you had gotten knocked up by some lousy piece of shit who left you high and dry afterward."

Ryker winced before I ever got the words out of my mouth. "Well, that part was a fact. I did get knocked up by some lousy piece of shit who left me high and dry afterward. So, I guess you were right to sleep with Monica on my behalf then."

"God! You're so frustrating!"

"Why are you here, then? You already left me. You should take a hint and stay gone."

"I'm not staying gone, Opal."

"Why the hell not?"

"Because I'm still fucking in love with you."

"Oh, that's rich! It was just two days ago that you were fucking someone else. That sounds an awful lot like you're really in love with me."

"Opal, I already told you that was a mistake, and don't try to be cute. You knew I thought there was another man involved in making that baby."

"Well, that just shows how little you think of me." My hands shook as his implication, his assessment of my character burned through my battered soul. "Your assertion that I would go out and do that, when I was literally balled up on the floor and dying of a broken heart instead, is insulting."

I moved forward and poked my finger into his chest with purpose. "It was *you* who wanted your freedom. *You* who wanted to fuck other women. *You* who wanted to know what it was like to date someone other than me. *I* never wanted any of that, so *you*, Marshal Kennedy, can go fuck yourself and stay far away from me while you do it."

"What happened to you?" He whispered.

"YOU DID! You happened to me. You broke me! Now get the hell out of my house!"

"Come on, man. You need to leave her alone. It's not good for her or the baby to be upset like this. She's already exhausted." Ryker – the voice of reason – spoke in gentle tones to his brother as he all but pulled him out of my apartment.

I had just enough energy to lock the door and make it back to the couch before I passed out into a fitful sleep of horrible dreams and tear-stained pillows.

"GIRL, I am never leaving town again without you," Bethany promised as I finally finished the recap of everything that had taken place in her absence. "Although," she said while glancing around the tiny little apartment. "I'm not too thrilled about your current living situation, either."

"I already told you, if I'm going to have a car payment and all the baby expenses to think of, then I have to be frugal with where we live for now. Maybe once I have the car paid off, I'll be able to afford something a bit bigger."

"Why isn't Mr. Marshal Kennedy going to be providing support for all of this baby expense you're going to have?"

"Seriously? There's no way I'm asking him for anything."

"But it's not for you. It's for your son."

I shook my head. "It's bad enough that he'll probably want visitation or something to appease his family, now that everyone knows."

"What's so wrong with that? As much as he's been a jackass these past six months, Marsh isn't a bad man. His family are usually good people too – if you don't count his despicable brothers."

"Uh-huh, and now I have to worry about whether Monica, or that pixie girl from the party that instigated our breakup, or maybe some other awful woman will be playing house with my son. Beth, I don't think I can handle it. Things were bad enough when I knew Marsh was sharing himself with those women, but how am I going to take it when he's sharing my son with them? Having them play mommy for him? I don't think I could handle it if my son came home and got mad at me and said he liked them better. His dad already chose them over me. How would I be able to breathe if my son did too?"

"Oh, sweetie," Beth cooed as she pulled me into a hug.

"I would never put you in that position," A deep voice called out by the door, startling both Beth and me.

"What are you doing in my house?"

"You didn't lock your door." He ignored the rest of the implied question, considering I told him I didn't want him coming around anymore the last time he was here. "And I said that I would never put you in that position with our son."

"Excuse me if I don't believe you, Marsh, considering you already put me in that position with you."

"Son of a..." he growled under his breath. "Beth, you mind stepping out for a bit, so Opal and I can have a conversation?"

"You mean the conversation you should have had with her a little more than six months ago?" She asked, while tapping her foot impatiently at him.

He glared at her for a minute, before he refocused all of his attention on me. "I'm sorry for how I handled every single thing. It was all stupid, and a waste of time."

"Well, I'm glad your waste of time was worth all the heart-break I suffered."

"It wasn't. If you'd just listen," He begged.

"What if you got Monica pregnant?"

"What? Where did that come from? I didn't even finish with her, so unless I have magic pre-cum…" he paused there and swallowed visibly as he realized what he just revealed.

"You didn't even use protection with her? It took us three years of dating to go without protection, and you're telling me that Monica…" I felt like I was going to throw up. "You know what, never mind, I don't want to know anything else. Get out of my house, and I'm serious as sin, Marsh, Do Not Come Back!"

"Dammit, Opal, just give me a minute to think things out. You know how I get flustered and say the wrong things when I'm put on the spot. I'm trying to make things right with you."

"Well, you sure have a funny way of showing it when you break into my house and tell me all about how you came inside another woman. Excuse me, 'didn't come in her', but you were still fucking her without protection. Maybe my son will have a sibling seven months after he's born."

"Opal, please," he begged.

"Get the fuck out of my house!"

Thankfully, he took me seriously that time. Marsh turned and left.

"Damn, that was a whole train wreck."

"This past six months has been nothing but a train wreck."

"Unpopular opinion?" She questioned.

"Nope." I had an inkling of what she was going to say, and I didn't want to hear it.

"You should at least hear him out. I'm not saying that he's going to magically tell you something that will make everything you've been through okay, but this anger you're holding onto isn't good for you or the baby, sweetie. It's time to get some closure and the only way you're going to do that is if you let the man have his say. Once he does, maybe he'll be more inclined to walk away, or maybe you'll want him to stay."

I scoffed at the last bit. "Are you serious? If someone did this to you, would you honestly ever trust them again? What happens if I get back with him, and in two years, his brothers are in his ear again? What happens when a new woman starts to work with him? Or another one pops up at a party who seems far more interesting than I do? What's to stop him from walking out on me again? Only then, it won't just be me he's walking out on."

"What happens if he stays?"

"That's just it, Beth, I don't see a scenario where that's possible anymore. Every time I close my eyes, I'm going to wonder if today will be the day it happens all over again. I don't have enough big pieces of my heart left to break. If he shatters the rest, there won't be anything to give my son."

"Oh, Opal!" Beth swooped in and wrapped her strong arms around me. That time, no one interrupted and she didn't let go until we were both worn out from crying. By the time she did, my tears had dried up and I felt sick to my stomach that my baby constantly had to put up with my sadness.

Chapter 16

MARSH

My visit to Opal's new place did not go like I thought it would, not by a long shot. I stared down at the money that I'd taken by her place, angry with myself for not just leaving it there. Truthfully, I'd been so caught off guard by her angry vehemence, that I'd forgotten why I showed up at her apartment that morning. It hadn't been to anger her further. I just wanted to make sure she had her portion of our savings account, plus a huge chunk of mine, to help with her expenses.

The sad part was, while she had Bethany there with her, I had no one I could talk to. My brothers were out and for very different reasons. The twins were the ones that wouldn't stop pushing until I ruined my relationship with her to begin with. Ryker was on Opal's side all the way. Truth be told, I was happy about that part because it meant she had someone from our family who had been by her side.

Then there was the man who was once my best friend. Crayfish had also been on the 'we hate Opal' train, but as of late, he'd dipped out of sight and hadn't really been coming around as much. I wasn't sure what was up with that, but it made me wonder if what my mom had said to me once wasn't true. She thought Cramer wanted me to break up with Opal because he liked her too much, not because he hated her, but because he hated that she was with me.

My oldest brother, Jimmy, probably didn't even know what was going on. He was stationed in Japan and wasn't due home for another few months. That meant, by the time he got back, I'd already have a kid in the world. Whether I was with my son's mother or not by then remained to be seen.

I leaned back into the pillows that were pushed up against the wall where the head of my mattress and box spring rested. I hadn't bothered to buy a new bed frame when I moved out of my old apartment because in the back of my mind, the only end to this scenario was going back home. To Opal. That should have told me everything I needed to know. It was only ever her, and I let the idiots in my life talk me out of what I always knew.

That left me trying to find a way to make things up to her, to make her life better. Never, even in my wildest dreams, did I foresee my actions having such dire consequences for her. Had I been able to predict any of it happening, I would have never left her the way I did.

My phone rang and pulled me from my thoughts. It was my mom.

"Were you able to talk her into moving in with us until you can close on the house?"

"Hello to you too, Mom."

"Formalities aren't important right now. Did you tell her what you were doing?"

"I didn't quite get that far." She must have been able to hear the hesitation in my voice, because she clucked her tongue and then pulled the phone away while she growled loudly into the air.

"Do I even want to know what you said to screw it up?"

"No, you really don't. Let's just say, I think I managed to make things even worse."

"How could you possibly do that?"

"She asked what I was going to do if I got Monica pregnant, too."

"Oh no!" My mother groaned.

"And I told her that I didn't even cu-uh-finish in her unless the um…" Shit, this was my mother I was speaking to. I couldn't exactly spell things out for her. It was fucking embarrassing. Beyond that, I knew she'd be even more disappointed in me when she realized what it all meant. I had been beyond irresponsible.

"Unless pre-ejaculate counts?" My mother guessed, though she used the more acceptable term to convey the thought.

"Yeah."

"I know I taught you to wrap your tool! What were you thinking? Dammit, Marshall, it's not like you don't already have a hell of a mess to clean up in your life, a baby on the way, and the baby's mother might never forgive you for how you treated her. But she's right. What if you got that other girl pregnant? You know you don't have to finish in someone for that to happen, right?"

"I know, Mom. But what are the chances of that happening?"

"What are the chances that you'd leave your girlfriend of seven years, who you claimed was the love of your life, for a damn stupid reason on the same day she was going to tell you that you were about to become a father?"

I sighed. As usual, my mom wasn't wrong and there was absolutely nothing I could do about the Monica situation except to wait and see. So, that would tack another month onto the timeframe for when I could ease Opal's mind about other women. It would figure that I held out on having sex with anyone else during all six months, even though that was what I originally set out to do, and at the last minute, I fucked it all to hell and back.

"Have you heard about how long closing will take?" My mom asked.

"Should be thirty days."

"Well then, maybe in a month you'll be able to deliver double the good news to Opal and earn some of her good graces instead of adding to her burdens."

"Mom?" I asked hesitantly.

"What?" The impatience in her tone almost made me keep my mouth shut. Almost. I wasn't kidding myself earlier about not having anyone to talk to about the mess I'd created.

"What am I going to do if she never forgives me?"

I thought my mom's sigh might be never ending at one point. Then, she finally answered. "Son, you need to prepare yourself for the fact that she may never forgive you. What that poor girl has gone through," she started to say and I could have sworn I heard a sniffle when her words trailed off. "I had no idea it was that bad for her, and then every time I turn around, I hear how much worse it has gotten, and not a bit of it is her fault. Marshal, even though none of it is her doing, she probably feels as though it is."

"What do you mean?"

"When everything happened with your father and his secretary, all I could think, the only thing that kept cycling through my mind, was: 'What had I done wrong? Why was I not good enough? Was there something I didn't do? Something I did do?' I wondered if it was because I was growing older, or maybe that my body had been ravaged from having five boys - two in one pregnancy." I could hear the pain in my mother's voice as she expressed some aspects of her troubles with my father that I never considered before.

"The doubt I heaped on myself was almost as bad, maybe worse, than your father's actions. But it was his actions that caused me to doubt in the first place. Opal's life has fallen apart since you left her. Your ex-girlfriend has a baby on the way while she's feeling as though she isn't good enough, doing enough, and is failing at life. I can't imagine how she could forgive the person who started that chain of events for her." My mother sighed as my heart was caught in a vice that squeezed tighter by the second. "She knew that you left to see if the grass was greener, if someone out there was better than her, and she's had that thought in her mind this whole time - that she wasn't good enough for you. You never came back. If you had come straight back, hell if you had the courage to talk to her like a grown ass man before you left, things might have been salvageable. With all the time that has passed, the amount of women you've dated, and the fact that she knows you were intimate with at least one of them without precautions…" Her voice trailed off as nausea swooped in to push my discomfort to the next level.

My heart sank even lower than I ever thought possible. I didn't respond to my mother at all because I was too lost in my thoughts. I'd lost her. My mom was right. What I had done to Opal was incomprehensible, especially now that I was seeing the whole picture with clear eyes. She would never take me back and worse - she absolutely hated me. How would that play out with my son? Would he one day hate me too because his mother couldn't stand to be in my presence? It would serve me right.

"Marshall, she also has seven years of loving you and knowing what a good man you can be. People make mistakes, sometimes big ones, and hopefully they learn from them. You just have to show her you learned from yours and that you're doing everything you can to make up for how those mistakes you made affected her."

After I hung up with my mother, I drifted off down memory lane, to better times, from before I screwed it all up.

There was a time, that no one knew about, when Opal tried to leave me. You wouldn't think I'd classify that as a 'happier time' but she did it for good reason. She did it for a selfless reason – for me.

"CAN WE TALK?" *Opal asked as I got ready to head to baseball practice.*

"*I have practice, babe. Can it wait until after?*"

"*Sure, I guess, it's just that…*" *her voice trailed off and she glanced around for a minute, watching all the other students pass us by in the hallway. "Well," she sighed, almost a defeated sound, "I guess it will be better if we talk in private.*"

"*Privacy is good,*" *I teased and winked at her before hurrying off. There was something sad in her voice, or maybe it was her eyes, that had me worried. During practice, the only thing I could think of was that Opal said the words every man dreads hearing from his girl.*

"*Yo! Crayfish, wait up!*" *I called to my best friend after practice was over. "I need some advice.*"

"*What kind of advice could you possibly need from me? You were coach's favorite out there, yet again.*" *He rolled his eyes, making it seem like he was just playing around, but for some reason it felt like everyone had a bone to pick with me that day.*

"*Opal asked if we could talk, earlier.*"

"*Why would she want us to talk? About what?*" *It was a little weird that he got excited about the prospect.*

"*She wants to talk to me about something. She stopped me before practice and said, "Can we talk?" Isn't that the line that everyone in a relationship is supposed to fear?*"

"*Nah, man. That would be if she said, "We need to talk."*"

"*It's the same fucking thing,*" *I argued.*

"*She gave you a choice. That means it can't be as bad as you're thinking, right?*"

"I don't know, man. I have this strange feeling." I rubbed my hand against the center of my chest, trying to get the pressure there to ease. It didn't.

"Well, if she's dumping you, it's probably about time," He huffed at me as he stripped out of his practice gear and headed for the showers.

"What the hell is that supposed to mean?"

"Dude, you just turned eighteen. The two of you have been dating for what? Three years? That's unheard of in high school. Besides, you're about to head to college. She's staying here and going to a state school, right? Those lunatic, hippy parents of hers probably can't afford anything better. You'll be off to Breakers U, and will no doubt have all the hot pussy you can handle. I bet you can't wait to sink into some strange, finally."

I popped the bastard in the back of the head. "Watch your mouth. First of all, wherever Opal goes, I'm following. Second, I have exactly what makes me happy. There's no need to chase any other women."

Cramer chuckled. "Yeah, okay man. Look," he glanced around. "She ain't around to hear you admit to shit, man. You're a guy with a swinging dick between his legs. You can't tell me that you haven't thought about other girls. What about Susan Barnes?" He said, naming the head cheerleader. I shook my head.

"Monica James is so into you she's gagging for that dick. I heard her trying to convince the rest of the pep squad to help her break you and Opal up. She would jump right on your dick, and you can't tell me you haven't fantasized about those tits of hers."

"Where do you even get this shit? I'm happy with Opal. I love her. She's my girlfriend and nothing is ever going to change that. Well, at least not until I put a ring on her finger and make her my wife."

"What the fuck, Marsh? You're eighteen-fucking-years-old. Live a little first."

I HAD FORGOTTEN about the locker room conversation I'd had with Cramer that day. It was overshadowed by what came next, but it also made me feel sick to my stomach to remember what he said about Monica. I should have remembered much sooner. Long before I ever agreed to a date with Monica James, because if Cramer was talking about her trying to break us up, that meant she had been giving Opal a bunch of shit back then to make it happen. Only, my girlfriend would have never laid that burden at my feet. She would have ignored it, dealt with it, and never let me know that something or someone was bothering her.

How in the hell had it come down to Monica? How had she become the only other woman I'd ever slept with, besides the love of my life? My mom might have been right. Opal couldn't possibly forgive that, even if she could find it in her heart to look past everything else I'd put her through.

"MARSH," *Opal started out with a slight crack to her voice, later that day,* "we need to talk about college."

"Yeah, we do. Where are we going?"

My girl shook her head slightly, as if to tell me 'no' about part, or all, of my question. I wasn't having it though.

"I think we should stay close to home, save some money by doing it, and then we'll be able to afford a house of our own sooner," I informed her.

"Marsh," *She called out to me again.* "Be reasonable."

"That is me being reasonable. Jimmy left college with so much debt that he had to join the military when he couldn't find a job right away. The twins are racking up more debt than STDs, which is a miracle between the two of them."

Opal winced at the mention of the STDs for some reason. My brothers were known to play it fast and loose with the women they encountered. One day, it would catch up to them and bite each of them in the ass, but until then, they were living it up and keeping good enough grades to continue going further into debt with student loans while they were at it. I didn't want that for myself. Even if Opal wasn't in the picture, it wouldn't be the path I took, no matter that my dad thought we'd all follow in his footsteps and go to his alma mater.

"Marsh, I think we should break up."

"Opal, do you love me?"

She swiped at a tear that had fallen down her pale cheek. "Of course, I love you. I think I've always loved you."

"Then why in the world would we break up? You are my everything, babe. I've loved you since the first moment I looked into your eyes after I knocked you down in the hallway." I grinned at her. That fateful fuckup of mine had been the beginning of us and there was no way I was ready for it to end. Hell, I'd never be ready for an ending with Opal. I meant what I said. She was my everything.

"Marsh, you are going to go to your father's school, and…"

"No, I'm not. We just talked about this. I don't want the kind of student loan debt my brothers have. Whether we were together or not, I wouldn't go there. I have scholarships lined up to help with a state school, where I'll come out after four years with barely anything to pay off. If I play things smart, I won't have any debt at all."

"Marsh, it's not just about cost, and you know it. It's been hard enough dealing with all the haters in high school since we've been together so long."

"What's that supposed to mean?"

"Well, half the female student body is perpetually pissed at me because they haven't had their shot at you yet."

"Who cares about them? They're just angry because I don't notice them, and why would I? You're all I see, babe. You're all I want to see. Why would I look past my own heart for something that would never compare?"

"Oh God! Marsh!" She hiccuped as she said my name because my silly girlfriend started crying. "That's the sweetest thing."

"No, Opal. The 'sweetest thing' is going to be the day you say 'yes' to marrying me. After that, the 'sweetest thing' will be the day that you really *do marry me. And just when I think we're all out of sweet, you'll give me a baby and that will be the 'sweetest thing' by far. Me telling you like it is, that's just being honest."*

"I love you, Marsh. So much, but I'm trying to do the right thing here."

"Telling me that we have to part ways, will never amount to doing the right thing."

"What about five years from now? Ten? Twenty? What about when you're older, and our kids are grown, and you look back on your life and wonder if you could have had someone different, something more than this?" She asked me in all sincerity. "College is the time everyone is supposed to explore other options."

"Do you want to explore other options, Opal?" She couldn't even answer through her tears, so instead, she shook her head. "Then what are you worried about?"

"I'm worried that one day, you'll get bored with me and I'll end up with a broken heart."

"Opal, I could never get bored with you. I'd choose you again and again, every day, for the rest of our lives. Never doubt that."

———

MAYBE THAT WALK down memory lane wasn't the best thing to do. I was not just an asshole, I was a complete piece of shit, and Opal had been right once again. She knew what our future would hold, what would happen with me feeling like we hadn't experienced enough apart. She knew it all along, and stuck it out with me anyway because I promised to always choose her. I wonder if she ever thought about that day, or my promises that ended up broken?

Chapter 17

OPAL

"I'M GOING TO LOVE YOU FOREVER, YOU KNOW THAT, RIGHT?"

"I hope so, because that's how I feel too," I whispered in his ear as he sank deeper into my body. Our heated skin brushed in so many places, lending a comforting sensualness to our lovemaking. Marsh knew innately how to bring me to the best orgasms. There was no denying that. We had our moments where we would simply get freaky and explore our sexualities with one another, but it was the moments like this one that I cherished the most.

"God, you feel so fuckin' good, babe."

"You fill me up just right," I answered back, as if he had asked a question. "I need you, all of you!" I demanded, and Marsh knew what that meant. I wanted him deep and hard. He had no problem obliging. His steady rhythm worked me into another approaching orgasm, as his cock massaged my g-spot on each downstroke, while his pubic bone simultaneously ground against my clit. "Yes, just like that," I cried out.

"Damn babe, you need to get there. The way your pussy is clenching me so tightly, I don't think I'm going to last." And then, he dipped his hand down between us and pinched my clit, giving me just enough added stimulation to tip me over the edge and trigger the release that I'd been chasing.

I AWOKE, panting and unable to catch my breath at first as my stomach contracted into a hard ball of tense muscle with my orgasm.

"What in the hell?" I asked my pillow.

I climaxed without even touching myself. Just a simple dream of being with Marsh set me off. It wasn't so much a dream, as a memory of a time we were together last year, before my world fell apart. Before Marsh tore it down, brick by brick, in his pursuit of something more.

Three weeks passed since the day he came to my apartment, and I figured that meant we were well and truly done. Especially since I was so close to giving birth, and he didn't seem to care about his son that I carried. Then again, maybe he was waiting until his son was actually here to give a damn. Who knew?

I'd warned him, years ago, when we were about to leave high school behind. He didn't listen then, and while I wish he would have, there's no way I'd want to change things, even the worst moments. If I did, there might not be a baby kicking at my belly so hard that I had to run to the little bathroom before I peed on myself – again. Poor boy. My dream must have triggered a reaction from my body that he wasn't used to experiencing.

"There is still no need to kick Mommy in the bladder," I scolded my enormous belly, playfully. "Once you get out of there, and I'm ready, I guess it will be time for Mommy to date and go explore her options too," I told my son. "I wish you never had to know a time when Mommy dated someone who isn't your daddy. It's not what I ever pictured for you, or me either, but this is the hand we've been dealt."

If I thought my son would argue, tell me I was stupid, or that I should wait for his father to pull his head completely out of his ass, I would most likely be waiting a good long while. My son settled back down as soon as my bladder was emptied. The couch was unforgiving as usual when I sat back down on it, and still there was no point in lying down again. I couldn't sleep after my brain tricked me into thinking Marsh was with me again. Stupid brain. Stupid memories. Stupid body. Stupid man. Why did I have to react to it?

The sun tried to stream in through the window of my shoebox sized apartment, but I had put thick, light blocking drapes up. Not that I necessarily wanted to block out all the light, but living where I did made me nervous. Most of the people that lived in the complex were wonderful and had introduced themselves. There was a single mother with two kids living on the floor above me who gave me a little pep talk about being strong enough to handle things on my own.

She also warned me about a few of the men in the area who tended to be pushy and intimidating. That was the part that scared me. There was no one who would come to my rescue if something happened. Bethany and her mom would, in a heartbeat, but they both worked a lot. The chances of one of them dropping in on any given day to check on me were not the greatest.

I slowly sat up on the couch, stretched some of the kinks out, and then took my time standing up too. I had been getting dizzy when I stood too quickly, but it was also awkward trying to get my pregnant belly to cooperate with the rest of my body. It felt like I had to do a damn backbend just to get up off the couch, and that sucked, especially first thing in the morning.

Once I peed again, showered, brushed my teeth, and got ready for my day, I realized there was nothing else to do except to wait an hour until my appointment. There was no way I was walking again. I'd already beaten myself up enough about having to spare the expense for a cab, yet again, but I just couldn't do it. Besides, Joe Marquette had become my regular

Uber driver, and he always managed to make me laugh before we got to our destination.

"What's on the agenda today?" Joe asked with a bright smile on his face as I got into his car. He was actually the only local Uber driver we had. The local taxi company was a bit too unreliable to keep calling on them, and that was how I met Joe.

"Doctor's appointment. I have to do them weekly now."

"That means you're really close, and probably plenty miserable," He surmised.

"And how would you know that, Joe?"

"I have two nieces, and my sister was miserable with both in the last month, and ready to just get it all over with."

I chuckled. "I think that's probably the case for any woman who has their bladder and ribs beaten on all day long." I squirmed in the seat, trying to get comfortable and finding nothing helped.

"You have anyone going with you?" It was cute that Joe worried about me so much. He was only about five or six years older than me, but he seemed more worldly and wise.

"The baby's uncle is supposed to meet me there."

"The uncle and not the father?" He asked with a questioning look in the rearview mirror.

"The father is absent. For about five minutes, I thought he wanted to be involved, but then he dropped off the face of the earth again. His younger brother is about to turn eighteen, and when he found out I was pregnant, he stepped up and made sure if I didn't have anyone else with me that he would be there. He's super excited to meet his nephew."

"He sounds like an awesome kid."

"He is. A lot like his brother used to be, if I'm being honest. I just hope he doesn't change the same way."

"Damn," Joe hummed as he shook his head. "Do you mind if I ask who the father is?"

I shrugged my shoulders, knowing it didn't really make a

difference in our small town. Most people already knew. "Marshall Kennedy."

"No fucking way!" He nearly shouted. "You're telling me Jimmy Kennedy's brother is the one who left you, even though you're pregnant with his kid?"

"You know Jimmy?"

"Yeah, we grew up together and used to be good friends, even started out college together until I couldn't afford it anymore. We don't stay in touch as much, since he's been overseas, but I guess that's to be expected."

"Yeah, but he should be home soon. Maybe you'll find that friendship again."

"Opal, for what it's worth, I'm sorry this happened to you. I just can't imagine anyone in that family dropping the ball like this."

"It's a bit of a long story," I admitted.

"Nah. Doesn't matter what the story is. You're pregnant with Marsh's kid. He should be by your side through this, even if the two of you aren't together anymore."

I swiped at a tear that trailed down my cheek. "The last time I saw him, about three weeks ago, I told him to stay away from me. He took me at my word."

Joe made a sound of disagreement and continued to shake his head. Then, as he pulled up to the curb in front of the doctor's office, he huffed out what sounded like a chuckle. "Well, I'll be damned. Looks like someone did not listen to you after all."

I glanced up in surprise, to see that Marsh was standing there waiting for me, instead of his brother. I pulled out my phone and shot a message off to Ryker.

> Opal: Why is Marsh waiting outside my doctor's office?

> Ryker: I couldn't miss school today and he deserves to go to at least one appointment, don't you think?

> Opal: He's had eight months to do that.

> Ryker: Technically, he's only had about a month since he found out. Let him do this, Opal. I think you both need it and before long my nephew will be here, and he will need for his parents to be able to have a conversation without yelling and anger involved. That has to start somewhere.

> Opal: Fine.

"You want me to go with you for support?" Joe asked, making me realize we'd been sitting there idle the whole time.

"I'm so sorry to keep you waiting, Joe. I was just hashing something out with Ryker."

He chuckled. "Opal, it isn't a problem at all. My offer wasn't meant to get you out of my car. It was a legitimate offer. If you need a buffer, I'll come stand by your side while you go through your appointment."

"Thanks, but I think I can handle it."

"Do you want me to wait until you're done?"

I shook my head. "There's no telling how long the wait will be once I get in there, so if you get another customer, you should take it."

"All right, just text when you're done, and I'll head back this way. If you need someone before then, let me know."

"Why are you being so nice to me?"

"Because you strike me as one of those people who deserves to be treated well, but it seems like everyone else has been dropping the ball. Maybe one day, when you're ready, you'll let me prove that there is someone out there who will appreciate and put you first. No pressure. You have enough on your plate right now, and I get that."

I blushed profusely. Was he saying what I thought he was saying?

"Yeah, Opal. I'm telling you that when you're ready, I'd like to take you out on a date."

"But, I'm about to have a baby," I argued.

"That might be true, but you're still a wonderful person with a great sense of humor, even when life has you down. I spend a lot of time with my nieces, so I'm not afraid to date a woman with kids. The ups and downs of parenthood aren't new to me."

I didn't know what to say, so I chose to remain silent, but offered a smile and a nod as I got out of his car.

"Who is that?" Marsh asked as he bent down to get a better look at the man who just dropped me off. I rolled my eyes at him.

"Seriously, Marsh? You can fuck whomever you want, and rub it in my face, but you're getting defensive because I got out of the back seat of some man's car?"

The tips of his ears turned red. Whether shame, embarrassment, or jealousy caused that, I didn't know and honestly didn't care either.

"It was just a question, Opal. He looked familiar."

"He's a friend of Jimmy's, so that's altogether possible." Marsh seemed relieved by that statement, and it bothered me, so I threw in the latest development in my life for him to chew on.

"He did ask me out though. He was a gentleman about it, and patient with my situation, knowing I wasn't ready yet. Who knows? After the baby arrives, I might take him up on it."

"Are you trying to hurt me?"

I stopped walking and turned to look him in the eye. "No.

I'm not trying to hurt you at all. It's just the reality of what's probably going to happen. Better that you have time to adjust now. I know what it's like to be blindsided by you telling me that you were leaving, so that you could be with other women. At least you have the chance to get used to the idea and figure out how to deal with it. Besides, you left me seven months ago. You couldn't possibly think I'd wait around on you to come back, could you?"

"Jesus, Opal," He breathed out while holding onto his chest. I wasn't a fan of hurting people for the sake of hurting them, or even out of revenge, but maybe Marsh needed a better understanding of what he'd put me through for all these months.

"I'm really not comfortable with you attending this appointment with me."

"That's my baby," He murmured.

"Yeah, and it's MY body that will be on display."

"It's not like I've never seen your body before, Opal."

"You haven't," I argued.

"We were together for seven years. I beg to differ."

"My body looks nothing like it used to. I wish Ryker hadn't told you about my appointment."

"And what were you planning on doing when you went into labor? Were you just not going to tell me?"

"I would have told you after our son was born."

"After? As in, you don't want me in the delivery room?" His eyes widened, and the shock there over me not wanting him in the delivery room was priceless.

"Why would I want my ex-boyfriend, who hurt me beyond any way words could describe, in the room with me when I'm at my most vulnerable?"

"Opal!" My name on his lips felt more like a plea for mercy.

"You can come today, but don't get your hopes up for

anything else, Marsh. After the baby is here, we'll work out something regarding visitation or whatever, but that's it."

"I would take it all back, if I could," He whispered.

"That's just it, Marsh. You can't take it back. It can't be undone." I turned toward the entrance of the doctor's office and made my way inside. It didn't even occur to me that I should be worried about confronting Monica until I was through the door. Thankfully, she wasn't there and check in was relatively painless. Too bad the wait wasn't.

"Do I even get a say in his name?" Marsh asked as he sat down beside me. I honestly hadn't even thought about that because as far as I was concerned, Marsh and I had already picked names years ago. I had planned to use one of them, despite how angry with him I was.

"HOW MANY KIDS DO YOU WANT?"

"Right now?" I asked with a laugh, because teasing Marsh was one of my favorite things to do.

"Obviously not, though it wouldn't be the end of the world if you happened to be pregnant now."

"If we have a girl, I want to name her Katrina Nichole," I told him.

"I like that. Wasn't your little sister's name going to be Nichole?"

"It was." My parents had a later in life child when I was fourteen. She was born early, after a complicated and risky pregnancy, and she only lived two days. I wanted to honor her memory, but didn't want to get lost in the sadness of missing all the times I should have had with her, so I quickly cleared the emotion from my throat and asked, "What about you?"

"If we have a boy, I want to name him Austin Jason Kennedy."

"Jason, for your dad's middle name?" I asked, to which he nodded.

"My dad is the best man I know, but I figure Jimmy, being the oldest, might want to have first dibs at naming a kid after him, so..."

"That's very considerate of you. I like the sound of it, so I guess we have a name for our first son and our first daughter."

WE ENDED up picking two more names for each gender, but Katrina Nichole and Austin Jason were the main ones we wanted to use. Marsh gently nudged my shoulder with his arm, bringing me back out of the memory.

"Where did you go just now?"

"I was remembering when our son got his name. You already picked it, Marsh."

He sucked in a quick breath, obviously surprised by my admission. "You're still going to use Austin Jason?"

"It's what we chose together, why wouldn't I?"

"I thought maybe you were so angry with me that you wouldn't do anything I had put any thought into."

"No matter what, we're both this baby's parents. He deserves to have something from each of us, something that represents a time in our lives when we were together and loved one another."

"I still love you, Opal, with all my damn heart."

I didn't return the sentiment. The love for him might have still been there, but it was buried under too much hurt, betrayal, and sadness for me to muster up the words. Besides, he didn't really deserve to hear them anyway after everything.

"Opal?" Tanya, my favorite nurse, called out from the doorway that opened up to where the exam rooms were. "We're ready for you," she added when I looked up.

Carefully, I did my belly-forward, backbend stand from the chair and then wobbled toward her. She grinned at me as I made my way to her. "I see your waddling skills are advancing," She teased.

"Paint me black and white and call me a penguin," I answered back, leaving us both giggling.

I didn't miss the way her eyes tracked back to Marsh and then to me before she leaned in to whisper, "Do you want him back here for all of this, or should we leave him in the waiting room and call him once you've changed?"

"Oh, gosh, I forgot about the changing part. Thanks for the reminder." I turned to Marsh then. "You need to wait here for now, they'll call you when I'm ready."

"Why?"

"I have to go pee in a cup, get weighed, and then change into the stupid paper gown that they give me to wear."

Marsh sighed, but for once complied with my demands without argument. It was almost like he'd been expecting it, so I assumed Ryker had filled him in on procedure and he'd just been hoping that the same rules wouldn't apply to him that applied to his brother.

Once I was ready, Tanya came back into the room and gave me a knowing look. "We could forget to tell him that you're ready," She suggested.

I couldn't stop the giggle that erupted from me. Not because I wanted to hurt Marsh that way, but just for the sake that it was nice to have someone on my side for once.

"Thanks, Tanya, but he needs to see that this baby is real."

"Honey, you're a small girl. Did he think you were smuggling a basketball under your shirt all this time?" She teased. Again, I had to laugh, because if I didn't, crying was my only option. She must have realized, as she came over and put her arm around me in a quick hug. "I'll go get him for you. You just sit tight, and the doctor will probably be in soon after."

"Thank you." The quietly spoken appreciation wasn't necessarily about her going to fetch Marsh. I truly appreciated the human contact.

A few minutes later, Marsh was escorted into the room and thankfully, the doctor came in right behind him, so there wasn't any awkward wait with my ex-boyfriend standing there staring at me while I only had the thin barrier of the gown between us.

"Opal, how has the little guy been treating you?" Dr. Burns asked, as he moved to the foot of the exam table and sat on the stool.

"The kicks to the bladder have lessened, but he's putting a hurting on my ribs these days," I complained.

"To be expected. He's getting ready for his entrance into the world. Sounds like he's turned head down now."

"Is that normal?" Marsh asked.

Dr. Burns turned ever so slightly to acknowledge him. "Well, we do like for babies to be born head first. The other way tends to cause problems for both mom and baby."

"No, I meant her being in so much pain from the baby kicking," Marsh clarified.

"Well, that's fairly normal. Babies move around in there, and they don't have a lot of room to do it, especially at this stage."

"How about everything else, Opal? Tanya said you mentioned something about being dizzy often when she was taking your vitals."

"I wouldn't say often, but whenever I stand up, if I'm not careful, and do it too quickly, I end up with a dizzy spell that takes a minute to clear."

Dr. Burns seemed a bit concerned by that. "Now, I know at this point in your pregnancy, getting up too quickly is pretty much out of the question, so that development concerns me a bit. Sounds like your blood pressure's been a bit low." He glanced down at the tablet in his hands and nodded his head. "It's not at concerning levels today, but I want you to be aware of how you're feeling and take precautions. Usually, we see low blood pressure as a norm before twenty-four weeks, but you're way beyond that."

"Is there something you can give her?" Marsh asked.

Dr. Burns shook his head. "I want you to take your time getting up when seated or lying down," He chuckled at the suggestion. "I know, you already have to, but take it a little slower if necessary. Don't stand or sit for long periods without breaks. You also need to drink plenty of water too. Hydration is always important. Don't wear constricting clothing, take hot baths or showers, and make sure you're eating small meals all day long, not just a couple of big meals." He thought for a minute. "And you really shouldn't be taking baths at all, just showers, if you can help it."

He glanced at Marsh and then back to me. "Do you have someone who can be around more for the next couple of weeks? I'd hate for your blood pressure to dip with no one around. The obvious concern is a dizzy spell that causes you to faint or fall. Pregnant women are already off balance enough. It's easy for accidents to happen."

"I'll see if my friend can stay with me when she's not working."

"Good. Now, let's take a listen, shall we?"

Dr. Burns moved my gown up and thankfully made sure that the little sheet across my lap was high enough that no one was flashed my goods just yet. The minute my belly came into view, Marsh gasped so loudly that the doctor and I both looked at him.

There were tears in his eyes. At first, I didn't understand why, and then it dawned on me. It was the first time he saw my pregnant belly, and not just the way it looked under a shirt. I supposed there was a difference when he was used to seeing my petite pre-pregnancy body.

I moved to cover my belly, self-conscious of the other changes, like the wicked red and purplish stretch marks that branched out from down near my groin up to my belly button. Dr. Burns clucked his tongue at me and moved my hands away.

"I'm not letting you get away with doing that in this office. There's nothing wrong with the way you look," He chastised, but I think that his warning was meant for Marsh as much as it was for me.

"No, there's not," Marsh agreed. "I just hadn't seen her belly before and it took me by surprise."

"Well, women's bodies tend to change a lot during pregnancy, and if you haven't been there, stands to reason it might be a shock to see it for the first time." Dr. Burns sent a wink my way, to let me know he had my back. It was appreciated, but wholly unnecessary. We all knew that Marsh had been absent this whole pregnancy. There really wasn't a reason to rehash it.

The familiar whooshing sound of my son's heartbeat came over the speakers after Dr. Burns ran the wand across my belly. "What is that?" Marsh asked.

"That is the little guy's heartbeat."

"That's my son's heart?" Marsh asked, with no small amount of wonder in his voice. For a minute, I let go of all the hurt and anger and just basked in that feeling. The one that should have accompanied me to every single appointment after that first one. The awe that he had for the son we'd made together, forced me to remember all the good things about Marsh. That realization came with its own burden of painful emotion.

Had he remained the same man, the one standing beside me, in awe of his son, then maybe things would have been so different for us. Happier. Like they used to be, or at least, like I thought they used to be. Obviously, Marsh hadn't been as happy as I had been with our relationship. That was the part that was so hard to swallow. I wondered again what I had done, or not done, to make him unhappy enough with our relationship that he just up and called it quits after seven years.

We didn't even fight that much. I turned away from the man and stared at the wall until Dr. Burns removed the wand from my belly.

"Okay, Opal, onto the part you hate." He pulled the gown back down over my belly and pulled the sheet up higher on my knees as he helped me place my feet in the stirrups. "I just need to check to see if there's any change in your cervix."

I nodded and bit down on my lip, completely uncomfortable with having an audience for this part. Feeling another man's fingers inside me, even for something as practical as checking for dilation, was unnerving as the only other man in my life that had them there stood by my side with a scowl on his face, watching.

"Hmm," Dr. Burns glanced up at me as he uncomfortably dug around.

"That doesn't sound like a good noise, Doc," I suggested.

"Well, Opal, how do you feel about going into labor a bit earlier than we predicted?"

"Terrible and overjoyed?" I spouted out my answer even though it sounded more like a question. Dr. Burns chuckled.

"That probably sums it up nicely. You are one of my most honest patients. It makes my job far easier. That doesn't change the fact that you're already dilated to three centimeters."

"What exactly does that mean?" I asked, with more than a little worry in my voice.

"It means that you need to stay off your feet as much as possible over the next couple weeks, if you last that long, otherwise you're going to go into labor sooner, rather than later."

"I'm not ready," I blurted. "There's still a week left of work before I'm out for the summer, and…"

Dr. Burns stopped me there. "Just breathe. I'm not saying

it's for sure going to happen early. Some women dilate like this and carry to term or beyond. Others go within hours or days."

"Hours? No. Nope. That can't happen. I still have almost four weeks to go!"

"The baby is going to come when he's ready, but we are well within a healthy time frame. You're only a few days shy of thirty-seven weeks."

I focused on being able to breathe as he spoke. "Remember when I asked earlier if you had someone who could stay with you because of the low blood pressure?" I nodded. "Well, this is an added reason to make sure that happens."

I glanced over at Marsh, who hadn't said a word during any of this. "Don't worry. I'll make sure you're covered, no matter what," He promised. If only I could believe in him. There was no way my blood pressure wasn't up at that point because I was honestly scared. What if I was at the apartment alone and went into labor? I didn't have a car, not that I'd be able to drive myself anyway.

"Maybe I should check with Joe about being on call for emergencies, just in case," I mumbled to myself.

"Who in the hell is Joe?"

"My Uber driver," I announced with little thought.

"The same Uber driver who asked you out on a date, today?" Marsh asked, exasperation clear in his tone.

I thought I caught Tanya sniggering over by the door as the doctor pulled off his gloves and threw them away. "All right, Opal, one final question for you, we never came to a decision about what you wanted to do for pain if you need help during the labor process. We're running out of time for those decisions."

"Not that you can't change your mind later, if you need to, but it does help to know up front," Tanya added for him.

"Tanya's right. You can always change your mind, but it's good to go in with a solid plan."

"I don't want any help unless it is absolutely necessary. I've read a lot about the effects of drugs and even epidurals on babies."

"Well, some of that..." Dr. Burns started to say, but I waved him off.

"I understand that the chances of complications seem to be slim, but I'd like to try to keep everything as natural as possible. I've already put my poor boy through so much with my emotions being all over the place and the amount of walking I've had to do."

Dr. Burns patted the covered part of my leg and smiled at me. "It's your show, Opal. We'll try everything natural, but if you decide you need help, I want you to ask for it. Don't be stubborn. Pain can add to stress, which can cause issues too. The good news is, you are in prime health. The walking, while not ideal amounts, means you're in better shape than a lot of pregnant women."

"The prenatal yoga too," I added.

The doctor nodded again and then stood. "Is there anything else on your mind? Any questions you need answered?"

"No. Just worried about everything happening sooner than it's supposed to."

"I assure you that you are in good hands. Now, we're going to get you up and out of here. Assuming nothing progresses, I'll see you again in a week. If not, we'll get to meet your baby real soon. Stay off your feet as much as possible and try to keep the stress down." The last part was said with a pointed look toward Marsh. "One more thing, since we did a vaginal exam, you might notice a bit of spotting and your mucus plug might also make an appearance. I don't want you to panic, if that happens. If you have more than a little bit of spotting though, I want you to call the office immediately. If it's a lot, go directly to the emergency room."

After that lovely spiel, the doctor and Tanya cleared out of the room. We were left alone, while I tried to decide how I was going to get dressed again with Marsh still present. There was a screen to hide behind, but hiding while pregnant seemed nearly impossible.

"You either need to leave or turn around," I said as I sat up on the exam table and carefully tried to get my feet down from the stirrups. Marsh came over and took hold of my arm when I had trouble maneuvering my awkward body.

"Please, let me help you. Once you're up and solid on your feet, I'll turn around, I promise."

"Stop promising me things."

"Okay, still, I'll honor your wishes. Just, let me help first."

"Fine," I huffed. After Marsh helped me up, it didn't take too long to get dressed, and then he walked with me to the checkout window to get my next appointment set up. Unfortunately, my luck had run out because Monica James stood there, smugly smirking at me before her eyes drifted over my shoulder and locked on Marsh.

"Well, maybe there's hope if I turn up pregnant. Seems you figured out how to step up after all." Monica was not being quiet about her pronouncement, as several of the other women working the front desk area and a woman who was checking in, all gasped and stared at us.

"I seem to recall you telling me that if you accidentally got pregnant, after the one time we had sex, even though I couldn't finish with you, that you would get an abortion. So, that really wouldn't be an issue for you, since you don't want to be pregnant, huh?" Marsh threw back at her. I was so embarrassed, especially when I realized Dr. Burns was within hearing distance of their little verbal sparring war.

"Ms. James? A word?" Dr. Burns called out. I couldn't hear what was said between the doctor and Monica, but she did not come back after he finished speaking to her. Instead, he turned back to me and offered up a sad excuse for a smile. "Someone else will help you arrange your next appointment, and you will not have to deal with Monica at any future appointment." He turned to leave, but Marsh stopped him.

"Can I speak to you, for a moment?"

Dr. Burns moved to the little window where we'd been standing during this awful scene, waiting to schedule my exam for the following week. "I'm truly sorry that happened," He apologized again.

"That's not what I want to talk to you about. A month ago, or close to that, Monica told me information about Opal's pregnancy that I wasn't aware of previously."

"What information was that?"

"She informed me that Opal's file said the father knew about the pregnancy and refused to be a part of it. For the record, that wasn't true, as Opal had been misled by someone else that I'd been informed. I never knew until that day when Monica and I were eating lunch and saw Opal outside the café. She told me things that were in Opal's medical chart, and led me to believe that someone else was the father. That is something I meant to discuss with you before now, but since I just found out I was going to have a baby soon, other things took precedence."

"Understandable," Dr. Burns stated. "I might need you to fill out a formal complaint, both of you, regarding the situation." He sighed. "Considering the timing, it can wait until after you've had the baby," He said while addressing me. "This falls under the realm of don't stress yourself out too much over the next few weeks. I'm sorry that one of my staff members contributed to that. It will not happen again. Considering you expressed concerns when you first saw her working here, and I assured you that wouldn't be a problem, you have my sincerest apologies."

Dr. Burns turned to Marsh after that. "I take your accusation very seriously, and she will be put on administrative leave while we handle the complaint.

Once we got my appointment straightened out, and left the office, I realized that I forgot the most important thing, securing a ride home.

"Dammit," I hissed under my breath while pulling my phone out.

"What's wrong?"

"Thanks to your bitchy girlfriend, I forgot to text Joe for a ride home, so that he'd be here when I got out."

Marsh put his hand over mine, so I wouldn't be able to text. "Stop. First, she's not my girlfriend. Never was. The only person who has ever held the distinction was you. Second, my truck is just across the street. I can take you home."

"No offense, Marsh, but I can't climb into your truck like this." I pointed to my belly for emphasis.

"I'll help you get in. Please, let me take you home. We have a few things to discuss anyway, don't you think?"

I sighed because it was true. We did have things to work out, especially since it looked like our son might make an earlier arrival, rather than a later one. "Fine. If you can manage to get my whale of a body up into your truck, you can take me home," I relented much to Marsh's amusement.

"You do not have a whale's body."

"Whatever," I huffed in response.

Chapter 18

MARSH

My heart soared when Opal agreed to let me take her home. It made what I had to do far easier, because the only other alternative was to kidnap her or make my brother pick her up under false pretenses. While I appreciated Ryker being there for my girlfriend – ex-girlfriend, I didn't want him there for what I had to show her. That was a memory I wanted to savor between the two of us.

"Where are you going? My apartment is in the opposite direction." Opal demanded.

"Maybe so, but your *home* is in this direction, and I told you that I'd take you *home*."

Her frustrated grumbling didn't go unnoticed, even as I pretended not to hear her. There was little hope left in my heart that Opal would forgive me for everything I'd put her through, especially after that confrontation with Monica just put what I'd done at the forefront of her mind again. If anything might help, it would be the surprise I had in store for my girl.

Opal took in another exaggeratedly deep breath. "Please,

Marsh, you heard the doctor. I'm not supposed to stress myself out."

"I know. You're also supposed to have someone stay with you, especially since you might go into labor at any time. I promise, this will all make sense when we get there."

Another major sigh that seemed to suck all the available oxygen out of the cab of the truck later, and we turned off onto the road that went to the school where Opal worked.

"You heard 'de-stress' and decided to take me to work?" She commented dryly.

I laughed. "Just wait, sweetheart."

"Don't call me that."

"What?"

"Sweetheart," She answered.

"Why not? That's what you are to me."

"No, it's not. I don't have a place in your heart anymore, Marsh."

"That's where you're wrong, Opal. You might not believe me just yet, because I let you down and screwed everything up, but you will."

She didn't think I noticed when she rolled her eyes, but I did. Eventually, she would believe me again. She had to because I didn't think I could live with myself if I saw her go off on a date with Joe freaking Uber driver, or anyone else for that matter.

Two minutes later, I pulled into the driveway of the house that I only managed to close on two days previous. It was two weeks earlier than the owners originally wanted, but my parents helped me finagle a deal to get them to approve getting it done sooner.

"Whose house is this?" Opal asked, her brows furrowed as I turned the truck's engine off.

"It's our house."

She laughed. It was a sound that I hadn't heard in forever,

and if there hadn't been a hard edge behind it, would have overjoyed me to hear it again.

"Right. Our house." She laughed again. "We are not even an 'us' any longer, so there's definitely no "our" in play with this house. Please, take me home. I'm not in the mood for whatever torment you have in store for me this week."

"Opal," I said, and waited until she turned to give me her attention. It killed me to see her warm brown eyes blurring with unshed tears. "I bought this house for us, but until you're ready for there to be an 'us' again, it's all yours. Well, yours and Austin's."

She shook her head in denial.

"Will you at least let me show it to you?"

We sat there for a few moments before she finally answered me. "We're already here, and I have to go to the bathroom. God, I hope you have toilet paper in there already."

I couldn't help laughing at her, but I honestly didn't know. My mom had been by the day before to stock what she called, 'the basics' in the place. Hopefully, that included toilet paper because it didn't look like Opal was joking about the bathroom thing.

I got out and moved around the truck to help her down. She looked so damn tired. Beautiful, but tired. I reached up and wrapped one of my arms around her waist. "Just hold onto my shoulders and I'll lift you down." She actually did as I asked and then allowed me to keep my arm around her as I guided us to the front door. I thanked every lucky star in the universe that she didn't immediately swat me away from her as I sorted through the keys on my chain to get to the correct one.

"I have a key for you too," I told her as I reluctantly let go to open the door.

"I won't need one," She argued in a quiet voice.

When I opened the door, and Opal walked inside, the gasp she made told me that my mom had indeed made sure everything looked perfect. What I didn't expect was the picture of Opal and me from two years ago that now hung on the wall, front and center, across from the door. It was blown up to portrait size and brought back so many damn memories.

"Is this where you've been living? I thought you were staying with your brothers?"

"No. I just took possession a couple days ago. I tried to get it sooner, when I realized you were walking everywhere, but this was as quickly as I could get into it."

"So, you bought a house because you found out I was walking to and from work?"

"Yeah, Well, no. I planned to buy it when I found out you were pregnant."

The little bit of light present in her eyes, dimmed immediately, and I knew I'd said something wrong, but couldn't for the life of me figure out what it was.

"I don't want your house," She said. "I just need to use the bathroom and then I'd like to go home."

"You are home, Opal. This is your home. I got it for you."

She pointed at the picture of us. "Do you think I'd want that hanging in my home? It is a literal reminder of everything I lost, everything you threw away. It's also a reminder of everything you stole from me."

"What? I didn't steal anything."

"Liar!" She accused. "When you left, you took every single one of our memories with you. Every picture. Every item we purchased together, outside of the crappy furniture, you took it all."

"No. That wasn't what I was doing. I just couldn't bear to part with anything."

"And you thought I could? I'm glad you had the comforts of our memories, because I was left with an empty apartment, an overwhelming emptiness in my soul, and a baby that you didn't want."

"I never said I didn't want our baby, Opal. That wasn't me. I swear to you, I would have never said that."

"No, but you did say that you didn't want me."

"No."

"Yes! You leaving and taking all our memories, telling me that we needed to explore other people, that more than said I wasn't in your heart any longer." She threw her arms up and spun around once in a rather clunky fashion that had more to do with her awkward waistline than anything. "Why did you even do this?"

"Because I love you. I never stopped loving you. You needed a house, space to move, and a safe place to raise our son. Plus, it will put you closer to work until I can get you a car."

She laughed again in that odd, non-humorous way. "If you were so concerned, you could have helped me get a car, paid my medical bills so I could get one for myself, or anything other than trying to buy me off with a house that I have to share with you."

"I don't have to stay here, if that's what you want. It can be just yours. I think, for now, considering what the doctor said, it would be wise if I stayed. But once the baby is here, if you want me gone, I'll leave."

"That's convenient," She mumbled.

"Make no mistake, Opal, I don't want to leave, but I won't force myself on you either. We're having a baby. You can't be left alone right now, and the first few weeks to months after he's born, are going to be a major adjustment. There's three bedrooms. We don't have to share."

"Well, that's certainly good news." She turned and went in search of the bathroom. Every time she came upon another picture of us hanging on the wall, I could hear her grumbling about stolen memories.

My mom thought she was doing something good when she

hung them. I was sure she thought it would help, but damn if it didn't backfire in the worst way. It was also a kick to the teeth. I hadn't meant to leave Opal with no memories of us. I'd never knowingly do that to her, but as I was packing that day, I would find another picture, ticket stub, or whatever else and then drop them in my boxes with everything else. I understood how angry she must be with me, since I wasn't able to leave without those things. I would have been ruined if she'd left and taken everything with her. Those memories were what kept me going. I knew one day I would end up back with her. My heart always knew what it wanted, if only my head - and everyone in it - hadn't fucked it all up.

By the time Opal made it back to the living room, I was fuming mad at myself. There was no denying I had been a fool for ever leaving my girl, but to leave her with no reminders of our happier times, was pure idiocy on my part. She no reminders of how good we were together, so she was stuck clinging to the last things about us that were true. I left. I took everything. She also believed that I never wanted our baby and left him too.

Chapter 19

OPAL

EVERYTHING LOOKED SO INVITING WHEN I WALKED IN. Honestly, it was the picture of what I wanted to do with the house we were saving for. Marsh must have remembered, or maybe he had all the things saved on his laptop from where we used to window shop online. Planning our dreams of not only homeownership, but making it truly our home, had been some of the most amazing memories with him over the past few years.

We were planning a future together and that always left me feeling exhilarated. Having it all ripped away from me in the course of one day simply left me weary. If he thought I would move into this house, under any circumstances, he was crazy. Why would I do that to myself again? My body sagged with the prospect of having to deal with any of it.

When I couldn't stall any longer, after actually taking care of business, I finally made my way out to the living room to the most unexpected sight ever. Marsh sat slumped into himself on the couch, face buried in his hands, and shoulders shaking as he cried. He wasn't just crying, it was full-on sobbing, the likes of which I had never seen him do. For a minute, my heart broke for him. Then, I remembered he had been the one to put me in the same position, only I was left crying for many days and nights, for months on end.

"Can you take me home now?"

He quickly swiped away the tears on his face with his arm before looking up at me. "I told you, Opal, this is your home. I bought it for you."

"Once again, you didn't give me any say in that before you went and made a decision that might affect me. You keep planning for my future, all on your own, without including me. So, my answer is no. I do not want to live with you again. I do not want to live anywhere that has your name attached to it either, whether you're here or banned from the place."

"Why not? You have to admit it is convenient as hell to work and by far a better neighborhood than the one you're living in."

"And again, it has your name attached to it."

"Opal," He started in a placating tone.

"No. Not happening."

"Give me one good reason."

"I've already been tossed aside like yesterday's garbage once, and left to pick up the pieces; I won't do that again. Dammit, Marsh, I have to worry about what else you'll decide is best for me without even asking. Maybe I shouldn't work because I have a son to raise, but then you decide that some shiny new woman at a party made you feel good, so you'll throw me out to make room for her and spare me the hurt of you cheating? Never mind that I have no income, because that doesn't affect you directly. What will it be next? What decision for MY LIFE will you dictate while I have no say?"

He sat there, taking in every word of my angry tirade before finally he huffed out a deep breath and stood up.

"Come on then, I'll take you back to your apartment." His agreement made it sound as though someone had died. I supposed for him, it was almost the same. He just lost all hope that our relationship could be salvaged. He was right in thinking that, because it couldn't be saved the way he kept trying to do it.

When I opened the front door to leave, Marsh stopped me in my tracks. "Do you want some of the pictures?"

I shook my head. "I've gotten by for seven months without those memories. I'm good now."

It might have been cruel, but no worse than the way he'd treated me. I didn't wait around for any other offer that might come from him to hold us there longer. Instead, I made my way out to the truck and stood there by the passenger side waiting for him to come help me back in. The whole time, I debated calling Joe to come get me instead. Though, I wasn't sure I'd be able to use Joe's services, knowing how he felt. He might think I'd be ready to get back out there in the dating world once I was no longer pregnant, but I didn't think that would be the case.

I couldn't un-break my own heart, and that was what it would take for me to change my mind about men and their place in my life. The only man who would get the benefit of the doubt from me would be my son, and I still had eighteen years of raising the boy until he got there. Did that make me a bitter woman? Probably. Knowing that didn't change my outlook though.

———————

BETHANY WAS THERE, waiting for me to get back, when I returned home.

"I've been so worried about you!" She damn near shouted as I opened the door. Marsh hadn't come up with me, because I forbade him to.

"Sorry, today has been a complete mess from start to finish."

"Sit down," She ordered as a bottle of water was thrust into my hand. "Now, tell me everything." And so, I did.

"Let me get this straight, the man bought you a whole house, furnished it the way you always dreamed about, and then you came back to this dump? No offense," She tacked on at the end. I'd be offended if she wasn't correct.

"He didn't buy the house for 'me'. He bought it for 'us', which means strings are attached. Even if he doesn't pull them yet, he will. Plus, it also means that the rug can be pulled out from beneath my feet at a moment's notice. Would you really move out of this dump just to jump into uncertainty with a baby possibly hours or days away?"

My best friend pouted as she contemplated my dilemma for a moment. "I see your point. Still, that's a huge thing for him to have done. Did you at least talk things out a bit? Get something settled about visitation and custody, or do you think we need to get you a lawyer?"

"We didn't get to talk about anything except all the pictures of us that were hung around the house like it was some kind of shrine to our relationship."

"Well, if he's trying to win you back, that's probably exactly what it was."

"It was in poor taste, considering."

"Yeah, I see your point there, too."

I laughed, after taking a healthy slug from my bottle of water. "The crazy thing is, he pretended like he didn't know he took everything with him when he left."

Beth listened to me rant and rave for another few minutes before she sighed. "Your whole situation sucks and I'm sorry you're having to go through it all while pregnant with his baby. I'm sure that makes it a million times harder."

"It does. No matter what, I'll have to deal with him for at

least the next eighteen years and then for special occasions after that involving our son." I groaned in misery as I pictured what that future might look like. "What if my son ends up with a step-monster like Monica?"

"Then we'll go out for target practice and make sure we're ready if she ever steps a toe out of line. We can start saving now for bail money, or get out of the country money, which-ever we can get away with."

I laughed at her suggestion because knowing Bethany, she was serious as a heart attack. She would go with me and my son to a foreign country to hide out after killing Marsh's wife, fiancé, girlfriend, fuck buddy, or whomever dared to mess with my boy. That was true friendship.

"So, Uber Joe asked you out?" Beth asked as she waggled her eyebrows at me.

"Stop! That is so not happening."

"Pshh, wait and see how you feel in a couple months. Time changes things. Besides, I think it would be good for Mr. Marshal Kennedy to see exactly what it feels like to watch the love of his life dating someone else."

"I'm not the love of his life," I argued.

"Agree to disagree."

"How can you say that?" I asked in all seriousness.

"Honey, I think the boy did something completely idiotic after years of being taunted, tormented, and worn down by his friends and family. They basically brainwashed him into believing that he wasn't meant to be with you until he got other people out of his system for sure."

I rolled my eyes at her assessment because if he really loved me, none of what they had to say would have mattered.

"Was he a moron? Yes. Did he do idiotic things? Yes, again. Did he break your heart to pieces and make me want to break his legs and his dick in much the same way? Also yes. Does any of that mean you aren't the love of his life? No. Anyone with a pair of working eyeballs can see that you two are soulmates. Hell, even a blind person could see it just by spending five minutes in a room with you. The energy you two put off is electric."

"A soulmate wouldn't do that to their other half," I whispered.

"Normally, I'd agree with you. I'm not saying you should forgive him, forget what he did, or not go on living your life and making decisions like he doesn't exist beyond his connection to your son. I'm just saying that the man never stopped loving you. It's obvious."

I shrugged my shoulders and changed the subject because it hurt too much to consider that Marsh might still be in love with me, despite what he'd done to destroy us.

"I could have this baby at any moment," I declared.

"Holy shit! Are you having contractions?" Bethany yelped as she jumped up and looked between my legs.

"What are you doing?"

"Checking to see if your water broke?"

We both started laughing so hard that I peed a little and that just made us laugh even more. It was something I hadn't done much of in a long while, and something about it was almost healing in a way.

"Ow, my stomach hurts now," I complained through the waning laughter. "You're going to make me go into labor from laughing too much."

"I'm pretty sure that's not a thing."

"You don't know," I challenged.

"I'm a nurse," She corrected, as if that meant everything.

"You work in a pediatrician's office."

"I moonlight two weekends a month in the emergency room. Trust me, we see everything there."

"That's true," I conceded.

Beth glanced around again and frowned. "Are you sure you can't take Marsh up on staying in the three-bedroom house?"

"What? No! Why?"

"Because, it's going to suck camping out on your floor until you go into labor."

"Aw! You'd do that for me?"

"I'd give you my left kidney if you needed it."

I stared at her for a moment before she asked, "What?"

"Is there something wrong with your right kidney?"

"Nah, I just thought having to carry around the extra weight on my dominant-hand side would be a bonus," She rolled her eyes at my ridiculous question, as if pointing out which kidney she'd give wasn't equally nutso.

"Thank you for being the best, best friend a girl could ask for."

"Thank you for being the same."

No matter what, I could rest assured that my boy would be born into a world where we had at least one good person at our back and I would teach him by example to make sure he always reciprocated that. It was something positive to look forward to.

Chapter 20

MARSH

"How did it go?" My mom asked immediately when I entered the house. Ryker was there, in the kitchen, baking cookies with her. He seemed a bit on edge, as if he was waiting for a full report too.

"It sucked."

"What did you do?" Ryker accused.

"The best part of today was getting to hear my son's heart beating."

My little brother's grin said it all. He had already experienced that and got to see my son on a sonogram too. That was something I'd never experience, since Opal was so close to giving birth.

"What else happened to bring you so down, Son?"

"Where should I start?"

"How about the beginning?"

"I fucked up and left the love of my life," I started.

"We all know that part. Maybe fast forward to when you were waiting at the doctor's office for Opal to show up. Was she surprised?"

"I don't think she had time to be surprised since her Uber

driver, who happens to be friends with Jimmy, asked her out on a date."

Ryker couldn't hold back his laughter, even as our mother smacked him in the back of the head. It was mostly a playful slap.

"What? It's not like he didn't deserve to see her with someone else after what she had to witness him doing while she was alone, heartbroken, and pregnant with his kid."

"Thanks for summing up just how stupid I've been, Ry."

"You're welcome," He tossed back with plenty of attitude.

"Anyway," I continued. "After that, I had to wait in the waiting room while Opal did a bunch of things and got into one of those paper-thin gown thingies."

"Of course, you did."

"I got her pregnant. I've obviously seen her naked before."

"That was before," My mother said as she waved off my observations.

"That's what she said." Again, Ry thought my statement was hilarious for his own juvenile reasons.

"Mom, we need to be prepared, because the doctor said Opal is already dilated to three centimeters and she can basically go into labor any time."

"Oh, she's a bit early."

"He didn't seem too concerned. Said she's in range at almost thirty-seven weeks."

My mom did some kind of calculation in her head, or at least that's what it looked like. "I suppose the doctor is right about that. I had the twins at thirty-five weeks and they only spent two days in the NICU."

"Maybe you shouldn't use the twins as an example of perfect health," I muttered.

"Oh hush. Your brothers might have led you down the wrong path, but you followed them willingly, and you were born at forty-two weeks." She gave me the look she always did that said she still wasn't over the fact that I was too stubborn to come out on my due date.

"Mom, why did you hang those pictures at the house?"

My mom beamed such a beautiful smile at me that I couldn't really be mad at her. I knew she had the best of intentions. Plus, she couldn't possibly know that my moronic behavior far exceeded what any of us previously thought.

"Oh! You took her to the house? How does she like it? Is she settling in? Wait! What on earth are you doing here? You said she could go into labor at any moment. You should be there with her, just in case."

"Mom, take a breath," Ryker admonished. "It doesn't seem as though it went that well, remember?"

For the first time in months, I think my brother actually felt bad for me and the situation I'd gotten myself into.

"What happened?" My mother asked as she quickly wiped her hands on a towel before coming to wrap her arms around me. That was when I broke, and for the second time, I fucking lost control of my emotions and sobbed into my mother's hair.

"Oh! My baby." Mom cooed as she rubbed her hands up and down my back in an effort to comfort me. "What happened?"

"She wasn't too keen on seeing the house to begin with. Refused to even acknowledge that I got it for her, but when we went inside and she saw the picture hanging there, she lost it on me."

"Why?"

I told them about how I took all the pictures and anything that wasn't bolted down or furniture that had a memory attached.

"Oh, Marshall, if I had known…" My mom started to say, but couldn't finish her thought because my brother broke in with his.

"That was cruel," Ryker added.

"I didn't do it on purpose. It never even... I didn't real-ize... Fuck! How did I go from living a happy life with her to this?"

No one bothered to answer because they didn't have to. We all knew how everything went down. We sat there silently staring at nothing until the timer on the oven beeped.

"Do you mind if I stay here tonight? I can't bring myself to go back to the twins' place."

"What about the house?" Mom asked.

"Can't go there either. It's hers. She made it pretty clear that she'll never accept it if I'm attached to it in any way, so I won't spend a single night in it. Not unless she invites me to."

"Oh, Marsh, what are you going to do if she never accepts it?"

"I don't know, Mom."

"Keep trying then. That's all you can do."

"Yeah."

Chapter 21

OPAL

"OPAL, I HAVE SOME BAD NEWS."

I stared at my best friend as she worked the kinks out of her neck. She ended up bringing an air mattress over to sleep on, which looked way more comfortable than my couch, but apparently wasn't.

"I'm afraid to ask," I admitted.

"There's no getting out of my emergency room commitment this weekend. There's some stomach bug going around and half the damn staff is out with it already."

"It's okay. I've made it through this week. I'm sure nothing will happen this weekend."

"Girl, you better knock on some damn wood, throw salt over your shoulder, or whatever those superstitious people do. You can't be saying things like that; you'll jinx yourself."

"Sorry, I just meant to tell you that it would be okay and for you not to worry."

"Now, I'm doubly worried. Maybe we should put Joe on alert, just in case."

I rolled my eyes at her as she tried to smooth her hair down.

"On second thought, just call an ambulance, that way you'll come straight to the ER, anyway."

"I will not call an ambulance to take me to the hospital to give birth. Do you know how much that would cost?"

Bethany picked her makeshift bed up and tucked it into the corner between my couch and the wall, so that it was standing up against the wall and held there by the unmovable couch.

"I worry about you. Can you at least call Ryker to come stay with you or something?"

"I don't want to put him in a bad spot with his brother."

"Then call Marsh." She held her hand up before I could adamantly oppose that idea. "Hear me out. He is the father, and should be there when his son comes into this world. If you take away your anger for how he treated you, then you know damn well you wouldn't forgive yourself for making him miss that. Besides, he should have to take at least some responsibility for that little guy you're growing. So, start letting him."

"You want me to invite him into my home for the weekend. That's something entirely different than just relenting on the whole delivery room thing."

"Sweetie, please, I can't stand the thought of you being here alone, especially since you've had two episodes of getting dizzy while I've been here."

"Fine. I'll text him." She stared at me, arms crossed over her chest, waiting for me to do just that, as if she didn't believe I'd actually follow through. Dammit.

> Opal: Beth has to work the ER this weekend. Could you come stay in case I go into labor or faint and fall or something?

"There. Happy?" I asked.

"Nope."

"Why not?"

"Because I know for a fact that you still have his phone

blocked, you little, lying, liar pants." She snatched my phone from me, unblocked Marsh's number, and then hit resend on the message I tried to fake my way through.

Asshole who left me: What time is she leaving?

Opal: In about ten minutes.

Asshole who left me: Be there in five.

Bethany chuckled and then handed my phone back to me. "Nice name you gave him."

I shrugged my shoulders.

"Silent treatment, huh?" She asked even though the smile never slipped from her face. "Whatever. He can use my air mattress, but I demand that he wash the sheets and replace them before Monday, and I better not hear that you took them to that ratchet-ass laundry room in this complex."

"How do you think I get my laundry done? Do you see a washer and dryer hiding in my apartment anywhere?"

"Girl, you should have taken that man up on staying in that house." I rolled my eyes at her. "Yeah, I know why you couldn't. Doesn't mean I can't wish you were in a better place."

"Maybe next year I'll be able to afford something more."

A few minutes went by as Bethany got ready for work, before there was a knock on the door. Bethany came flying out of my tiny bathroom with a makeup brush in hand. "Sit your booty down. I got it."

"You know I am allowed to move, right?"

She sniggered at that. "Oh, I know, but it takes you forever to do it."

"Jerk," I tossed the taunt out even though I didn't really mean it.

"You love me," My best friend declared as she swung the door open.

"I like you. I love your best friend," Marsh said before Beth opened the door wide enough for him to come through.

"Watch yourself, smooth talker, she's in a mood."

"Let me guess, you had to steal her phone to text me to get here?" He asked.

Bethany simply shrugged her shoulders without actually validating the truth of his statement. "I'll be out of your hair in just a minute," She told him as he took over making sure the door was shut and locked, despite the fact that Beth would be leaving any minute.

"I wish you had been the one to text," Marsh admitted, while taking the seat next to me.

"Didn't want to bother you."

"Don't you understand that you couldn't ever be a bother?"

I didn't dignify that with an answer, all things considered, but only because I didn't have the energy to fight. Instead, I told him he was welcome to use Beth's air mattress.

"You know, there are a couple of actual beds over at the house that I bought for you."

"You didn't buy a house for me. You bought it hoping to buy my forgiveness and for us to use it together. There's a world of difference between the two."

He shrugged, not denying that fact. "I never said I didn't want us to eventually be a family in that house, but it's yours until you decide you're ready to let that happen."

"And what if I never decide to let it happen? What if I decide that you aren't any good for me, especially after I've had enough of being jerked around, and tossed aside for other women? Do you kick me out? Leave me no time to find a new, acceptable place? Do you take all of my memories again?"

"Christ! Opal, I swear to you, the whole time we were apart all I could think of was you. I wished away the six months, in hopes that we could get back together sooner."

I scrunched my nose, whether in distaste or disbelief I

couldn't be certain. Probably a mix of both. "That is the grossest thing you could have ever said to me."

"What? Why?" His voice grew excited, and I could see it plain on his confused face that he had no clue what he'd just implied.

"All you could think of was me? So, you went out on dates with a bunch of other women, and you thought of me?" He nodded his head. "Did you think about how knowing you were with other women made me ache like my heart was going to beat right out of my chest and I would die?"

Marsh's mouth dropped open in shock. I continued to stare at him, not allowing him the opportunity to escape the pain he'd put me through. No answer came from him, but it didn't need to. I was going to make my final point to him, so that he understood just how completely he had ruined us.

"You keep mentioning these six months, like there was some sort of hallmark event that was supposed to happen. What did you think would happen after six months trying to find an upgrade for a girlfriend?"

"I was never looking for an upgrade. That could never happen," He denied.

"Then why were you looking at all? If you already had the best person for you, then why were you out there searching for something else?"

"I thought we needed to both experience the things we never did when we were younger, so that neither of us would have doubts later, like my father did. I meant what I said, I only thought of you during that time."

I scoffed at that. "So, when you were fucking Monica unprotected you were thinking of me? Thinking of the diseases you would bring home in a couple days? Thinking of the baby that you'd have me raise if you knocked her up?"

"I wasn't thinking about anything, except how angry I was that some other man put a baby in your belly and you didn't seem to wait very long before you went there with someone else," He yelled at me.

I shook my head. "It never occurred to you that you were the asshole who left me with a baby in my belly to go off and sleep with other women? You thought so little of me that you left without so much as a conversation, and your first thought upon seeing me pregnant was that I was somehow more of a whore than you were, and slept around the minute we broke up?"

"Opal, that's not fair. What was I supposed to think?"

"I don't know, Marsh, maybe that you left me so fucking heartbroken that I couldn't function for months on end, especially since I was carrying your baby and having to listen to the gossip about your latest dates around town. You couldn't even respect me enough to go on your dates somewhere else. No. I had people sending me pictures of you. Did you know I had to block half the damn town to get it to stop? And all the while, I was sick every day because the baby we made together didn't like the smell of food, or my anxiety, or my sadness."

"Opal," his voice broke as he spoke my name with so much anguish that I almost felt bad for him. Then I remembered how much I had endured so he could have his freedom and not live with the regrets of 'what if'.

I shook my head again. "No. Marsh, just no. You don't get to feel bad about that. It's what you wanted."

"It's not what I wanted. It's never been what I wanted! I didn't want to see you in so much pain…"

"What in the hell did you think would happen when I got home that day to find the apartment cleaned out? What did you think would happen when I wasn't even given a chance to speak as you took less than five-minutes to tell me that you needed six months away to date other people? Did you think I would be happy about that?"

"Opal, I swear, I thought I was doing right by us."

"Doing right by us would have been you realizing that we were happy already. It would have been you putting your friend and your brothers in their place instead of standing back, quietly letting them insult me for years while they belittled our relationship. You put yourself in that situation and kept yourself there, Marsh. No one else. And now, you have regrets about your decision. Imagine that. You went from not wanting to have regrets about staying with me to having regrets about throwing me away and losing me forever."

"No! Don't say that! How can you say that?"

"Because it's the truth. You think I want a man who would so easily cast me aside for others? Who would think the worst of me and go sleep with another woman as an act of revenge when I did nothing wrong? You think I want a man who values everyone else's opinions above our relationship? I don't want you anymore, Marsh. If I hadn't been pregnant, I would have already been dating, or moved to another town to start my life over without you. That would have been the better option for me. Since you left me with child, I don't even get the dignity of a fresh start in a town where I haven't been made a mockery of."

"Fuck!" Marsh hissed under his breath as he turned away from me.

Chapter 22

MARSH

THERE WERE MOMENTS, SINCE I MADE THE DECISION TO TAKE A break from my relationship with Opal, where I felt like there might be no going back. I'd always talked myself out of those thoughts. I knew, deep down, that we were always meant to be together, and for whatever reason, I never really thought about the situation from her perspective of hurt and anger. There was only the inevitable result that she would want us back together just as much as I did.

"I don't want you anymore, Marsh." I wasn't sure if I heard anything else she'd said since coming into her shabby little apartment. Those words were on repeat in my head just as the pain of their meaning stabbed me in the heart. Repeatedly.

"I don't want you anymore, Marsh."

She couldn't mean that. It couldn't truly be over. My eyes drifted back to her belly, the one cradling my son as he grew inside her. We were about to be a family in the way I'd always dreamed of, but I'd already missed so much. Missed holding her hair back as our son made her sick. I missed all those doctor appointments, getting to see my son move around on ultrasound. I missed finding out, with her, that we were having a boy. And now, she was telling me that I'd miss out on nights snuggled up with them. I'd miss out on the happy family meals I always dreamed of having with her and our children.

There weren't going to be any family moments to hang on the wall of the house that I purchased for us. She was telling me, in so many words, that I would have to settle for every other weekend visits, a few weeks in the summer, and maybe every other holiday and birthday. We wouldn't be doing those things together. Our son's first Christmas would be spent at one house or another, not enveloped in the love of his two parents as he joyously opened gifts. Okay, a baby probably wouldn't be joyously opening gifts, but that wasn't the point. By the time he got to the place in life where he bounded in early in the morning before the sun even rose, to wake his parents for present time, it wouldn't be to a bedroom I shared with his mother.

I wanted to argue with her, tell her something that would magically wipe out the past six months of my personal stupidity. Six months of suffering that wasn't worth it. Well, shit, seven months now. I didn't consider the past month as part of that period though, since I had been dedicated to winning my woman back.

My thoughts drifted to Jimmy's buddy, the one who asked my Opal out on a date. Could I even bear the thought of another man stepping in and playing dad to my kid? No, not really. That was mostly because I think I'd rather die than ever have to see Opal in the arms of another man. That's when the rest of what she'd admitted hit me.

"Someone showed you pictures of me out on dates?"

"That's what you took from everything I had to say?" She sassed.

I shook my head. "No, I was hung up on the fact that you said you didn't want me anymore, but I just realized you also said someone was sending you pictures. Who? Who would do that?"

She rolled her eyes. "As if you don't already know." She must have seen the question in my eyes, because my girl blew out a frustrated breath and reached over to where she'd set her phone down. "I never deleted any of them. I needed the images, just in case I ever forgot exactly how much I hate you now."

She handed the phone to me, after pulling up a string of texts. The name of the person texting her was 'The Biggest Asshole to Ever Breathe'. I looked and the first image was of me and Tandra, the little pixie girl that I met at the party before I left Opal. Jesus. She knew then. She knew that the woman from the party was part of the reason I'd left. My interest in her had been the thing that sealed my decision. If I could be that intrigued by another woman, then I was doomed to repeat my father's mistakes.

"Nothing ever happened between us," I explained as I stared at the picture. Opal scoffed again, something that seemed to be a new habit when we spoke these days. It was another one of the changes I had brought about in her. A change that I absolutely hated.

"Sure. You just left me because you felt something more for her at that party. Nothing happened between you two, though." She rolled her eyes as her accusation settled in with its heavy weight, right on the middle of my chest.

"Nothing. Never even kissed her. When we went out on our date, it didn't even last through the meal. She said some shitty things, and I replied in kind. That was the end of it."

"Oh, so you left me for a chance to date her and it wasn't worth it? Congrats!" Her sarcasm hit harder than it normally would because I could damn near taste the anguish hiding behind those words.

I continued to scroll and saw as at least one picture from

every one of my dates showed up on Opal's phone in this string of one-sided texts. The last one was of me with my hands on a woman's breast as we made out in the apartment I shared with the twins. I had to look really hard to see where the picture might have been taken from, as there hadn't been anyone home that night. It was the one time I made out with anyone else. I hadn't even remembered taking her back to the twin's place. We hadn't been there long before I felt like a complete fucking joke and told her I needed to take her home. There was also that hate fuck with Monica after that, but I already knew that Opal knew about that one first hand.

"That was when I blocked his number," She admitted.

"Who?"

Her eyes met mine, and I could see her trying to find some truth in mine that I didn't really know. "Cramer."

"That son of a bitch," I muttered. He was going to get what was coming to him, and soon.

"Why are you angry with him for showing me what you were up to?"

I snapped my attention back to Opal for a moment. "He caused you more pain than was necessary."

"No, he didn't. You did that. He wasn't the one out with those women. And if he had been, I wouldn't have cared. It was you who was with them. All of them. He just showed me the truth of what was happening."

"You just said you had to block him because it was too painful to see that truth, Opal."

"Yeah, Marsh. It became a bit too painful when I saw you with your hand on another woman's breast, your mouth on her skin."

Anger boiled inside me. Not just at Cramer for making Opal have to witness my idiocy first hand, but at myself for being such a fucking fool.

"I'm sorry," It was all I could say; even as I knew it would never be enough.

She didn't respond, but I deleted the entire string of texts between her and Cramer so that she wouldn't have those images to look at anymore. If she was able to look back and see them, she would have more reason to stay angry and there would be less chance she'd ever forgive me.

"I can never unsee those pictures or Monica delivering your underwear to you on the street in her robe." She shrugged her shoulders. "You can delete the pictures, just like you did the ones of our relationship, but you can't delete the memories that are already there."

I knew that.

There was no denying I'd fucked up beyond repair. That didn't mean I was going to give up. Not on her. Not on us one day being a family. Not on anything.

We sat in silence for a long time. Internally, I was going back over damn near every memory we shared together, trying to figure out how I had gotten to the point where I was able to accept a break away from her. Things had been kind of status quo with us for a while, but we were still content. Happy even. I allowed my fears of ending up like my father and the taunts from the people close to me to make me feel like there was something missing when truthfully, I had everything.

'Had' being the operative word. Opal would barely look at me these days and only tolerated my presence because we were having a baby. 'Together' should have been tacked on the end of that sentence, but it was more like we were having a baby that would tie us in some way, but we would be raising him separately. There was no 'together' involved in her future plans anymore. That was entirely my fault.

"How are you feeling?" I finally asked. It was high time I started thinking about her and our child, rather than what I wanted or needed. They had to come first because nothing about what I'd already put us through had been about her or them. It had all been about me and what I thought I needed in order to prove that I'd never become my dad. The crazy thing is, looking back, what I did was far worse than what my father put Mom through.

Far. Far. Worse.

"Collectively, or just physically?"

"Any of it. All of it. You're getting closer to the delivery date," I suggested.

"I'm achy and tired all the time."

"I guess that's to be expected?" I asked because honestly, I didn't know. I just figured it had to be draining and maybe a bit painful to grow a whole human in your body.

"Yep," She mumbled.

I had the sudden urge to get away from Opal. Not because I wanted to be away from her, but because there was zero chance she would let me hold her. "Have to use the bathroom," I mumbled as I slipped back toward the door that hid the space that was barely big enough for a stand-up shower, sink, and toilet. In fact, you could probably wash your hands while sitting on the toilet, everything was that tight. How my pregnant girlfriend – shit, ex-girlfriend – managed to shower in there was beyond me.

When I came back out, my eyes drifted to the room that would house my son once he arrived. There was a box lying on the floor with a picture of a crib on it. "What's this?" I asked as my feet guided me the few steps across the narrow hall to the bedroom.

"The nursery?" She asked, not moving from the couch where she had parked her butt earlier.

"No, I mean, why is the crib still sitting in the box?"

"Because I haven't had the energy, or the tools, to put it together yet."

"Why didn't they put it together when it was delivered?"

I stepped back out into the hall to look her way when she didn't dignify that question with a response. When our eyes met, hers just stared at me, as if I was stupid. Maybe I was. No. I definitely was. She had been mine and this could all be going in a completely different direction, if only I hadn't... No use dwelling on my mistakes or what could have been.

"Where are your tools?" I asked.

She shrugged. "Beth was going to borrow some of her mom's this weekend. I don't have any. The ones we used to have at the other apartment, you took with you."

Son of a bitch. There were so many things that I never thought of when I left her. So many ways that she had been left with a giant 'fuck you' from me, and none of it had occurred to me because it didn't affect me. It had all, always, been about me and never her. She was right to not want me back.

I was a selfish asshole. That knowledge stung something fierce too. The least I could do was to find every way possible to make her life easier, since I'd all done before was make it more difficult.

"I'll make sure you have a set of tools to use when you need them." It was my first response to make sure she had everything she needed to take care of herself and our son, since she wouldn't move into the house I bought.

"No need. Beth and I will get it done in a few days, like we planned."

"I didn't mean to imply that I wouldn't put the crib together. I'm getting you the tools for when you're too stubborn to ask for help on other occasions. Beth is working the ER this weekend. She's going to be too tired to put a crib together, and you're in no condition to do it either, so I'm going to get it done for you."

"Knock yourself out then," Opal said with a lengthy sigh. I could have sworn that I heard her mutter a not-so-sarcastic, "Please," at the end. Couldn't say as I blamed her. There had been many days, since the reality of the shitstorm I caused finally sunk in, when I wished that knocking myself out was a viable option.

I ran down to my truck and grabbed the tools I would need and then I got to work building a crib. You wouldn't think the damn things would be that difficult. I laughed as I screwed it up, once again, and had to take the damn thing apart by three steps and flip the stupid piece upside down. It didn't look right like that, but then again, according to the picture, that was how it was supposed to go.

Fucking crib!

The fleeting question I asked her was, *"Why didn't they put it together, when it was delivered?"* She hadn't given me an answer, just stared at me like I was a moron. It was then I realized why. As I sat there, living through the headache of being the one trying to put a crib together without another set of able-bodied hands to help out, that I realized the only reason I was able to do it was because the walls were so close together and basically holding parts up for me. She rented this shit hole of an apartment because she didn't have a lot of money to spare. It stood to reason that she wouldn't want to spend the extra on having people come in and put shit together for her.

There was no way I could have felt any smaller. It was like I kept opening my mouth and rubbing salt in a wound that was still very much raw for her. If we were together, the damn thing would have been assembled already – whether by me and my family or after I hired someone else to do it. The one that I had set up at the house that I bought for Opal was put together because I'd paid extra for assembly on delivery. Wasn't that just a bite in the ass?

There I was, flaunting my money. Some of which, Opal didn't even know existed yet. She didn't understand that I had inherited a huge chunk of change from my mom's parents when they died. I didn't even know about it until a couple months after we broke up. Mom and Dad hadn't told any of us about it until we were able to collect the money. She swore each older child to secrecy. We weren't allowed to tell the next in line that they had money coming.

It was after learning about the inheritance, that I finally understood how the twins had been able to buy their condo. I always pissed them off by calling it an apartment, but in truth, they owned the space they lived in. Up until a few months ago, I thought they were renting and that they lived together because they couldn't afford it separately. Turns out, they both wanted to get in on something cheap while they were living their best bachelor lives and save money for the future whenever they decided to settle down and start families.

That was still something I couldn't imagine either of them ever doing, but then again, stranger things had happened. Look at me. I had trashed the best relationship I would ever have for the stupidest of reasons. If I could fuck up a good thing, surely my brothers would be able to hold onto one, once it presented itself.

I just finished tightening the last screw, and stuck my head out into the hallway to call Opal in to take a look at the crib, when I heard her groan.

"Opal?" I called out as I set my screwdriver down and made my way to the living room. She was bent, almost double – if that was possible for a woman who was in her eighth month of pregnancy. "Opal, are you okay?"

She shook her head. "Get my bag," she hissed.

I glanced around and didn't see anything special. Thinking she meant her purse, I brought it over to her. She huffed, but didn't say anything for a solid two minutes. "In the little closet next to the front door. I have a bag packed for me and a diaper bag for Austin. Please, grab them. We need to go."

"Go where?"

The heated glare she sent my way froze me in place. Then,

before either of us could say another word, the floor beneath Opal's feet started forming a puddle. I cocked my head to the side as Opal glanced down in horror.

"Oh my God! Get the damn bags, I'm in labor you idiot!" She yelled at me.

"Shit!" I rushed to get the bags and then came back to help her waddle-walk out of the house. "I'm so sorry, but getting you in the truck probably isn't going to feel great."

"Don't care," She huffed through clenched teeth. "Just get me to the hospital and we'll call it good."

"Wish you were talking about everything when you say that," I muttered as I helped her into my truck.

"You probably should have gotten a towel. I think I'm still leaking," She moaned.

"Don't worry about the truck. As long as we get you to the hospital in time, that's all that matters."

Chapter 23

OPAL

"BREATHE THROUGH THE CONTRACTIONS," MARSH COACHED AS he drove us across town to the hospital.

"I'm trying," I groaned.

"Come on, breathe with me. In through your nose." He paused as I did so. "Now, out through your mouth in slow increments." When I eased my hold on his hand, he smiled. "Better?"

"For now," I agreed, and for some reason, I didn't let go of his hand. Marsh and I might not have been in a good place, but the strength he offered was desperately needed. I was afraid of going into labor, had been for months now. What if something happened to me? I knew Marsh and his family would take good care of my son, but it hurt my heart to think that he might not have his mother to guide him as he grew up.

The other possibility just wasn't something I cared to imagine. If my baby didn't make it, they might as well let me go too. I knew plenty of people were able to cope with the loss of a child, stillbirths, and whatnot. Eventually, anyway. I didn't think I'd be able to get over the loss of my child with Marsh though because there would never be another one.

"Stop worrying, you're going to be just fine," Marsh said as he squeezed my hand. "Both of you will be."

It seemed he still knew me well enough to know what was going through my mind. "If anything happens to me," I began to say when Marsh squeezed down on my hand even tighter. A contraction took my breath before I could say more.

"Breathe," He reminded me. I followed along with him, wondering when he had learned the breathing exercises they taught in Lamaze classes. "That's it. If you stay calm, you can work through the pain of the contractions a little easier. And stop trying to plan for an eventuality in which you are no longer here to care for our son. That shit isn't happening."

"You." Quick breath out. "Don't." Another quick breath out. "Get." I tried to breathe in, but it hurt like a mother… A whip-like pain lashed out at me, spreading from my back to my front, fast as a wildfire on a windy day. "Ouch!" I cried.

"No, I don't get the 'ouch' part," Marsh agreed with a chuckle while trying to bring some levity to the situation.

"Shut. Up." Those two words were a growl as the contraction finally eased back a little.

"They're about five minutes apart now," He insisted.

"You've been timing them?"

"Of course, I have."

I didn't know what to do with that information. I hadn't even been able to wrap my head around the fact that I was about to give birth, beyond dealing with the contractions and sitting uncomfortably in my soaked pajamas.

"You know you can't dictate how everything plays out," I quickly stated, trying to finish my thought from earlier. "Even I don't get a say in whether something goes wrong or not."

"You're a fighter, Opal. You managed to get through the things I put you through – the things I didn't even understand I was doing to you. You can do this. You're going to show our son what it means to be tough, loyal, and loved."

Loyalty. That was something Marsh wouldn't be able to show him. Not if he was supposed to lead by example. The bitter thought took me right into another contraction.

"Think," breathe, "coming," breathe, "quicker." I huffed out an exhausted sigh and relaxed for a minute as the last contraction passed and we pulled into the hospital parking lot. Luckily, they had what the hospital called 'stork spots' so that when someone pulled in, the staff would send a nurse out immediately with a wheelchair to help the woman directly into labor and delivery.

It was something new they were implementing after having one too many women come in through the emergency room, where all sorts of other concerns would arise.

"Have you done all the pre-check-in paperwork?" The nurse asked as she came over to help me into the wheelchair.

"Yes, I did it a couple weeks ago when Dr. Burns said I might go early."

"Good. How far along are you?"

"Thirty-eight weeks," I replied.

"And how far apart are your contractions?"

I couldn't answer as another one whipped me from back to front and squeezed until I didn't think I'd ever breathe again.

"In through your nose, out through your mouth," Marsh coached. "She's about three to four minutes between contractions now. Her water broke just before we left, and that was about twelve minutes ago. She was only about eight to ten minutes apart then. It seems like things are progressing really fast."

If I could have thought clearly through the pain, I would have been impressed with the way Marsh not only kept his cool, but rattled off all the pertinent details as if he brought a new baby into the world every day.

Then I made myself sick with that thought, because one day, he'd do this again, only it would be at another woman's side. The pain that realization caused my heart, made the contractions pale in comparison. How in the world would I deal with seeing Marsh in love with someone else? Dating was one thing. Knowing he had sex was another, but to see him in love with or marrying someone else, let alone having a baby with another woman… That might just kill me.

My son and I might have to move. That was a selfish thought, but one that felt necessary for my self-preservation. Then again, that wouldn't be an option now that he for sure knew about the baby and the fact that it was his. When I thought he knew and didn't care, it had been an option that I was willingly looking into. There was no way he'd let us go without a fight. Besides, I couldn't take my son from his family. My parents were never going to win a 'grandparents of the year' prize. They'd probably see him once every two years, and that was if we traveled to them.

There was a large part of me, when faced with that uncertain future, that wanted to give in and take Marsh at his word that he got it all out of his system. That we could go back to being us, or maybe a better, wiser version of what we once were. We could be a family.

Just as the thought broke free, and felt right, I was pushed into the delivery room, where I would hopefully give birth to our son, very soon. Only, when our nurse turned around, I felt like throwing up.

"Hi," She called out in a friendly voice. "I'm Gabby and I'll be your labor and delivery nurse today." She glanced over my shoulder, and I knew the moment the recognition appeared on her face that I hadn't been wrong in thinking she was the same woman whose picture was on my phone. The one Cramer sent me of Marsh making out with another woman. The one that forced me to finally block his best friend because I couldn't take the updates any longer.

"Marshal! What a surprise," She stated before bringing her

attention back to me, while still speaking to him. "Are you here supporting your sister?"

She couldn't have known him that well. If she didn't know his family dynamic better than that. The gleam in her eye told me she was just throwing out a hopeful suggestion. Marsh didn't get a chance to speak up.

"You need to leave and have a different nurse come tend to me," I told her in a quiet, even tone.

"Oh!" As the word came out of her mouth she left it hanging there with a surprised little pouty "O" on her lips too.

"Marshal?" She questioned.

"Nope," I countered immediately. "I'm the one giving birth here, and very soon," I yelped as another contraction hit me. Once it eased a bit, I glared at her for having not moved. "I will not do that with you in this room."

"I don't understand," She feigned ignorance still, and that pissed me off even more.

"Gabby," Marsh finally called out. "Please do as Opal asked."

"Opal?" She cried out in shock. "As in the ex-girlfriend you couldn't stop talking about that almost ruined our date?"

Marsh sighed, but it was an agitated sound.

I wheeled myself over to the bed and pushed the nurse's call button repeatedly until a disembodied voice came over the little speaker system in the room.

"Please, come remove Nurse Gabby from my room and get someone in here who can catch my baby before he falls out of my vagina!"

There. That should get people moving.

A flurry of activity happened after that. Gabby was pushed out of the room, but no one had time to ask the all-important question of why. Instead, I screamed bloody murder as the doctor and two nurses helped me from the chair onto the bed and quickly assembled it into something akin to what Dr. Burns had in his office.

"Dr. Burns," I requested through clenched teeth as the urge to bear down hit me hard. There was no way I could form a full sentence.

"He's on the way, sweetie. We notified him the minute you gave us your information."

I nodded and then started crying. "I really need to push," I told the older nurse who looked down at me with a bit of sympathy in her eyes before they skated over to Marsh and then the closed door where Gabby had been shuffled away.

"Let us check you first. Please, don't push. We need to make sure the baby is in the right position and everything looks good first."

"I wonder what women did before there were hospitals," I muttered unhappily.

"Be thankful that we check on things first, these days," The nurse answered back with a bit of a chastising tone. I didn't mind. She was at least doing her job and not demanding answers from the baby's father. Speaking of…

"I don't want him in here," I told the nurse.

"Who, dear?"

"Him. I don't want him to see me."

She didn't hesitate to turn around and tell Marsh that he needed to leave the room.

"No way." He turned from her to me with a grief-stricken expression. "Don't send me away, Opal. You were fine with me being here five minutes ago. Don't do this because of *her* being here. That's not fair. I'm not with her. We had one date, a little over two months ago."

I shook my head and then all hell broke loose because the baby wasn't planning on waiting a minute longer for me to push. I could feel him moving.

"Arg, too late," I growled to the nurse. "Can't check. Please, help!" Then, I pushed with all my might to get my baby free of my body.

Fifteen minutes later, I was holding my son in my arms for the first time. "Hello, Austin, my beautiful baby boy. I am going to love you with everything I have left in me," I promised him.

"He's perfect. That was amazing, Opal. You did so good." Marsh gushed, and when I looked at him, there was a part of me that wanted to reiterate my original wish to have him banished from the room. The other part couldn't take the moment from the man. He had just as much right as I did to welcome his son into the world.

I tried to hold our son up higher, an offer for him to take the baby. "You want to hold him?" I asked as my arms dropped. Luckily, it was a gentle drop, but Marsh stepped right in and took our son from me. He cradled him against his chest and grinned down at our boy so widely that I should have felt his joy. I didn't. All I felt were bittersweet regrets.

"We need to get the baby down to the nursery for a few minutes so we can get him cleaned up."

Panic, like I'd never known before, overwhelmed me. I got ready to stand up, but the doctor gently pushed me back down. "We're not done here just yet."

"I don't know her," I fussed at him. "She can't just take my baby. He doesn't even have one of those tags on his foot yet."

"Calm down. That's what they're taking him to do." He turned to Marsh. "You're the baby's father?" He asked, to which my ex-boyfriend nodded. "You can go with him and they'll give you a matching bracelet to wear while he's here in the hospital."

Marsh looked to me, for permission or what, I didn't know. "You good with that?" He finally asked.

"Don't let him out of your sight."

"I won't."

Marsh turned from me to the doctor then. "What are you doing? Is there another baby in there or something?"

The doctor – who was not Dr. Burns – chuckled. "No. Opal needs to deliver the placenta and once she gives me a quick push, we'll have that over and done with so she can get cleaned up and rest a bit."

Marsh nodded and turned to follow the nurse out of the room. She was pushing what looked like a portable glass bassinet in front of her and Marsh, true to his word, had a finger on the damn thing. Taking his eyes off the baby wasn't even a question when he refused to relinquish hold of the bassinet as they strolled out of the room. I could trust him with that. I could trust him with my son. I just couldn't trust him with my heart. Nurse Gabby had been an awful reminder of that, and just when I was weak enough to beg him to come back to me.

Over an hour later, when I finally woke up, it was because they were transferring me to the room I would be staying in for the next night or two. Shortly after they got me there, Marsh came strolling in with the rolling bassinet and the biggest grin on his face. He had one of those special security bracelets on his arm and it made me angry that he had one and I didn't until I looked down and saw that someone had stuck one on me while I was sleeping.

"I hope you don't mind, they asked if we had a name picked out yet, so I told them."

"What exactly did you tell them?" I asked, afraid of what he might say.

"Austin Jason Kennedy."

With a sigh, I nodded my head. In my mind, there had been a tossup over what last name my son should carry. Mine or his. It should have never been this way. It should have never been a question. We were supposed to be married before we ever brought a child into this world, and suddenly the grief for the loss of that future hit me like a ton of bricks and I couldn't hold the tears in any more.

"Hey! Hey, hey, hey," Marsh called out gently, almost soothingly. "If you changed your mind, we can fix it." He sat beside me on the bed then and tried to wipe the never-ending tears away. Eventually, he realized it was a futile effort. "Opal?" My name was a question on his lips, and a desperate one at that.

"We were supposed to be married before we had kids. The last name the baby got should never have been a question in my mind," I sobbed out almost unintelligibly.

"Fuck," He hissed low, under his breath. "Opal, there aren't enough apologies in the world to undo the damage I caused us. I'm so damn sorry, baby. If you want him to have your name..." The offer was left hanging there in the room between us as I shook my head.

"It's all lost. My son's name won't ever match mine. I'll have to watch him interact with a stepmother eventually, and have to see you with more women. I wish I could just disappear," I admitted. It was safe to say that I was feeling my lowest.

"Oh!" A feminine voice called out in distress from the door. I looked up to see Marsh's mom and Ryker standing there. Ryker looked angry enough to kill his brother on the spot. Kathy only had sad eyes for me, though. "Sweetheart, it's hard after you give birth. Your emotions are all over the place. I promise, that feeling will pass."

"How would you know? You were happily married when Jimmy came along and the rest of the boys too. You have no clue what it's like to have a space built in between you and your child because there was a question of whose last name to use and the decision was made for you while you were resting after giving birth."

"Tell me you didn't," Marsh's mother hissed at him.

"I thought that was what we agreed to," Her son admitted, looking sheepish under his mother's scornful glare.

"We agreed to Austin Jason. I wasn't sure about what to do with his last name yet."

It was Marsh's turn to give me the same look his mother had just landed on him. "I think you're just punishing me because of Gabby."

"Gabby?" Kathy asked. "Who is Gabby?"

"Cramer sent me pictures of your son, and all his women, every time he went on a date. Did you know that?" The color drained from Kathy's face. "The last one he sent, before I finally had enough and blocked him, was of Marsh and Gabby making out. Marsh had a handful of her breast. When they rolled me into labor and delivery, guess who my nurse was?"

Kathy gasped and turned to her son, the disappointment on her face was clear. The loathing rolling off Ryker for his brother grew to suffocating levels. "What were you thinking?"

"I wasn't aware that my dating life was being sent to her in vivid pictures," Marsh spat out at his mother. "That was something I only learned today, and it will be dealt with later. My son's birth took precedence over that, for good reason."

"There are so many things I want to say to you, Son. Unfortunately, we can't change the past, so it's pointless to say them." Kathy turned to me. "I understand that would have been incredibly hard to handle, especially today of all days. Opal, it is all in the past, though."

I laughed quietly. "It's only the past until it gets shoved in your face at the worst time all over again, Kathy. Those pictures are burned into my mind. I can't even unsee them."

"I hate this for both of you," She admitted. "This isn't the time or place to hash anything out. I came to meet my grandson." Kathy turned her back on me and moved to the bassinet that was tucked into the corner of the room between the end of my bed and the wall. "Can I hold him?"

I didn't want her to. I glanced over at Ryker, and knew there was someone else who deserved to meet my son more than his grandmother.

"Actually, I would very much like it if Ryker was the first to hold him. He was there with me during so many of my doctor visits and just to help me out whenever he could. He deserves to meet his nephew before anyone else."

Ryker beamed at me. "I promise, I'll be careful with him."

"I know you will," I told him. I thought Kathy might be angry with me for shutting her out from being the first, but the pride in her watery eyes as she took in her youngest son while he gently picked up my son, told me that she didn't find fault in my decision.

"He's so tiny," Ryker said reverently as he looked down at his nephew. "Hey Aus, I'm your Uncle Ry. We're going to be best buddies, little man."

I was so enraptured with the sight of Ryker holding my son that I didn't even notice when Marsh shifted and kneeled beside the head of my bed. My hand was wrapped in his before I noticed. "That was really cool of you," He whispered. "Ryker deserved that honor."

"I know he did."

"Ryk?" Marsh called out. His brother lifted his eyes for a moment, giving Marsh his attention. "Thank you for being a better man than I ever was, especially since Opal needed you."

Ryker nodded his head and then shifted his attention back to his nephew.

Chapter 24

MARSH

"Marshal, can I speak to you in the hall for a moment?" My mother asked, after she got her turn to hold Austin.

"Are you good?" I asked Opal. She was sitting up, holding our son, and feeding him a bottle. Her milk hadn't come in yet and she was afraid that our son would starve if he didn't get something to eat. The nurses had laughed at her and brushed away her concerns, but honestly, I felt the same way.

"What's up?" I asked as we left the room and shut the door to give us some privacy.

"I'm sure this is a bit of a delicate situation, but the twins are here and wanted to know if it was okay for them to come up and meet your son."

My face flushed with heat as I thought about what Opal's reaction might be to the twins' presence in the hospital. "I don't know if that would be a good idea."

"Austin is their nephew. They deserve to meet him, same as Ryker," She insisted.

"Really, Mom? You don't see a difference? Ryker, has always worshiped Opal, and was there for her when none of the rest of our family was. The twins have always taunted her and tried to break us up, but you think they deserve the same consideration?"

"They messed up. If she can forgive you…"

"She hasn't forgiven me anything," I shouted at her before I pulled my anger back. "The only reason I'm here is because I'm that baby's father and she can't really shut me out." I choked out an awful sound then that was half laugh, half sob. "She tried to get me thrown out of the delivery room after we walked into the awkward situation with Gabby. She would have succeeded too, if things hadn't moved so fast that the nurse didn't have a chance to do her bidding."

"I can't stand the strife in our family right now."

"I get it, Mom. I think we're all strung a little tight right now. It's a shitty situation and one of my own making, no matter the shit the twins did. I made my own decisions, but this isn't even about me leaving Opal. They have been awful to her for years. Years, Mom. She's not going to want them up here."

"Then bring the baby out in the hall so she doesn't have to see them."

"Do you hear yourself? Do you know what will happen if I go against her wishes, take her son, and introduce him to two of the three people she hates most in this world?"

"They're your brothers!" My mom yelled at me.

"And they made their bed with Opal. Now, they get to lie in it. I can't live with my family because of what I did. They can't meet my son because of what they did. When she changes her mind on that, then it will happen."

My mom turned her back on me. It hurt to see her shoulders shaking, but then she surprised me and stomped back into the room and faced down Opal.

"It's not right that our whole family can't meet the baby!" It wasn't quite a shout, but there was enough passion in my mom's voice that Ryker stepped between her and Opal, ready to protect the mother of my child from our own mom. If it was possible, my respect for my little brother grew by leaps and bounds that day.

"I don't know what you're talking about," Opal said as she shifted our son to her shoulder and started patting his back.

"The twins are here, and you won't let them come meet their nephew," My mother accused.

Opal's eyebrows shifted upward at a high arc toward her hairline. "I wasn't even aware they were here," She tossed back to my mother in a deceptively quiet voice. I was sure it was just to keep an even tone so as not to startle our boy.

"Well," Mom huffed. "They deserve to meet him."

Opal sighed at length, waited for our son to release the gas that built up, and then cradled him in her arms again to feed him the rest of the bottle he was rooting around for. Only once he latched onto the thing like a ravenous little monster, did she look back up to where my mother stood.

"They don't deserve a thing from me. Let's get that straight right now. Those two have only ever tried to take my happiness from me. They succeeded. So, don't you dare come in here and get an attitude with me on the day my son was born, a day that should have been the happiest of my life. It's because of your sons that this day is clouded in misery for me." My mom started to speak, with her chest puffed up, ready for a fight. Opal cut her off.

"I never said they couldn't come meet their nephew. I wouldn't take any of my son's family from him. He's going to need every one of y'all in his life at some point. Hopefully, he's smart enough to know the twins are morons when it counts."

Ryker chuckled at that and stepped back a little, realizing the threat was no longer there as my mother deflated a bit.

"Kathy," Opal called as my mother went to move to the door to go get the twins.

"Hmm?" Mom turned back to Opal with tears hanging in her eyes.

"What you're doing here, it's going to cause damage between us that won't be easy to repair. Those boys have tortured me for years. Your insistence, your venom toward me when I didn't deserve it, it all boils down to me losing any respect that I once held for you. It breaks the trust that I placed in you years ago."

Mom gasped, her hand rising to cover her mouth to hold in the emotion trying to escape. "I'm sorry." She told Opal and then she left.

The twins never did come up after that.

Chapter 25

OPAL

It had been two weeks since I was able to bring my son home from the hospital. Marsh hadn't pushed for an overnight visit with him yet, at least not away from me. He made use of Bethany's air mattress a few times since then. I couldn't say anything bad about the visits either. He was helpful and let me get some sleep, taking the nighttime feedings for Austin without complaint.

I felt like a failure of a mother because my milk never came in like it was supposed to. There were issues that made it impossible for me to feed my son properly, so he always required extra nourishment from a bottle. Eventually, I gave up trying. The one time I managed to get my mom on the phone, she told me she had the same problems with me. That might have been good to know sooner. My parents made their excuses for not coming out to visit.

"Maybe once he's a bit older and can appreciate our visit more," My mother said during our call. It made me wonder if I wanted them to meet my son at all. The fact that they could abandon me here and then not even care to come see their first, and probably only, grandchild made me angry. It also made me incredibly sad. My own family couldn't love me or my son, how could I expect anyone else to? Yeah, the baby blues were a thing, especially with the whole breastfeeding situation, the Kathy situation, and then there was Marsh in the middle of it all.

I hadn't forbidden Kathy from coming to see her grandson, nor had I done so with the twins, but I think they were all giving me a bit of space after Kathy's disturbing display in the hospital. She had sent flowers and a gift basket with an apology. Honestly, I didn't even blame her. The twins were her children, and I know she was feeling the strain of her family being at each other's throats. Marsh explained that his mom hoped the baby would bring everyone back together.

Kathy was delusional. She had stuck her head in the sand for years about the way the twins treated me. The way she ignored the problem then was coming home to roost for her now. That wasn't my problem, and I was done trying to bend over backward to make everyone else around me comfortable.

It was one of the rare days when both Marsh and Beth were out, at work or doing whatever, that there was a knock on the door. Sadly, I had just managed to get Austin down for a nap and sat my butt on the couch to fold the laundry Bethany had been kind enough to do for me the day before, so I wouldn't have to take Austin with me to the laundromat.

With a heave and a sigh, I hefted my butt up off the couch and went to answer the door. The twins were standing there with gift bags in hand.

"Marsh isn't here," I informed them.

"We know," Brixton said as he continued to stare at his feet.

"We came to see you," Bastion added.

"I don't see why," I countered, which caused both boys to look at me, for the first time since I opened the door. Oddly enough, I didn't see what I thought I would. Brix looked stricken by the sight of me, as if I was lying on my deathbed or something. I realized then that I'd been crying for hours over the conversation with my parents and the fact that I was a loser who couldn't breastfeed her baby, even though I really wanted to.

Bastion had tears in his eyes as he pleaded with me, with only that look, to hear them out. I didn't have any fight in me, so I opened the door wider to let them in.

"Make yourself at home," I said while extending my hand in reluctant invitation. There really wasn't anywhere for them to sit though. I had laundry on every spot of the couch, except where I'd been seated moments ago. The two chairs tucked up close to my little kitchen table were overflowing with diapers and stuff for the baby that I had nowhere to store in our little space.

Both men looked around, horror-stricken at what they were seeing. It nearly made me kick them out, because what I didn't need was more judgment, especially from the two of them.

"Why are you living like this?" Brixton asked. "You're a teacher. You make decent money."

I laughed at him. "I make shit money since I took a twelve-month payout, so that I could take the summer off, knowing that I would have the baby in June. Insurance only covered so much of my medical expenses, and I had a ton of stuff to buy for the new human being I gave birth to."

The twins exchanged a strange look. "But Marsh has money."

"And I'm sure Marsh spends his money how he wants to. In case you missed the memo, we are no longer together," I snapped at them.

"Yeah, but the baby is his kid. He should have been paying the medical stuff," Brix argued. I tapped my foot on the floor, growing more impatient with him and his brother.

"Someone failed to tell him that I sent a text letting him know I was pregnant. Someone thought it was funny to send me a text back acknowledging that it was received and letting me know he wanted nothing to do with me or the baby."

Brixton hung his head lower on his shoulders, if that was possible. Then, when he looked back up at me, he had tears running down his face. "You'll never know how sorry I am for that. I honestly thought it was just a last-ditch effort on your part to keep him in your life when he finally left."

"Why are you here?" I asked after completely losing my patience.

"We came bearing gifts and apologies," Bastion answered. He held out his bag to me. When I didn't take it, he set it down on the only free space available on my tiny kitchen counter.

Brixton offered his bag too, which I also didn't take. He set his down on the floor and then glanced around the apartment once more before he shocked me with what he had to say next.

"Mom said you won't take Marsh up on the house he bought for you because it comes with strings and expectations from our brother." I didn't dignify him with an answer, not that he asked a question, but he had the gist down, so I didn't see a point.

"We have a different sort of deal for you," Bastion added.

Brixton took out a stack of papers and handed them to me. "These are the papers for our condo. We decided to sign it over to you. It's yours. Free and clear. It will be in your name only. You owe nothing."

I glanced down at the papers he still held out, as if they might bite me. "What exactly are you saying?"

"We are giving you our condo. It's been cleaned out and we'll help get your things moved over, or get you better things that will fit there."

"Why?" I asked, not understanding their offer.

"It's our fault," Bastion told me. "This whole mess, the fact that our family is falling apart and barely speaking to one another. You – living here in the worst apartment I've ever seen – it is our fault."

I shook my head to deny that. The assholes might have been bullies to me and the reason their brother ultimately decided to do what he did, but they never held a gun to his head.

"No, Bas is right. This whole thing started with our jealousy and it just snowballed out of control. Now, our nephew's life is completely fucked because we refused to grow up and see the damage we were causing."

"Jealousy?" I asked, not understanding what the twins had to be jealous of.

Brixton sighed as he once again stared at his own feet, almost like he was afraid to look me in the eye. "At first, when Marsh hooked up with you, we thought you were a cool chick. He was having fun with you, and honestly, we thought it would end quickly. That was our experience with girls in high school."

"Only, he never stopped having fun with you. We would ask him to hang out, do things with us, and he was always busy. Ryker was too young and Jimmy ran off to college and eventually the military, so we didn't have him."

"You had each other," I suggested.

"Not the same. We always have each other," Bastion explained. "We wanted our brother to go out chasing women, going to parties, and hitting up bars with us, especially once he was old enough," Brix added.

"It pissed us off that he didn't come to college with us, and that's when we got it in our head that you were the problem."

"And we thought it was a problem we had to solve for our brother because we thought he was missing out on life to be with you," Brixton chimed back in. It was weird having a conversation where the twins talked because it was like one person talking, only there were really two. They just kept starting up where the other left off and it was really disconcerting.

"Okay, well, congratulations!" I told them with mock enthusiasm. "Your plan worked."

"That's just it," Brix said as his eyes met mine again. Oddly enough, I could see the sorrow and regret there. "It worked, eventually, and that's when everything fell apart."

I scoffed. "Seems it worked out well for you two. Your brother didn't just hang out with you, he moved in and left me in the dust."

"He moved in and became a shell of the man he was when he was with you. We had to force him out on those dates, Opal. He wouldn't hang out with us, barely spoke to us unless it was something about keeping the noise down, or to leave him alone. We pushed him into those dates and when we found out he wasn't even giving any of them so much as a goodnight kiss, we pushed even further and made sure that Gabby was ready to give all the nudging he needed to get back in the saddle with another woman."

I felt sick to my stomach at the mention of Gabby. "He made out with her, but that was it," Bastion tacked on quickly where his brother left off. "And he got sick that night afterward. We were going to leave him alone after that, and not push anymore because it was obvious how miserable he was with the whole experience."

"We honestly felt bad for him at that point." Brixton added. "Had we known what you were going through, we would have done more, sooner to get the two of you back together, rather than pushing to keep you both apart. We're so fucking sorry."

I laughed at him then. "You're sorry? You feel bad for making your brother miserable. So, now you want to give me a condo, and you think that makes up for everything you did?"

"No. It's not about making up for anything or asking

forgiveness for our part in everything that happened to you. It's about taking responsibility for our actions though, and well, taking care of family. That should have been our priority from the beginning. We didn't take very good care of Marsh. We were awful to you. Our nephew will know that one day. Please, let us do this one thing and make something better for you."

"What does Marsh have to say about this generous gift you plan on giving me?"

Brixton and Bastion made eye contact with one another, and not for the first time, made me wonder if they were truly able to communicate telepathically. Eventually, they both admitted that their younger brother did not know they were offering up their condo.

"How do you think it would make him feel, if I accepted the condo, but didn't accept the house he offered for us to live in?"

"Mom said you wouldn't accept that house because there were strings attached. Marsh wanting you guys to all be a family and whatnot."

"That's all true," I agreed while tapping my chin to seem deep in thought. Then, I turned a hard glare on both men, trying to figure them out. There was honestly no way to tell if they were being sincere or playing more games. Who knew? Maybe this was a gold-digger test. A little late for that, considering I already had Marsh's baby. There was also the fact that I hadn't asked their brother for a damn thing and had turned down his house.

Then again, there was a third possibility hanging in the wind too. They were doing this to torment me further.

"Well, if its something you'll consider, we have our lawyer on standby to make all the necessary paperwork happen to change things over for you," Bastion tacked on helpfully.

"So, let me get this straight…" I took the empty – mostly empty – seat on the couch and started folding laundry again.

"You want to gift me the condo where your brother moved to after leaving me with nothing but a mostly bare apartment and no warning that it was about to happen?"

When Brix started to speak, I held my hand up to hush him. "The same condo where Cramer took pictures of him fooling around – maybe more – with the nurse who was working the labor and delivery department the night my son was born?"

Both of their eyes grew wide.

"I allowed you into my home and thought you were being sincere, but apparently you're still both hell bent on making me miserable." Angry tears fell freely from my traitorous eyes that refused to hold them back any longer.

"What did I ever do to either of you to make you hate me this much? Seriously? You said you were jealous, but all I ever did was love your brother. I never stopped him from hanging out with you. I encouraged it, even after you started saying hateful, awful things to me."

I shook my head. "I always told him, when he wanted to stop talking to you guys for the way you treated me, that it wasn't right and you were his brothers. I never wanted to come between you. None of you. So, what was it? What did I do?"

"You didn't do anything," Bastion offered in a pleading tone. "I swear we were just being stupid and thought we knew what was best for our brother."

Brixton stood by quietly, and no one said anything else for quite a while before I heard Austin stir. The twins both looked toward the nursery with a longing expression on their faces. I stood up and went to get my son while they stayed rooted to their spots.

When I brought him out, I moved to stand in front of his uncles. "Austin Jason Kennedy, these are your uncles, Bastion and Brixton," I told my son. "You will never again see them in the same room with your mother for any reason. If you see them again, it will be because your father took you to see them. I hope you never hold that against me and know that it's a rule I'm setting in place to protect myself from the two people who have bullied me for years — for no apparent reason – other than it was entertaining to them."

"Opal!" Bastion gasped.

Someone knocked on my door.

I moved to go open it, as the men stood there staring at me with abject horror written on their faces. When I opened the door, it was to see Marsh, his mother, and Ryker all standing there with huge grins on their faces.

"I see you forgave my boys," Kathy expressed gleefully as she pushed past me and tried to take my son from my arms as she went. I stepped back, not allowing her to do so.

"My apartment is not big enough for everyone here."

"Well, that's not really going to be a concern for long, is it?" Kathy asked while eyeing the baby. "I brought the other boys to help you pack up."

"Pack up?" Marsh asked.

"To move. Your brothers gifted her their condo," She told Marsh, as if it were already decided. "It's perfect really because it will put my grandson much closer to the house."

"And a lot further away from where Opal works," Marsh argued, his face turning red with anger.

"Mom," Brixton choked out, and when I turned, he had tears streaming down his face. The mood shifted completely as Ryker shut the door, and seemed to stop all the oxygen flow in the small space with the gesture.

"She didn't accept," Bastion informed her as he put his arm around his brother's shoulder.

"Didn't accept?" She glanced around my place and wrinkled her nose at the space. "Why in the world would you turn down not one, but two, good housing options for you and the baby? If you're holding out for something more," she started to say when Brixton stopped her.

"Mom! Stop."

"No!" She huffed. "I will not stop. That is MY grandson and I will not see him living in squalor like this."

"Get out!" Those two words were said almost whisper quiet, but the tone behind them let everyone crowded inside my apartment know that I meant business.

"Excuse me?" Kathy snapped at me while once again reaching for my son.

"Do you have multiple personalities?" I asked Kathy. "One minute I think you're an amazing mother figure and the picture of what I want to be one day. The next, you are a fire-breathing dragon who I want nothing to do with. I suggest you pull yourself together, and when you're around me, you don't act like you have any right to demand a single thing from me." I physically shook with anger as I spoke to her, though I never raised my voice. When she seemed ready to argue, I carried on with my point instead.

"Austin might be your grandchild, but he is *MY SON*! You walked in here, and because you didn't get your way, you proceeded to insult my home, me, and my decisions. I worked for this place and everything in it. It might not be much to you, but I did it all on my own, while pregnant with my son. No one helped me. No one paid my medical bills, for any of the baby's things, or for anything else. I was the only one providing every-thing we needed."

"Opal? Why are you speaking to me this way?"

"Mom, please, stop. She's already told us she never wants to be in the same room with either of us again. Do you really want to add yourself to that list?"

"She did what?!" Kathy yelled. My upstairs neighbor stomped on the floor. Kathy rolled her eyes at the noise. "The nerve," She said to the ceiling.

"Get Out!" I demanded once more. When no one moved, I picked up my phone. "If you are not all gone in the next three minutes, I will call the police and have them sort you all out for trespassing."

"What the fuck did you to my woman?" Marsh yelled at his brothers.

The baby started crying.

I had enough.

I started dialing, only I didn't call 9-1-1, like I planned to. Instead, I called Mr. Kennedy. "If you do not get your family to leave my apartment, you will need bail money for every single one of them because they're about to be arrested for trespassing, harassment, and any charge I can lob at them. I won't tolerate being treated like I'm some evil person for one more second by any of you damn Kennedys. Not ever again!" I yelled into the phone as the hot tears continued to stream down my face and my son cried in my arms.

"I'll be right there, Opal. I promise to get everyone on their way and they'll sort this mess, whatever it is. No need to call the police."

He hung up, and immediately Kathy's phone began ringing. She stared at me, as if she had never seen me before, as her phone rang through to voicemail and started back up again. I punched three numbers into my cell, and got ready to hit the phone icon to initiate the call when Kathy finally turned her back on me and walked out the door. All of her boys followed quietly. None of them looked back as Marsh set the lock and closed the door tight. Then I crashed down on the couch and cried with my baby.

TWO DAYS WENT BY, and I hadn't heard a peep from the

Kennedy household when my phone beeped with an incoming text.

> Ryker: Just a heads up – Mom has been trying to get Marsh to file an injunction against you, claiming you are unfit and mentally unstable. She wants him to take Austin from you.

> Opal: Thanks for letting me know, I guess.

Son of a bitch. My mind frantically began planning how to afford a lawyer, or better yet, how to pick up our lives and disappear. Marsh had returned my portion of our savings money when he stayed with me before I had the baby. It had been set aside, in addition to the other money I managed to save up, for me to purchase a vehicle. I hadn't done that yet, because I was waiting on Beth and Vi to take me to a dealership to go look. If I was frugal, I could get something that would fit most of what we needed, and then run.

It shouldn't have come to that, but I knew what it was like being the odd duck going against the Kennedy family's wishes. They knew everyone in this town and had their respect. I was just the daughter of some crazy hippies who took off and left me alone in this town years ago. It wouldn't matter that I was a good mother, and the Kennedy's had all dived off the deep end. It would only matter who believed the lies they told.

> Ryker: Accidentally hit send with my thumb. I wasn't done.

> Ryker: Marsh told her, if she kept her shit up, she would never see Austin again, no matter what you decided. He threatened to take you and the baby out of this town, so you wouldn't have to deal with any of us ever again.

> Ryker: And my dad threatened to divorce my mom if she didn't settle down and stop causing problems.

I did not know what to say to any of that, because I hadn't seen those responses coming. Apparently, Ryker wasn't through filling me in, as another text beeped through while I was trying to process the last few.

> Ryker: Dad laid into the twins for going to see you with that ridiculous offer, to Mom for insulting the home you worked hard to put together on your own, and me and Marsh for allowing Mom to go over to your apartment at all after the hospital fiasco.

A couple minutes went by before the next message came through.

> Ryker: I told Mom that if she kept it up, I would go stay with you and that I would testify in court that you are the best mom, the best person I know, and that if anyone in all this mess is unstable, it's her.

> Ryker: Dad went to check her into a clinic to get some help. The twins put their condo up for sale, since you wouldn't take it. Don't know where they've been, but they chewed Mom out for her behavior and I haven't seen them since the other day. They told her they deserved every bit of what you said to them and more, and told her that you were even respectful when you spoke to them.

> Ryker: Are you getting these?

Ryker: Hopefully, you didn't block me. Here's your other warning. Marsh is coming over in a bit. He wants a chance to apologize for our crazy family. He also wants to see his son. Please, don't turn him away because my mom and brothers made you cry. He deserves to see his son. I know he broke your heart, but...

Opal: I would never keep Marsh from his son. You either.

Ryker: Didn't know I had a son, but I appreciate you!

Opal: Smart ass. Sorry for kicking you out with the crazy. I just couldn't handle anything else that day.

Ryker: Don't apologize to me. I understood. So did Marsh, and he's back to being angry with everyone for upsetting the balance.

I set my phone aside after that. Why did it feel like I was the girl who broke up the band? There wasn't any one thing I did to cause any part of what was happening with the Kennedy family. Logically, I knew that. Still, it felt like I was at the epicenter of their problems and my heart hurt to know that an entire family fell apart because I was once involved with Marsh. What kind of family would be left for my son, when all was said and done?

Chapter 26

MARSH

My family was bound and determined to make my life as difficult as possible. There was little doubt that Opal hated me, my family, and her life in our town. We were all taken aback by my mother's behavior. My father blamed himself. She hadn't been the same since his little indiscretion with his secretary. My mother had been drinking, and hiding it from everyone so successfully, that we didn't even notice she had become an alcoholic.

It made me step back and wonder what kind of damage I'd really done to Opal. She'd been pretty upfront about most of her struggles. She also never held back when she chewed me out about how my actions had consequences for everyone, whether I realized it at the time or not. I worried for her, even though I thought she was handling everything in a healthy way. There was only so much a person could take before they came out of a situation completely broken.

Seeing Opal so close to the brink, as she held our crying son that day, while my family continued to pick away at her fragile pieces, destroyed something inside of me. I had done that. I had allowed my brothers to continue to treat her like crap, for years, without really putting my foot down in any kind of meaningful way. Granted, I thought if I had spoken up, it would have made their behavior worse.

It shouldn't have mattered. Opal should have been my priority, not the twins. It was a lesson probably learned far too late, but I was going to prove to her that things would change from here on out. That started by respecting her decisions. If she didn't think my brothers were good enough to come around her, or our son in her presence, then they weren't good enough period and they would have to work at changing her mind on their own time. Opal had been right. My brother's might not have been at fault for my decision, because I could have ignored them. They were responsible for bullying her, for years, to try to get her to break up with me and that was what they had to overcome.

I was done with them. They had good intentions with the condo, but it backfired because of their history with her, and there was no coming back from that scene. Especially after my mother added to the mix of drama.

I was going to see Opal again today, for the first time since everything went down. I'm not ashamed to admit that I begged Ryker to send her a message or call and explain what had been happening and that I was on my way. He wasn't the gatekeeper to my son or the woman I made him with, but he was the only member of our family who she still respected enough that she would hear him out.

Our family had a lot to atone for, eventually. That started with me. Ryker made me promise to put any talk of Opal and me getting back together on the back burner for now.

"Just support Opal in any way she needs, Bro. Right now, she needs to know that you're there for your son. She needs to know that she won't be pressured to do something she isn't comfortable with. After Mom's very vocal decree that you should take your son and have her declared unfit – that had occurred on the very busy street outside of the twin's condo — she's probably afraid of what our family might try."

It killed me to know that Ryker was right. The seventeen-year-old in the mix turned out to be wiser than all the adults he was supposed to look up to. It wasn't the first time that I'd thought of my little brother that way, and probably wouldn't be the last. The boy made me damn proud to call him family.

I stared at Opal's door for the longest time, debating on whether or not she had enough time to decompress from the events the other day. Truthfully though, I missed my son. I missed Opal too, but I could stay away from her, if that's what she wanted. The same wasn't true of Austin. I'd already made the mistake of disappearing from his mother's life. There was no way I'd disappear from his life as well. Even if it was just for a few days.

I took a deep breath, and then knocked softly on the door, in case he was asleep. It only took a moment for Opal to open up and stand aside to allow me in.

"Hey," I said as I passed by her.

"Hi," She offered back. Dark smudge marks looked like bruising under her eyes. It was obvious she hadn't been getting much sleep.

"You doing okay?"

Her answer was a shrug before she turned away and moved into the sparse kitchen. "He should be up soon. I was about to make a bottle. If you want to feed him, I'm sure he'd love to have you do it."

"Opal, what about you? Is there anything I can do for you? You look tired." Her head shook in answer and I wasn't sure if it was okay to push the point or not. Fuck, I hated walking on eggshells around her, but at the same time, there was no part of me that blamed her for being standoffish.

"If you want to take a nap," I started to say, but she immediately crossed her arms over her chest and turned to face me.

"Why? So you can abscond with my baby once I fall asleep?"

"Abscond with your baby? What the hell?" It took a minute for her meaning to really settle in, and then it was my turn to shake my head. "If it would make you feel better, I will sign a custody or visitation agreement with you. What my mom said, she was so far out of line that she's now in a rehab facility working on getting sober."

"Getting sober?" She asked, her surprise evident by the physical step she took away from me, as if the shock of that revelation needed more space. "What do you mean?"

I sighed deeply and took a seat on the only free chair at her kitchen table. "Ever since my parents had that shit happen with Dad's secretary, Mom has apparently been coping with a bottle."

"And no one realized before now?"

"No. There's been so much going on and everyone is always coming and going. No one really noticed that Mom was falling apart. Now, Dad blames himself for literally everything. He's promised that the bottle and drugs aren't his escape of choice. Unfortunately, he's been spending just about every minute that he's not at work in his shop. He might be able to retire and start a business selling whatever it is he's been making out there."

"I'm sorry to hear about your family's troubles," She offered politely. That was my Opal, always sweet, even to the people who hurt her so much.

"Don't feel bad for any of them. There's no excuse for all the bullshit that's gone down. Not from my Mom, Dad, brothers, or me. No matter what, you never deserved to feel an ounce of pain or anguish because of our bullshit."

"That's life, Marsh. Every action triggers another one. Some are just less pleasant than others."

I stood and moved toward her. She allowed me to pull her

into an embrace. We stood there hugging and swaying back and forth for a few minutes before I heard Austin start to squirm around in his nursery. I leaned in and kissed the top of her head. "I'll make it all up to you, if it's the last thing I do, Opal."

"Save your promises for your son, Marsh. If you want to do me any favors, I only ask for one."

"What?" I asked before tacking on, "Anything."

"Don't break them. If you make a promise to him, follow through. He should never have to know the heartache that comes with a broken promise, and he needs to know that his words have power. One day, it's going to be important for our son to know that his word means something. You need to help teach him that."

I nodded and understood where she was coming from. It wasn't even something I could disagree with, even if I had come here feeling contrary. She was right. My word didn't mean shit to her because I'd promised her forever, to never hurt her, to never leave. I'd broken them all. The result had far more reaching consequences than I ever imagined.

She nodded again and then left the room to go retrieve our son. Considering the size of her apartment, it didn't take her long to come back with him. "You might as well have a seat while I finish making his bottle. You two can catch up."

I chuckled at her suggestion.

"I'm sure he has a lot to tell me."

"He's grown already," She said so wistfully it almost took my breath away. Our son was meant to be a tiny thing a whole lot longer. What did she mean, he'd grown already? I soon found out. It was evident, at first glance, that his cheeks had filled out more and his eyes were wide open and seemed so much more alert.

"You weren't kidding," I huffed.

"I stopped trying to breastfeed at all and just switched

completely over to formula. Without all the fussing and struggle, he's flourishing. I might be a failure, but he shouldn't have to suffer for it."

"You're not even close to being a failure. Look what we did." I quickly corrected myself, because I'd only had a part in his creation. Everything else was down to Opal. "What you did! You made sure he came out healthy and happy even though you had a horrible time throughout your pregnancy. I think you deserve a damn award for it."

I could see her blush, while keeping my eyes downcast for the most part, so as not to embarrass her further. It hurt to know that she thought of herself as a failure for anything. The woman was probably one of the strongest people I knew. She spat in the face of adversity and carried on like nothing ever happened.

"I meant what I said, if you want to take a nap, I have him."

She glanced over at me and then shrugged her shoulders. "It would be weird to try to sleep on the couch while you're here."

"Why? I've slept here before."

"Yes, but it's the middle of the day and you'll have nothing else to do and nowhere else to sit while I try to dream and drool all over my pillow.

"I see. So, you're afraid I'll watch you while you sleep?"

She shrugged. "Can we just leave it at the fact that it would be weird?" Opal handed me the freshly made bottle, and despite knowing she would never give me something that was a temperature that would hurt our son, I still tested it out on my wrist to be sure. "I'm glad you're extra cautious with him."

"I know you would never give me something that wasn't just right, but I was reading about potential hot pockets of milk in bottles and…"

Opal giggled. "Those generally occur when people try to

microwave bottles. I never do that." She went back to the sink and started washing out the saucepan she'd just used.

"Don't know how you could ever consider yourself a failure when you go the extra mile for everything."

"My body didn't work the way it was supposed to," She admitted sadly.

"Opal, you know that happens to lots of women, right?"

"Yeah, but if we were living back in the olden days, our baby might starve if we couldn't find a wet nurse to help him out."

"It's a good thing we're not living in the olden days then." I laughed as I said it because sometimes, Opal could be just as weird as her mother. It was endearing most of the time. When she glanced at the clock on the wall for the fourth time, there was no holding back my curiosity.

"Do you have somewhere to be?"

"Sorry, it's just that I have a ride coming to get us at two, so that I can go to the store and grab some more formula. He goes through a lot of it."

"I could take you. I'm here and the truck is just outside."

"Actually, would you mind staying here with him and giving me a few minutes to shop without Austin? I haven't been able to go anywhere by myself, and could use a bit of a break."

"Sure." I carefully leaned over while cradling Austin in one arm and dug my wallet out of my pocket while anchoring his bottle with my chin. It was probably a sight to see, considering Opal was standing across the room chuckling at me.

"Here," I called out to her as I tossed my wallet onto the little coffee table in front of her sofa. Then I dug out the keys to my truck from another pocket. "Take the truck, and please, use my credit card for whatever he needs, or anything you need, for that matter."

"I don't want your money," She argued.

"Opal, he's my son, too. It's my responsibility to take care of him and we haven't set up any kind of child support or whatever. Save yourself a few bucks and use my money."

She relented and grabbed my card, but left my keys. Her phone beeped with an incoming text and she smiled down at it as she read. "My ride is here. Call if you need me to come back." Just as quickly as she looked at the text, the woman was out the door. It took a couple minutes for me to realize she hadn't taken the truck keys. Then, it hit me, she said she had a ride coming to get them.

Once I finished feeding, burping, changing my son, and laying him back in his crib, I pulled out my phone to text my younger brother.

> Marsh: Did you by chance come pick Opal up?

> Ryker: No. I thought you were heading to her place and gave her the heads up in a text, like you asked.

> Marsh: She left me with Austin while she went to the store. Said she had a ride lined up.

> Ryker: Probably Joe.

That's exactly what I was afraid of. She had mentioned him asking her out, before she gave birth to our son, but I hadn't taken it as seriously then. Opal was no longer pregnant with another man's baby. She was no longer pregnant. Period. Her body had seemingly snapped back to its pre-pregnancy shape, for the most part, and if she didn't have those dark smudges under her eyes, she would look just as gorgeous as ever.

I never thought about what I'd do if Opal started dating. While we were split up, before I knew she was pregnant, I figured what I didn't know wouldn't hurt me. My mind immediately thought that if I was having trouble dating other people, so would she. Then again, my brain forgot to factor in the part where our breakup hadn't been her choice. It had been mine, meaning I broke her heart and she hated me.

What if she started dating Joe? What if they decided to get married and create their own family with my son in the mix? I went to check on my boy, more nervous than ever that I might have truly pushed Opal away for good. If I hadn't, my family's behavior certainly hadn't helped push her back in my direction. If anything, the way my mom had treated her, that would have sent her running far away if she'd had somewhere to run to.

Almost an hour later, I was in the middle of changing a particularly nasty diaper when Opal came through the door laughing at something.

"I'm serious," A man tried to convince her. "You should have seen it. I was standing there with my hands up, and…" Joe finally noticed me sitting there on the floor with a shitty diaper beside me and a baby wipe midway between the dispenser and my son's ass. "Oh, hey man. How's it going?"

He really tried for casual, knowing exactly who I was, and that he'd walked through the door making my ex-girlfriend let loose and laugh like I hadn't seen her do in almost a year.

"Joe," I deadpanned and continued to clean my son up while keeping one eye on what was going on.

"Thanks so much for shopping with me and then helping me in with all this," Opal gushed.

"I told you before, glad to help. You already know that I understand how tough it can be to be a single parent without help."

I cleared my throat to indicate that she had plenty of help. Opal blushed, but Joe seemed put out by my interruption.

"Anyway," Joe carried on like I wasn't still sitting there in the middle of the floor with my son. "Would it be possible to get a babysitter Friday night? If not, you can always bring the little guy along. I don't mind."

"Oh," She thought for a moment. "I'm not sure. I'll check with Bethany and see if either she or her mom are free."

Were they really setting up a date right there in front of me? Fuck!

"Great." He leaned in and kissed her cheek, but pulled away as his phone beeped. He pulled it out and shook it in the air. "Gotta go, duty calls. Let me know one way or another and I'll be here Friday at five with my phone off so we don't have any interruptions," The asshole confirmed before heading out the door. Opal moved behind him to shut the door and lock up before turning with her hand pressed to her cheek, right over the spot where the asshole had kissed her.

She was in a completely blissed out daze before Austin's squeal for attention pulled her back to present. Her cheeks pinked in embarrassment when she realized I had been watching the whole thing play out.

"Was this some sort of revenge?" I asked quietly.

"What? That's ridiculous, Marsh."

"Is it? You never dated before, now you're suddenly making plans to go out on a date with some guy while I'm sitting right here to witness it."

She huffed. "I never dated before because I was pregnant and also heartbroken at first."

"And now?"

"Now, I'm no longer pregnant or heartbroken. I'm just a struggling, single mom who thinks it might be good for me to begin moving on."

I couldn't look at her. Instead, my eyes stayed trained on my son. Our son. Maybe the only thing we would ever have linking us together again. "Can you…" I tried to get out as I stumbled back from where Austin was lying on the mat on the floor. The minute I got to the bathroom, I heaved up everything I'd eaten that day. It took me a few extra minutes to get my shit together enough to go back out to the living room.

"That happened to me the day I came home to find you'd cleared out any trace of yourself from the apartment we used to share," Opal said, forcing me to look up and find her sitting there on the floor with Austin, waiting for me to come back out.

"What happened?"

"The vomiting," She replied without an ounce of emotion. "Funny thing, I thought it was just morning sickness, but judging by your reaction, maybe it truly was the first stage of grief."

"Grief?" I asked. It felt like I was swimming in a fishbowl full of sludge. Nothing was processing the way it was meant to.

"Yeah, Marsh. You probably never really experienced it because in the back of your mind, I've always been an option to come back to. From where I stood when you left me, my whole future – the one we'd planned together – was wiped out completely without any hope of getting it back."

"We *can* have it back." Opal didn't look as though it would be easy to convince her.

"How do you imagine something like that might be possible? You wanted to use your mom and dad as the reason for why you left me. So that one day, neither of us would have regrets about being the only people we'd ever had a relationship with. What about now?"

"What do you mean?"

"Your mom is in rehab. Your dad is a mess. The whole Kennedy family is at odds with one another and according to you, it all stemmed from your dad's regrets. Look at the mess your family is in and tell me that anything can ever go back to what it once was. Your dad didn't even sleep with his secretary, and it destroyed your mother completely. How do you think I feel knowing you were with someone else?"

She had a good damn point. My parents pretended that their marriage was still pristine and the picture of perfection, minus that one blip. It had all been a lie though. The one thing I'd counted on when I left Opal was that my parents were able to go back to that picture of happiness after the mistakes my father made. That picture was a carefully constructed lie. You couldn't go back.

Just like Opal couldn't go back because the results of my mistake continued to haunt her. The same mistakes that stared her in the face the day she gave birth to our son. She couldn't even go to her doctor's office without worry of having to face my worst mistake – the one that went too far.

And if she went out with Joe, it would change everything for me too. Even if it never worked out with them. Knowing that she was with someone else, building memories with them, that he could make her laugh when I no longer could... Those things were almost worse than picturing anything intimate happening between them.

"I'm so sorry for everything I put you through," I admitted.

"I appreciate that, but 'sorry' doesn't erase anything, Marsh. I still see those pictures, those moments when I thought I'd die. Sorry doesn't undo the moments that made me die inside, like when Monica gave you your underwear on the street in front of our old apartment. When she said what she did at the doctor's office, or when Gabby was there in the delivery room. Those are all permanent memories that are burned into my mind. I'm not the last person you kissed, touched, or even had sex with. I'm not the last person you took on a date, and the funny thing is, I can't even remember the last date you took me on before you left me. I remember the dates you went on with other women in vivid detail, though."

"I get it, Opal. There are things I did that can't be undone. It's a lesson I'm pretty sure my dad is coming to terms with right now as well. As you said, those decisions he made had a ripple effect. I honestly thought that I was saving us from my parents' future."

She laughed. "You took away our future."

"I'm realizing that, even if I still don't want it to be true."

"Marshal?" She questioned.

"Yeah?"

"I will never keep you from your son, but we're going to need that paperwork signed and filed with the courts about custody and visitation schedules."

"It's really over," I mumbled.

"It's been over since the day you walked out on me."

"Can I come back tomorrow to see him? I promise not to get in your way or put pressure on you for more."

"Of course."

I nodded, kissed my son's head, and said goodbye. Then, I left Opal's apartment, knowing there was no more hope for the two of us.

Chapter 27

OPAL

"Are you sure that you've never done this before?" Joe asked me as I leaned over and took aim at the ball in front of me again.

"Positive. I always wanted to, but…" I had to stop myself from finishing the sentence because there was just something tacky about bringing up your ex-boyfriend while on a date.

"It's okay to talk about him, you know? It's not like I don't know the family or your history. Plus, you share a son. Stands to reason, if I'm dating you, he's going to be in your life."

"I know, it's just weird to tell my date that my ex-boyfriend never took me to play putt-putt golf because he thought it was lame." I shrugged my shoulders.

"Well, shows what he knows because you're a natural, and if I'm not mistaken, having a blast."

I grinned at Joe. "I am having a great time, thank you for doing this with me."

"Anytime, Opal." Joe's grin was sexy as sin. There was something about him that made my heart pitter-patter more excitedly than usual. It was nothing compared to the way

Marsh made me feel when we first started dating, but I'd chalked that up to first love.

"Opal?" I turned to see Bastion, Brixton, Jimmy, and Ryker standing off to the side of the golf course. It was part of an entertainment complex where there was an old arcade, thirteen seat movie theater, and even a go-kart track out back.

Jimmy hopped the fence and came over to give me a hug. He also gave one of those half hug, half back slap bro-greetings to Joe. "Joey, my man, good to see you." He told him before turning back to me. "Opal, it's good to see you too. I was hoping to stop by and meet my nephew sometime soon, now that I'm back." It didn't escape my notice that his eyes continuously bounced between Joe and me.

"Well, if you get done hanging out here early enough, you can stop by Marsh's house to see him. He has Austin overnight tonight. He'll be bringing him back sometime tomorrow before noon, I think."

After our recent talk about the state of our relationship, and the fact that I didn't see us ever getting back together because too much damage had been done, Marsh had finally moved into the house he claimed to have bought for me. He did it because the twins were apparently selling their condo, and he needed a place where he could have our son over for visits. His parents' house hadn't been an option for so many reasons.

"My brother has the baby overnight?"

"That's what I just said."

Jimmy then waggled his finger back and forth between Joe and me. "What exactly is going on here?"

"That's really none of your business," I answered at the same time Joe said, "We're on a date."

"You're on a date while my brother, your ex-boyfriend, babysits your kid?"

My brow rose at that. "No. I'm on a date while your

brother spends his visitation time with his son - being his father. It is his child too, therefore he's not babysitting. He's being a parent."

"Does he know you're out on a date while he's being a parent to Austin?" Jimmy asked. The only thing stopping me from walking away and ignoring him was that his tone wasn't accusatory, just curious.

"It's not really his business what I do when he's spending time with Austin, Jimmy. We're not together anymore. Marsh left me almost a year ago."

"No offense, man," He said to Joe before addressing me again. "I just thought the two of you would work your shit out and get back together, especially after having a baby."

"Maybe your family needs to fill you in on some things, but this is a really inappropriate time and place to have this discussion, Jimmy. Not to mention, it's still none of your business."

"Fair enough," He finally relented as he took a couple steps back. He started to turn and then glanced back at Joe. "Sorry for the intrusion on your date and for what I'm about to say." Then he turned to me, "For what it's worth, Joe's a good guy, but you belong with my brother. Always have, always will."

"Well, shit," Joe said as we watched the four Kennedy brothers take off.

"I'm so sorry." The apology left me immediately. "I've been enjoying myself for the first time in a very long time, so I guess I should have known a Kennedy would come along and ruin the night. I wouldn't blame you if you wanted to end things here."

Joe chuckled. "I've waited four months since I asked you out that first time to actually get you out on a date. There's no way I'm throwing in the towel because Jimmy came back confused about family dynamics after his deployment."

"I highly doubt he was confused. Those boys see causing

me trouble as an amusing pastime. The twins probably put him up to it."

"I doubt it, Opal. Jimmy doesn't play games like those two do." He was serious while defending his friend.

"Maybe."

"What do you say we give up the golf and go grab that dinner now?"

I offered Joe a grateful smile. "That would be wonderful."

"Good, because I want that easy vibe we had back and I don't think we'll get it here with those four wandering around."

I nodded because if I said anything, it probably wouldn't come out right. Ruining my first date, since Marsh broke up with me, was not on the agenda. We ended up at a restaurant I hadn't been to in ages, Angelo's Place. They served typical Italian-American food, from pizza and pasta to burgers. They were also very popular with the date crowd on the weekends.

It seemed to take forever for our waitress to show up to get our drink order, let alone the food. When she did, the woman did not appear too happy.

"Hello, Joe. I guess I see why things didn't work out between us, huh?" Our waitress glared at me, like I'd personally wronged her, only I had no clue who she was.

"Sheila, this isn't the time or the place."

"So, we dated for the past three months, then out of the blue you decided we're done, and a week later, you're out with this woman? Were you seeing her the whole time we were together?"

She seemed truly distraught, as I was left sitting there doing the mental math that made my face flame red in embarrassment. The first time Joe asked me out, I had still been pregnant and maybe he had been single at the time, or at least hadn't been with Sheila yet.

When he asked me out two weeks ago, he was still with

Sheila. It was then I turned an accusatory glare on him. "You were dating someone else when you asked me out?"

"No, I dated her after I asked you out. And when you finally agreed to go out with me again, I ended things."

I scrunched up my nose. "So, she was what? A placeholder until I was ready?" He shrugged and poor Sheila was standing there taking everything in with tears in her eyes. Apparently, she thought there was a lot more between them. "Did she know that?" I asked him. He glowered her way before focusing his attention back on me.

"It's not really what it looks like. Sheila might have gotten the wrong idea, but I wasn't looking for anything serious with anyone else, except you."

"You're a pig!" Sheila yelled at him before she stalked off. I couldn't blame her.

"Did you think I would be okay with this?" I asked him.

"Look, Opal, I know you were only with Marsh and that you don't have a lot of experience dating other people, but did you really think I'd be a monk while I waited for you to figure out whether you ever wanted to date again? I liked you and wanted to try something serious with you, but after a month, I knew it might be a while."

"Did you know that when a woman gives birth she isn't even supposed to have sex until after her six-week checkup?"

"O-kay?" He dragged the word out as he questioned what my point was.

"You couldn't even wait a month before you had to go find someone to meet your needs. I'm assuming that's what Sheila was about, since you don't seem to care that you hurt her feelings. She was a hookup, right?" He nodded. "So, you couldn't even wait a month. What am I supposed to think will happen if we got together, got serious, and had a kid together, down the road?"

"I'm not following."

"You couldn't even wait a month to hook up with someone else when you were trying to get me to date you, after I gave birth, so what's to stop you from doing the same thing to me later on and cheating because your needs aren't being met."

"That would never happen." The growl in his voice made it clear that he'd been insulted by my accusation.

"I'm sure Sheila felt the same," I replied.

"Look, I'm not sure why you're upset. Sheila knew the score and I stopped seeing her before we went out on our date."

"You were still seeing her when you asked me out again."

"Well, did you expect me to break up with her first? Then if you had said no…"

"Say no more. That's just disgusting. If you were serious about something more than a hookup situation with me, then yes, you would have broken it off with her before ever asking me out again." I stood.

"Where are you going?"

"Home."

"Oh, come on, Opal! At some point, you're going to have to grow up and realize that adults who date have baggage. You have a kid, with a man whose family is always going to be in your business, but you don't see me holding that against you." That did not even warrant a response. I turned and started walking out of the restaurant.

"Opal!" He called out. I ignored him. "How are you getting home? I'm your Uber driver and your date for the night too."

I laughed at the thought that I would have to go back to taking the more unreliable taxi service in town, until I could purchase my own vehicle, because there was no way I'd ever get in a car with Joe again. His nice guy act was just that – a show. He had just shown me, and Sheila, exactly who he was and there was no part of what he did that said he was a nice guy. Even if I had been perceived as being on the "winning" side of that nightmare situation, all I could think of was how soon I'd be the woman in Sheila's shoes. If he'd treat her that way, he'd do the same to me – eventually.

I started to walk home and got about a half mile from the restaurant when a car pulled up. To my complete and utter humiliation, it was Ryker and the twins.

"Need a ride?" Ryker asked.

"No, I'm fine, thanks."

"What happened to Joe?"

I scoffed. "Joe happened."

"Did he hurt you?" Ryker asked in a menacing tone. That boy really was going to be the best man a girl could ask for one day.

"My pride maybe, and Sheila's feelings, otherwise, no, he didn't hurt me."

"Son of a bitch," One of the twins hissed. "I told you I thought they'd been dating."

"That moron will pay," The other twin agreed.

I wanted to turn around and tell them both that they were idiots, but truthfully, I couldn't face them. I was certain they were happy about my humiliating date experience.

"Let me give you a ride home, Opal. It's late, and I'll be worried all night."

"I appreciate it, Ryker, but there's no way that I'm riding in the same seat with either of them," I pointed out.

The car door opened and Brix got out and moved immediately to the back seat. "You can have the front seat with Ry, since you don't mind his company, and Bas and I will remain quiet for the whole ride. I promise, we just want to make sure you get home safe." Ryker grinned as his brother seemingly made it easier for me to accept his offer of a ride.

"Where's Jimmy?" I asked.

"He's hanging with Marsh and Austin," Ryker replied.

"Fine." My feet already hurt, so I relented and got into the car. "Why are you the one driving?"

"They couldn't agree over whose vehicle to take tonight, and when I ended the argument by telling them that I'd just drive myself, they hopped in and told me I could be the designated driver."

One glance back at the twins told me they weren't inebriated. They both smiled at me, as if we were old friends. "Ended up not drinking after all, since Jimmy decided he wanted to just go hang out with the baby."

"Why didn't you all just stay together and hang out there?" I asked.

Both twins gave me an odd look, but it was Ryker who answered. "Bas and Brix aren't allowed to go over there when Marsh has Austin."

"What? Why?"

"Because Marsh said that they haven't earned your trust or approval yet, and he wasn't going to go against your wishes."

I stared at Ryker, dumbstruck. All this time, I'd been thinking that the twins were able to see my son when he was with his father. I hadn't realized that he had forbidden them to be there when he had the baby.

"You still haven't met your nephew, outside of that awful day in my apartment?" I asked them. Both shook their heads as their twin sorrowful expressions attacked my fragile heartstrings. I turned back to Ryker. "Take us to Marsh's house, please."

His grin grew by a mile and the boy did not argue.

Chapter 28

MARSH

"Hey man! Good to see you. I thought you weren't going to come by until tomorrow?"

"Well, I wasn't planning on it until I ran into Opal at The Parks."

"She was at The Parks?" I asked, immediately wondering who she had been there with.

"Yep," My oldest brother answered. "She told me you had the little squirt here, so I figured I'd stop by. Had Ryker drop me off once they explained why the twins weren't welcome here today."

I nodded, not willing to face down the argument about why the twins couldn't come to my house. Apparently, they'd told him enough because Jimmy didn't push the issue with me.

"So, where is my nephew?"

"Just got him down for the night, but you can come back to the nursery and see him. Quietly," I tacked on with a bit of warning.

"I gotcha, Bro," He teased as we made our way back to the nursery. He looked in on Austin and shook his head before we turned and moved to the living room once more. "Never thought I'd see the day when one of my little brothers had a baby, but I guess if I had to pick one of us to go first, it would have been you." He nailed me with a solid look as we sat.

"What the fuck happened with Opal? The only reason I pegged you to have a kid first was because you always had a rock-solid relationship with that girl." He glanced around at all the pictures of us together still hanging on my walls where my mother put them. I couldn't bring myself to take them down. It hurt too much to think that they might be all I had left of our time together, aside from my son.

"She was out with Joe tonight." I had my suspicions, but the confirmation from my brother was just like receiving a surprisingly swift kick to the balls.

"I was an idiot." That admission seemed to surprise Jimmy, but then I went on to explain everything from beginning to end. When I got to the final stages of the crap fest I'd created, Jimmy whistled long and low.

"Well, shit. You make me angry with myself for going away when I did."

I shook my head. "Nah, you had the right idea. Maybe I should have joined the military too and took Opal out of this place. Then, we wouldn't have had family drama and the twins in our faces the past few years."

Jimmy laughed at me. "No, you would have had deployments, time apart, and the possibility of coming home injured, with PTSD, or not at all on your shoulders. You can't trade one set of problems and think there won't be another set waiting for you. You should have already figured that out by now. You went looking for the greener grass and found that you had the best lawn out there before you stomped all over it."

"Thanks for the recap. Where were you a year ago before I stupidly agreed with Brix and Bas?"

"That was dumb on your part. Of all your brothers, those were the two you chose to listen to? No wonder Opal wants nothing to do with them, and as little as possible to do with you."

And there went another hammer to my nuts.

"Did she look happy?" I asked, almost afraid to know the answer.

Jimmy nodded. "Seemed to be, until she noticed us standing there watching them. She had been laughing and having a good time playing mini golf."

I scoffed at that. "She always wanted to do that, but I thought it was stupid."

"Maybe you should have thought more about what would make her happy, rather than yourself."

"Yeah, I'm getting that."

"A bit too late though, huh?"

"Any more salt you want to rub in my wounds, or should we take a trip to the store next time Austin wakes up?"

"Calm down, little brother," Jimmy ordered in his polite way. "Just want to make sure you never fuck up so epically again."

"Trust me, that won't ever be a problem."

"So, how do you plan on bringing women home when it looks like a shrine to your lost relationship in here?"

The sigh I heaved out was almost answer enough, but when Jimmy's stare became unrelenting, I finally capitulated. "I don't plan on bringing any women back here."

"You just going to give up on dating?"

"No, I guess not. I'm not ready right now."

"What about when you are?"

"There will never be another woman, who I'm not related to or who isn't Opal, that will walk through *that* door."

"You're serious?" I glanced up to see I had well and truly stunned my oldest brother.

"Yep. If I ever have a chance to get her back, I'm going to take it, and the last thing I need is for this house to have memories of someone else being here. I already told you about all the other shit Opal went through. She's already had enough of having the women I've dated being shoved in her face, and at the worst times."

"I get it, but it seems like she moved on already. She's got the entire night without a kid. Do you think she'll grant you the same respect, and not take Joe to her place, when their night winds down?"

I laughed. "She doesn't even have a bed at her place."

"Well, then I guess they'll end up at his."

He shrugged his shoulders in such a nonchalant way, as if Opal and Joe ending up in bed together was a forgone conclusion, that it made me rage inside. I stood, fury riding me hard as I thought about Joe putting his hands on my woman. I picked up a lamp and got ready to chuck the thing across the room when Jimmy stood and caught my hand before I could release it.

"Did you really try to give her this house?"

I nodded, my anger still rode me hard as we talked.

"She might have accepted. I felt like she was going to, at least thinking about it, but then we walked in and the pictures were everywhere thanks to Mom trying to be helpful." I explained to him why the pictures were a big deal and my brother simply hung his head.

"Man, when you screw shit up, you go all out."

"That's the damn truth."

"What are you going to do to try to get her back?"

"I'm giving her space."

"Considering she's out on a date tonight, maybe that wasn't the wisest plan."

"Jimmy, I took six months off from our relationship, to date other people, all the while thinking I could just walk right back into her life. She didn't get the same opportunity I did to date other people during that time because she was pregnant. The least I can do, after all the shit she had to put up with, is offer her the same thing I asked for."

"I know Joe. He's a genuinely good guy and has had a thing for her for years. We talked about it before I left because he used to ask how serious you two were. I think he was hoping you would rush off to college and leave her behind."

"He was like twenty-three when she was graduating high school." That rat bastard. Jimmy chuckled and shrugged his shoulders.

"She was legal and hot. You think he was the only one sitting back waiting on you to screw up? Half the town wanted in that girl's pants, your best friend included."

"He's no fucking friend of mine," I shouted.

"Well, you know that now. You let him get inside your head first, and then fuck with Opal's too, before you finally realized that." Jimmy sat back down and put the lamp down out of reach. It looked like I might have broken the cord on it when I snatched it up, so I guess I needed a replacement.

"That asshole always rubbed me the wrong way. I used to tell Mom to make you pick better friends. She laughed at me and said you'd figure things out, eventually."

"I've come to the realization that Mom hasn't been in the right frame of mind for some time."

"Well, this was before the shit with Dad and the drinking." We sat quietly for a bit, each of us lost to our own thoughts before Jimmy spoke again. "What are you going to do about the twins? You can't keep them from your son forever. I realize they were assholes, but they tried to make up for it — however stupidly. If you're forgiven for your part enough to have a place in your son's life, why can't they be?"

"They're not his dad," I said. "Trust me, if I wasn't Austin's father, I wouldn't have a place in his life either. They have years-worth of bullying her to try to overcome whereas I don't.

Even so, Opal still tried to kick me out of the delivery room, remember?"

Jimmy laughed. "Yeah, that's some funny shit."

"Didn't feel all that funny," I grumbled at him.

"Just in a funny, ironic kind of way, Marsh. What are the odds that one of the chicks you dated, and made out with, was the nurse meant to deliver your kid?"

"Fuck, it's like the universe was set on delivering Karma to me directly, but Opal was the one that kept getting hurt by it."

Headlights in the driveway caught both of our attention and we stood to see Ryker and the twins coming up the walkway. It looked like someone was behind them, but I couldn't see who. They fucking knew better than to be here when I had my son. They also should have known better than to bring a guest to my house this late.

I raced to the door and threw it open. "What the fuck are you two doing here?" I bellowed.

"Chill man," Ryker insisted, but I wasn't having it.

"You know they're not welcome here when Austin's at my house." My eyes were narrowed on my younger brother because there was no way I would allow him to start disrespecting Opal's wishes now. He had stood by her this long and needed to keep his promises to her.

I heard Austin squeal from the nursery and cursed under my breath that he had been woken up. Then, a voice I never thought would be on my doorstep again, pulled my attention back to the people on my lawn.

"I told them it was okay to come," Opal said as she moved around my brothers and stepped into the light. I couldn't help glancing around, further behind them, to see if her date for the night was lurking somewhere. There was no way that son of a bitch was going to waltz into my home with my girl on his arm. Then again, maybe he should come inside and see the pictures of us when we were happy together.

"What are you doing here?"

"Can we all come inside and have this conversation where the neighbors aren't hanging out with their cell phones ready to either dial 9-1-1 or shoot some video?"

"That's one of the few times I've ever heard Brix say something smart, you might want to listen," Opal teased. I didn't miss the way my brother tried to hide the grin on his face over my ex tormenting him.

I stepped back and held the door open for all of them to come inside. Opal tensed slightly when she noticed that the pictures of us were still hanging up.

"Oh, I hear Austin," She stated and immediately headed in the direction of our son's wailing. I followed behind her, but my brothers all congregated in the living room to wait and see how everything would play out.

"Not that I'm not happy to see you but, I'm a little confused," I told Opal as she picked our son up and scrunched her face at the smell he was putting off.

"Well, I guess it wasn't the noise that woke him after all," I commented dryly as I got a diaper and the wipes together on the changing table. She relinquished her hold on our son after placing a little kiss on his scrunched up forehead. I changed him as she stood back and watched with a content little smile on her face.

"So, how is it you came to be here, with three of my brothers, two of whom you banished from your life?"

"They stopped to give me a ride when they saw me walking home."

"Why in the hell were you walking home this late at night?"

"Bad date," She said and turned her back on me to head toward the living room as I picked our son up to follow behind her. *Bad date?* Well, that certainly worked in my favor, and it appeared it worked in the twins' favor as well, since she wasn't sending them on their way. They all brought her here, instead of taking her straight home, and that was something to be encouraged by as well.

The minute Opal walked back into the room ahead of me, the hushed conversation my brothers had been having ceased. I was positive they were filling Jimmy in on why exactly Opal was with them instead of on a date with Joe. While that was information I also wanted to know the answer to, it didn't seem like the most important aspect of the night.

The twins appeared to be holding their breath while both sets of their eyes were glued to my son.

"Brixton and Bastion, this is your nephew, Austin Jason Kennedy." Opal informed them. They both stood there in awe of my little boy, yet afraid to make a move toward him. "Who wants to hold him first?" Opal finally asked.

I don't know whether he did it to break the ice or because he genuinely wasn't going to let the twins hold Austin before he got the chance, but Jimmy jumped in and took him from Opal's arms.

"I'm your Uncle Jimmy. We'll forgive your mom for her rudeness at not introducing me too because she didn't know you were asleep the whole time I've been here."

Opal blushed profusely. "Sorry, Jimmy. I didn't realize."

Brix had legit tears falling from his eyes as he pushed forward and grabbed hold of Opal. "I'm so fucking sorry for everything. You have always been a far better person than any of us deserved. What we did was unforgivable."

Bastion took over with the hug after shoving our brother away. "He's right about everything. Thank you for this. It means the world to us, especially because we never deserved your kindness."

Before Bas let go of Opal, Brix was already claiming Austin from Jimmy. Having been informed about what a momentous occasion this was for the twins, Jimmy relented his hold on his nephew. Brix took Austin in his arms and moved to go sit on the couch.

"Hey, little man, I'm your favorite uncle."

"Nope. He already knows it's me. Besides Opal's doctor, I was the first to see that he was a boy," Ryker boasted.

"How was that possible?" Jimmy asked.

"He came with me to my doctor appointments," Opal explained. My other three brothers watched for my reaction.

"And I'm thankful that he was there for her when I couldn't be." Everyone left it alone, but I knew there would be more questions later. I'd filled Jimmy in earlier, but there were probably some things that got left out in the re-telling. Some of that was simply because I didn't know all the details about what happened between our youngest brother and Opal to put them on the path where Ryker ended up being her protector.

I stood back and watched as my brothers all cooed and baby talked my son, who was eating up all the attention.

"Sorry to show up unannounced," Opal said as she made her way over to me.

"Don't ever apologize for showing up here, Opal."

She glanced at my brothers and then up at the picture of us hanging on the wall above where they sat on the couch. "Why haven't you taken them down yet?" Her question was whispered in an obvious attempt to not have my brothers overhear.

"Because I still have hope," I explained. Opal nodded her head and then moved to my kitchen.

"Where do you keep your glasses?" She asked when I followed behind her. "I need some water."

I reached above her and pulled a glass free from the cabinet and then filled it with cold, filtered water from the fridge. "Why were you walking home tonight?"

Once she pulled the glass away from her mouth, her eyes met mine. "I told you, bad date."

"So bad that you had to walk home?"

"Apparently, Joe had been seeing someone else when he asked me out again. She happened to be our waitress after we left mini golf to go to dinner."

"He was cheating, and made you the other woman?" My eyebrows had to be solidly in my hairline. "Jesus, what the fuck was that idiot thinking?"

Opal shrugged her shoulders. "I think it was a bit more complicated than that. He had broken things off with her before our date, but that didn't erase the fact that he asked me out again while he was still seeing her." She shrugged again. "Joe claimed it was never anything serious between them. He even agreed that she was a placeholder, someone to do, while waiting on me to recover from having Austin."

"What the fuck?" Jimmy stood there in the space between the kitchen and living room, fury clear on his face. "I'm sorry, Opal. I told you earlier that he was a good guy, but apparently a lot of shit has changed around here since I've been gone. More than I was aware of," My brother added at the end with a pointed look toward me.

"It's okay, Jimmy. I've learned that you never really know a person. Not truly. Besides, people change, so even if you did get to a point where you know them well, things happen that change the way they think and handle situations."

"Still, I thought you were in good hands. Had I known my old friend had grown to become a slimy bastard, I wouldn't have left you there with him."

"Had I known that in advance, I would have never gone on the date with him," She admitted. "Hindsight is a bitch like that." Her comment made me wonder if she regretted our relationship. She must have felt my intense stare because her eyes searched mine out and then she smiled.

"Don't worry, I wouldn't wish you away like that. If for no other reason, than I could never wish Austin away."

I didn't get a chance to respond because Opal left the room and went to sit with the twins and Ryker who were still playing with Austin. His sleep schedule was probably going to be screwed seven ways to Sunday, but there was no way I'd break up the moment my two brothers got to meet my son and Opal was willingly sitting in the house I bought for us.

"You going to pull your head out of your ass and stop waiting around for her to come back to you now?" Jimmy asked me. I turned my attention back to him.

"She's here, isn't she?"

"Yeah, brother, she is. You're a lucky bastard if she gives you another chance. Don't waste it."

That was something I never planned to do again. I just had to figure out a way to get her to want to come back to me and stay.

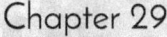

Chapter 29

OPAL

THE WARM FEELING THAT ENCOMPASSED ME WHILE WATCHING all of the Kennedy boys engaging with my son was something I couldn't stop thinking about. It had been a week since that night. I'd stayed for another hour, until Austin grew cranky and tired, and then asked Ryker to take me home. He promised the others that he'd be back for them once he dropped me off.

When we got to the apartment, Joe was sitting outside my door waiting on me. He was none too happy to see that it was Ryker dropping me off.

"Did you trade one brother in for the younger model?" He asked snidely.

I ignored him as I unlocked my door. Ryker didn't though. By the time I turned around, after hearing the sound of flesh meeting flesh, it was to see Joe standing there holding his busted nose.

"I don't care how pissed you are that you fucked up the only chance she was liable to give you. That doesn't give you reason to disrespect Opal. Don't give a fuck what you insinuate about me, but you say one more out of line thing about her and that nose won't be your only problem tonight."

Joe shook it off while using his shirt to staunch the flow of blood. "You're right," He told Ryker in a nasally voice before turning to me. "I'm sorry. The kid is right. I'm angry with myself, not you. I was just surprised to see one of them dropping you off."

"He saw me walking home and picked me up."

"That was hours ago," Joe insisted.

"Yes, because we went by Marsh's place, so I could check on Austin first." It was none of his business who else had been there or why we really went by Marsh's place. It wasn't even any of his business how I got home. Still, I was too tired for conflict.

"I see. Look, Opal, I think you got the wrong idea back there at the restaurant."

"Nope. I got the gist of what was going on. I sincerely hope that you apologize to that woman and do something nice to make it up to her. She didn't deserve that. You had to know she worked there," I added, because it was something I'd been thinking about since I started my walk home.

"Actually, I didn't. She apparently got fired from her last job when she didn't show up for a few days." He looked guilty as he mentioned that part, and I guessed that it was because she hadn't dealt well with their breakup.

"You're right, though. I didn't handle things the correct way. I never should have asked you out again while she and I still had something going on. We were never in a monogamous relationship. I promise you, I didn't lie when I said we were just hooking up and hanging out."

"Isn't that how all relationships start, in a way?" I told him. "That girl caught feelings for you, and the longer you continued hooking up and hanging out, the more hope she had that you would make things official with her. She couldn't help the way she felt any more than you could."

"Where does that leave us?" He asked.

"It leaves us nowhere, Joe. You went about things the wrong way. I'm not inclined to wait around for that to happen to me when something better comes along."

"Opal, don't punish me for what Marsh did."

"I'm not. You just showed me exactly who you are and what I can expect."

"Everyone comes with baggage," He tried to remind me again.

"You mentioned that earlier. It's also my choice to accept it or move on because I don't think it's something I have time to handle." I groaned. "I appreciate the fact that you came here tonight, to try to work things out and explain, but I'm tired Joe, and I'm done. We tried a date; it didn't work out."

Joe stood there for another minute before his shoulders slumped and he walked away. I turned to Ryker then. "You didn't have to punch him in the nose."

"Yeah, I did. You don't deserve to be talked to that way. He's lucky he only got one."

"Come on, Hulk-boy, let's go get your knuckles tended to."

"They're fine," He argued.

"You need ice or they'll swell."

"Fine, Mom!" He teased.

"The weird thing is, I am a mom now. That's still tough to get used to some days."

Ryker laughed and pulled out his phone, no doubt texting his brothers about what happened, as I got some ice into a freezer bag for him.

Despite Joe thinking I brushed his comment about baggage off, it was on my mind since I left the restaurant. Everyone I would meet, from here on out, would have baggage. There would be exes, maybe kids, damage from being cheated on or being the cheater. The crazy thing was, I wouldn't know what I was getting into, no matter who I attempted to date in the future. It wasn't like meeting the love of your life and starting to date your sophomore year of high school.

Neither of us had come into our childhood relationship with anything else. We had been blank slates and that would never happen again. I wondered if maybe I would always be too picky, or if something else was holding me back. Something, like the fact that I never got over my first love. Sure, I was angry with him. There were things I still hadn't forgiven, and others that I'd never be able to forget. It meant that Marsh and I now had baggage between us, that we'd have to maneuver around.

That was something I'd been thinking over for the rest of the week. Was the proverbial devil I knew better than whatever else was out there? Had I been spoiled by Marsh for the seven years of our relationship prior to him leaving me? We never really had any major arguments and never split up before. I had so many questions, but the main one was 'why?'.

Why had he left? Why had he done it the way he did? Why didn't he come back sooner, if what he said about not being interested in any of his dates was true? Why would he make out with Gabby, if he didn't really want to? Why would he sleep with Monica?

I knew some of those answers, but others were just a vague understanding of why he did things the way he did. There wasn't any real clarity to them.

Sure, his parents had issues, his brothers were pressuring him and treating me badly, his best friend was an absolutely unforgivable dick, who Marsh unfortunately listened to back then. I knew all those things. What I didn't know was how all that equated to the way Marsh left. Some might think that wasn't important to know, but it was the one thing holding me back from forgiving him. I knew better than anyone that if you couldn't forgive, it was hard as hell to move on.

My thoughts shifted, as I glanced at the clock. I hadn't

heard from Joe since our date night. I wasn't surprised by that, but it was rather disappointing that I would no longer have a reliable mode of transportation, especially one who didn't get impatient when I had to put a car seat in the vehicle. That was unfortunate, since my son needed to get to his doctor's appointment, and I couldn't get a ride to take him there. Finally, I had to relent and call Marsh.

"Hey, what's up? Everything okay?" He asked immediately upon answering.

"I hate to bother you, but Beth has been bogged down with work during normal business hours, and I haven't had a chance to go look at cars."

"I can take you to pick something out," He offered.

"No, thanks. That's not what this is about. I need a ride, and the taxi drivers get testy with me when I have to put a car seat in their cabs. Austin's checkup appointment is in an hour."

"Why didn't you tell me sooner? Why were you looking for a ride? Dammit, Opal, that's something I would prefer to go to anyway. I'm not some absent father who doesn't care about his son's well-being."

The deep sigh I exhaled said everything I couldn't while biting my tongue.

"Sorry, I get it. You've been used to going it alone and it's hard to change direction. I'll be there in fifteen minutes, and I already have a car seat installed, so taking the time to do that won't be an issue."

"Thank you." I hung up immediately because crying on the phone wasn't something I wanted to do.

True to his word, fifteen minutes passed before there was a knock on the door. I answered and let Marsh see himself in while I continued to get Austin ready. "Sorry for the late notice," I called out.

"After his appointment, I think we need to sit down and have a conversation about what we're doing in the future. I don't want to continue being left out of things. You might still be angry with me, but I have…"

"I'm not angry with you," I told him as I carried our son from the nursery to the living room. "That's not what this was about. Life is hectic right now. I have to go back to work, and I've been trying to find a daycare to take Austin to where I feel comfortable with the staff, and the appointment honestly slipped my mind until I got the reminder."

"What's going on with the daycare thing? You know that my mom," He started to say and I cut him off before he could even suggest what he was about to.

"Look, Marsh, two years ago, if we'd had a baby I would have been the one to suggest your mom take care of our child while we worked, if that's what she agreed to do. The fact is, she is not the same woman today that she was two years ago. She's only just recently returned home from a stint in rehab, and no offense to your mother, but I think she needs time to prove that things will stick. The last time I saw her, she was completely erratic and out of line with me. There is no way I would entrust my child to her."

"She's doing much better," He insisted, but I could tell that he had his own reservations. "I understand you feeling the way you do. I'd like to help find a suitable arrangement for Austin. Maybe, we can look into getting a nanny instead?"

I laughed. "A nanny? Really? Who is going to pay for a dedicated nanny and where is she going to stay? Under my sofa?"

"The nanny can keep an eye on him at my house, since there's more room. When you get off work, you can pick him up there. It won't be much different than dropping him off at a daycare, except we'll be able to control things better this way. I can even install some security cameras in the house so you can check in on him throughout the day."

"Again, who is paying for this, because unless you got a hell of a raise at work, you don't have that kind of money either, especially not with a house payment."

"I don't have a house payment, Opal."

"What? How is that possible?"

"Inheritance from my grandparents. I have to swear you to secrecy about that because Ryker isn't allowed to know that he has money coming to him when he reaches the designated age."

"Oh. No problem. That's not my business to tell your brother." I moved to grab the diaper bag, but Marsh beat me to it. "If you don't have a house payment, then I guess you can afford the nanny, but I want to interview them with you."

"I wouldn't have it any other way."

I nodded my head. "We really do need to get going."

"You have everything?" He asked. When I offered my agreement, he picked up the infant carrier our son was already strapped into with one hand while placing his other behind my lower back to escort me out of the apartment. It was a gesture that was such a normal thing in our relationship through the years that my heart clenched tightly in my chest at the feel of the innocent touch.

He must have felt me stiffen in reaction because he retracted his hand and turned me so that we were facing one another. "Are you okay? Did I do something wrong?"

"No, you didn't. I just remembered how you used to always guide me with your hand on my back when we were together. It was something so normal back then that I took it for granted." I shook the sentiment off. "It was just a bit of a shock after not having someone do that in so long."

"We better go," Marsh choked out, and the emotion in that sound made me regret flinching at his touch and the memories it brought back. I nodded and made my way out to his truck wishing that I could feel his hand on me once more. There was no denying that I missed his touch, the way we used to talk, our friendship, and so much more. It was hard not to miss it.

On the one hand, I got to witness him being the father I always knew he would be. On the other, the rest of the picture I'd always held in my heart was missing. The picture of us together while being the best parents we could be was just an illusion, or at the very least, a dream. For that brief moment, it almost felt real.

We were both quiet all the way to the doctor's office. Once we were in the parking lot, and Marsh turned the car off, he turned to me with a solemn look on his face. "I'm sorry if I made you uncomfortable. Sometimes, I forget that I don't have the right to do things like that anymore."

"You didn't make me uncomfortable. It was simply a shock to my system, considering I'm no longer used to it. You didn't do anything wrong, Marsh. I promise."

"Okay," He said before getting out of the truck and going to the back to grab Austin.

OUR LITTLE BOY was not too happy with us when we left the appointment. He had been due for another immunization, and was cranky, not that I could blame him.

"What do you say we grab some food and head to the house to eat and talk?" Marsh suggested above the wailing our son was doing in the back of the truck.

"That sounds fine, though you might want to think about ordering something from delivery once we get there, because I don't think anyone in a drive thru will hear you over that racket," I pointed out. Austin had a set of lungs on him that would impress anyone.

Marsh chuckled. "Fair enough."

Once we were settled at his house, I stood while rocking

Austin until he finally wore himself out enough to fall asleep in my arms. It was still odd that Marsh had pictures of us up all over his house. I had none of him displayed anywhere in my apartment. There were only pictures of Austin, Beth, and me. I didn't even have any of my parents, but that was for an entirely different reason.

All the pictures of my previous life with Marsh were in electronic format and I refused to print any out because it felt disingenuous to me, since we were no longer together.

"Food should be here in about fifteen minutes. Do you want to go lay him down in the crib?"

"Sure," I offered as I moved toward the nursery Marsh had set up in his house. It made me a little jealous because it was the nursery I would have given my son, if I had been able to afford a place with the space and all the things I really wanted to furnish it with. I laid my son down in his crib and turned to find Marsh right there behind me. His hands flew to my hips to catch me when his proximity threw me off balance.

"Sorry, I was looking down over your shoulder to make sure he was okay. I hated seeing him in pain today. Truthfully, that nurse was in danger the moment he started screaming like that," He admitted.

"I have to agree."

"I saw your fists clenched." Marsh teased as he grinned at me before taking a slow step back without releasing his grip on my hips.

"Well, she basically bullied and assaulted our son. Did you hear her telling him to stop whining about it? I almost jabbed her with that needle and asked how it felt."

Marsh laughed and then slipped his fingers free of my waist and down into my hand. He then guided me out of our son's nursery and back to the living room, so we wouldn't wake Austin with our spirited debate over wanting to hurt the nurse who so callously hurt our son.

"Seriously, I get that it was her job, and he needed it to protect him from something worse, but I've never been so angry with someone, so quickly, in all my life."

"No, I get it. I was right there with you. He's still so tiny. It's not okay that we're expected to just sit through someone poking him like that."

"It wasn't that bad the first time," I admitted. "I'm not sure if it was because he was younger or what, but the last time he needed shots, there were only a couple of tears and a bottle right after worked to calm him immediately."

Marsh grew serious then. "I don't want to miss those things, Opal. I already missed so much with your pregnancy. There's a part of me that absolutely hates my brother because he got to be there to find out that I was having a son before I even knew you were pregnant." He held up his hand, to stifle any reaction I might have.

"I'm not blaming you for that. I know that falls on the twins and what they did. You thought I knew and didn't care. Not going to lie, the fact that you thought I would ever react that way about my own child angers me a bit."

"Put yourself in my shoes, Marsh. You didn't even talk to me about our relationship, problems you thought we were having, what was going on with your parents. Nothing. I just came home to find the apartment cleaned out and you telling me that we were separating for six months, so that you could date other people. None of that sounded like the man I thought was going to propose to me. I was completely blind-sided and questioned everything after that."

Marsh took a deep breath and then let it out at length before responding. "I know. I'm sorry. No matter what, every-thing that happened is on me. Opal, you didn't do a damn thing wrong. There was never anything wrong with our rela-tionship, except that maybe we'd grown a little stagnant in our interactions. That is on me too. We both got busy being adults and I think it was a bit of a rough adjustment for me to go from our teen years, and even our college years, where we went out and had fun and explored new things. Instead, we were both working a lot and bringing work home as well."

I nodded because I understood. Where he was missing the action of all our dates, I only missed the closeness we once had before we sat around working until we were too tired for conversation with one another. He missed the excitement. I missed the intimacy. Somewhere in the middle, we simply didn't think to communicate about what we were each missing in our relationship. Why would we? It was a first for us, and neither of us understood how to handle it.

"We should have talked more," I mumbled.

"Everything seems easier in hindsight."

I chuckled. "That's the truth."

"Moving forward, I want us to be able to communicate more effectively. If something's going on with Austin, I want to know. I'd tell you if he was here with me and needed to go get shots or had a diaper rash, or a snotty nose."

"I know. I'm sorry. Truthfully, I've been on autopilot a lot lately, especially with work about to start and being stressed about what to do with Austin."

"We talked about that, but I wish you would have mentioned it sooner. It's not something you should worry about alone. I'm not some deadbeat dad who just left you swinging in the wind."

I was saved from further chastising by the doorbell. Marsh got up to go get the food he'd ordered while I thought things out. If only we'd talked like this sooner, maybe… No. I had to stop living in the past and thinking about scenarios that never happened. It wasn't healthy.

"Food's here," Marsh declared as he brought the bag full of containers to the kitchen table. I joined him before realizing there were no drinks.

"I'll grab some water. Do you want some too, or something else?"

"I'll take water too. There's filtered in the fridge."

"I remember." Once we were settled, and had our food laid out before us, curiosity finally got the better of me. "Are you still working?"

"Of course. What made you ask that?"

I shrugged. "You said you got some money and no matter what's happening, you seem to be able to take time off work."

"I can take time off because my boss understands the situation I'm in right now. He's a single parent, and respects the fact that I share custody with you, so when I say something came up with Austin, he's pretty good about sending me on my way. I make it up to him by working different hours when necessary, and when you have our son."

"I see."

"What about you?"

"You already know. I had the summer off, for obvious reasons, but I need to go back, now that the school year is in full gear, and my maternity time has run out."

"I meant that we always discussed you staying home for the first few years once we had kids. How do you feel about the change?"

I shrugged. "Honestly, Marsh, what can I say about that? In a perfect world, that's what I wanted to do so that our children would have one hundred percent of my focus instead of splitting it with a career. I'm not in a position to be able to do that now, so I've had to adapt. At least, I'm trying to. It's going to be hard to leave my boy with a stranger – whether at a daycare or with a nanny – no doubt about it. But that is the hand I was dealt."

"It doesn't have to be," He said quietly.

"I haven't won the lottery recently, that I know of, so there really aren't any other options."

"Please, just take this as something to consider, and know there's no pressure. If you moved in here, and we started working on us again, we could still make it happen."

I sat quietly, staring at my ex-boyfriend for a few minutes before I was able to respond. "Please, don't take this the wrong way, or as me being combative, but even if I was inclined to do that, there's no way I could take you up on that offer. Even if we were trying to work out how to have a relationship again, there's still no way I'd agree to that anymore."

"Why not?" He asked as his brows furrowed down to form a point toward his nose.

I sighed before explaining something I didn't think needed to be pointed out, but for the sake of argument, he really did need to understand where I was coming from.

"Do I need to remind you of what happened when you left me?"

"What do you mean?"

"You blindsided me. You took all your things from the apartment in secret when you knew I wouldn't be home to see you do it. Then you didn't even have a real conversation with me. You simply told me it was going to be that way and left. I didn't get a say. I didn't have time to prepare for what was happening or what came next. I didn't even get to tell you to your face that I was pregnant because you didn't think anything I had to say was important. You didn't factor me into your decision at all."

"We've been over that," He said grudgingly.

"Okay, well, considering how you've already done that once, what's to stop you from doing it again?" I shook my head to keep him from answering just yet. "What if something happens, like with your family, and you have doubts again? What if you meet someone like that girl from the party and want to explore it? What if you just get sick of me, or things become stagnant again? What if you're just unhappy and want a change? I have to worry that you might come home one day and kick me out. I won't have a job, money, a vehicle, or even family that is willing to help me until I can get back on my feet.

"I won't have anywhere to live, let alone to take my son to, so then I'll lose access to him. I hope you understand that I can never put myself in that situation again. Not ever, Marsh. Even if we were to get back together, I'd have to insist that all our finances stay separate, because I would need that security, especially after you took all of the money we were saving for a house with you when you left - my part of the savings included. I know, you said you didn't even think about that, and eventually gave my half back, but it still happened and I still struggled as a result. That means I would need a job, even if I lived here. Otherwise, my fear of 'what if' would keep us from being truly happy."

"Dammit, Opal. I'd never leave you high and dry like that." My eyebrows rose in indication that he already had. "I made sure your rent was paid up last time. I thought it would be enough because you being pregnant wasn't even on my radar then. Had I known…"

"It doesn't matter what your intentions were. What matters is what actually happened, and that I can never take the chance of being unprepared for the unexpected again."

We sat silently for a few minutes, both of us having lost our appetites along the way. "Okay, I get it. Again, it's all my fault because I did everything wrong when I left, starting with ever even thinking of leaving you. I screwed up so fucking much. You have to know how badly I want to make things up to you. I know that I can't ever take away the struggles, the things you saw, the impact my decisions had on you. I understand that. I don't want to start over, because that means going back to a damaged relationship, one that my actions chipped away at relentlessly. I need to know if it would ever be possible to start something new?"

"Like dating?" I asked, unsure where he was going with that.

"Well, I'd have you move in tomorrow if you'd agree, but that's not going to work until I've put in the work to prove to you that you and Austin are my only priorities now. Everyone else, and their problems, aren't going to be put ahead of you two ever again. That's where I went wrong before. Since I have to convince you of that by proving it, yeah, why don't we start slow and date?"

I giggled at the thought. "We already have a son together, don't you think that will make dating weird?"

"No. I think it just adds another dimension to our relationship."

"What if it doesn't work out? I don't want to end up being enemies, because at the end of the day, we have to co-parent no matter what happens."

"I could never be your enemy, Opal. I know you probably haven't felt the same over the past year, but I promise you, if it doesn't work out, we will do whatever it takes to co-parent our son in the healthiest way possible for him. We're already working on doing that. Let's work on getting to know one another again, and take some time to date."

"I would only agree to that if we were both going to remain exclusive, and that doesn't mean sex will be involved right away. So, if you can't stay celibate and promise me…"

He cut me off. "I promise you, I've already been celibate since the one and only other time I was ever with another woman."

I cringed at the reminder that he had indeed slept with someone else, when he was still the only man in my heart.

"I know it hurts you to hear, but I can't make it untrue, and I refuse to hide behind lies, even ones of omission. There hasn't been anyone else since. Not even a date, or thought of one."

"But I went out with Joe," I added.

"And it killed me to know that, but I felt it was only right to give you time to explore those options while not pregnant. When you finally agreed to come back to me, I didn't want you to do it with any regrets that you never had time to explore dating other people, since I was given that same opportunity."

"I never wanted to date anyone else."

"I know," Marsh hung his head and shook it back and forth as if he could rid himself of the decisions he made. "I'm sorry that I ever let other people confuse me, or that I ever thought it would be necessary. Opal, I hated it."

"Then why, Marsh? Why did you do it? Why did you keep doing it? Why didn't you ever just talk to me?"

Chapter 30

MARSH

Opal wanted to know 'why', and I wasn't sure my answers would do her any good. She already knew most of them.

"I'm not going to lie, so you have to be prepared to hear the truth." She nodded; so I continued. "You already know why I even thought about doing it. I had the twins and Cramer in my ear about needing those experiences outside of you. There were the issues with my parents that seemed to point to make what the guys were telling me feel like the truth. I honestly felt we needed that time apart to make sure we were both what each other wanted and that we wouldn't have regrets later on that would destroy a whole family instead of just the two of us."

She squirmed uncomfortably in her seat. "I already had all that going through my head, plus what I said to you earlier about there being no excitement left in our relationship. I realize now, that was my fault. If there was something either of us felt was missing, it was up to us to communicate that or plan something to change it. Instead, I allowed myself to entertain that new and exciting feeling with someone else that night at the party."

"Did you cheat on me with her? Is that why you were afraid to talk to me about everything?"

"No, Opal. I swear to you that I never cheated. We only talked, you saw that for yourself while you were at the party and that didn't change after you left. But it was exciting, at first. And with everything else going on, and everyone in my ear, I thought that feeling of excitement meant they had all been right."

"I see," She all but whispered.

"The girl from the party was the first date I went on after we separated, and it was a complete disaster. That initial feeling of excitement disappeared pretty quickly. We didn't even make it through dinner before we called the whole thing off."

"Then why did you keep doing it?"

"Because by then, I had already told you that we needed to take the six months, so that we could both be sure."

"What would you have done if you wanted to come back and I had already moved on with someone else?" She asked.

"I would have hated myself forever for letting you go, but if it made you happy, then I suppose that would have meant that the break was the right thing after all."

"You're an idiot. Anyone can move on and end up happy with someone else. People do it all the time after a spouse dies or one betrays them. I was already happy with you and you took that away from me."

I bowed my head in silent agreement. "You're right."

"And the other part? Why didn't you talk to me before you put this plan of yours in place?"

"I was a coward. I knew if we sat down and talked about it, that you would talk me out of going through with it. I didn't want to end up resenting you for taking that decision from me, when I had finally convinced myself that we needed to try it." We sat quietly while she absorbed what I had to say.

"I know what I did, and how I did it, was wrong. I never stopped loving you, Opal. I think that was the reason none of my dates ever worked out."

"Obviously, some of them did. I had the proof, after all."

"Are you sure you want to hear this?" She nodded. "With Gabby, the first woman I touched or kissed in any way, it was nearing the end of the six months. I think we were rolling into month five and Cramer and Brix yelled at me before my date. They both told me that I hadn't given dating a real chance yet, and how would I know if I was doing the right thing still, one way or another, if I didn't ever get intimate with any of the women."

"So, once again, you listened to someone else, rather than listening to your heart."

"I did. And that's exactly what it was like. I tried being intimate with Gabby. That image Cramer sent you was literally as far as it went. Right after that, I disengaged from the situation and told her it wouldn't work." I sighed before continuing. "Gabby made a comment that made everything so uncomfortable, that I couldn't go any further, even if I'd been more into what we'd been doing."

"What was it?"

"The comment?" I asked, trying to delay her from hearing something that would sound awful. Opal nodded her head, for me to tell her, and with my heart in my throat, I did.

"She said, 'I want you to fuck me like you never fucked your ex-girlfriend.'"

Opal's face scrunched up in distaste. "That's gross. Who says something like that?"

"She did, and that's when I couldn't go any further. I wasn't that into what we'd been doing to begin with. I'd been forcing myself, to prove a point. That wasn't fair to Gabby, but then again, neither was her demand fair to me."

"So, you just ended things there?"

"When she asked me why I refused to continue, I told her the truth. It felt like I was betraying the love of my life, even though we weren't together anymore, and her request was nothing more than an in-your-face reminder of that fact." Opal looked away and I felt a lead weight in my stomach at the thought that this conversation might be what put the final nail in the coffin for us. I don't know that I could sit through her telling me about dates she went on with other men, let alone where intimacy was involved.

"I tried to do things the right way, Opal. I left you so there would never be any cheating between us. It didn't stop me from feeling like I was doing exactly that, because you were still the woman who owned my heart."

"And Monica was because you thought I had moved on quickly with someone else and was having a baby with another man?" She reiterated the reason I'd told her that I went there with the other woman.

"Yes," I offered in a quiet response. "Monica was me trying to forget that I loved you, since I thought you had already replaced me in a way we'd never come back from." I shook my head. "There wasn't anything sweet or nice about that encounter, Opal. I need you to understand that. It wasn't even Monica on my mind at the time. My frustration, anger, and hurt all bled into that encounter and I guarantee you, it wasn't a good time for Monica. It definitely wasn't for me either. In fact, it was one of the worst, and most regretful experiences of my life."

A shiver ran through Opal's body and I wanted to take her in my arms and hold her until the cold, hard truth of our separation seeped away and was replaced with the heat of what we once had, or maybe something new. I couldn't touch her after just talking about being with another woman. Something about that felt like the wrong thing to do.

"I miss you," She finally said. "I miss what we once had as a couple, Marsh, even the boring times. I'd be lying if I said that I didn't often dream of us being a real family." The tone in her voice made me stifle the excitement I felt over her admission. The 'but' that was coming on the trail end would be what I had to contend with.

"But?" I finally asked when she said no more.

Her eyes came up to meet mine, and the glossy sheen in them hurt to see. It killed me that my decisions had wrecked her the way they had. I deserved every bit of hurt that she heaped on me because all of this had been my doing, but she never deserved even a second of it.

"I'm scared. I know you didn't betray me by cheating, but you betrayed me by leaving the way you did. I don't know if I could ever trust being with *that* version of you again." We both sat silently for a few more moments before she offered me a sliver of hope.

"I also know that we had seven good years together, some great years, and that our son deserves to see that too. We deserve to still have that. I just can't jump back in, full-steam ahead. That trust has to be rebuilt."

"I understand that, and I'm willing to do whatever you need me to."

"I need to go slow, so that we don't end up screwing everything up for our son." She huffed out a breath of frustration before adding to her thought. "And because my heart can't handle losing you again."

Chapter 31

OPAL

IT HAD BEEN ONE WEEK, SINCE MARSH AND I HAD OUR HEART-to-heart about the state of our relationship. We both agreed to go on a date, but only once we found a suitable nanny for our son. I still wouldn't allow Kathy to babysit Austin. She had spent time with him, while Marsh was present, but that had been the extent I was willing to allow her into our son's life, and thankfully, Marsh agreed with me.

"I think I should meet this nanny." Beth stated, once again, as I was getting ready for my date with Marsh.

"Beth, we ran background checks, and she came highly recommended."

"Well, she's staying at Marsh's place, and you're not. What if he decides to bang the nanny? It's a cliché because it happens so often."

I giggled at the thought of Marsh banging the sixty-two-year-old grandmother. "She's old," I admitted.

"How old? Like, sexy late thirties puma, early forties cougar territory or shit… What do they call the older ones?"

"I wasn't even aware there were different terms for

different ages. Aren't all older women with younger men called cougars?"

"Nah girl. There's a system. Jaguar is the other one. Is she a jaguar?"

"Is a jaguar a woman in her fifties?" I asked, laughing at Beth's ridiculousness. She nodded. "Then no, Mrs. Gliden is in her sixties. She does look good for her age, though. I thought for sure she couldn't be a day over fifty."

"Hmm," Beth hummed in thought, much to my amusement. "Do you have a picture?" I showed her a picture of the woman that had come with her background check. "Oh! I see. She does look like someone's granny."

"That's because she is."

"How does Kathy feel about this other woman watching her grandson when she's not allowed to?"

"Marsh said she threw quite the fit about it when she found out the other day."

"And? Girl, stop leaving me in suspense."

"And, Marsh told her that the outburst she just had was proof enough that she wasn't ready to take on the responsibility of babysitting his son."

"Damn, I bet that didn't go over well with Kathy."

I shook my head. "No, I'm pretty sure she ended up going to talk to her sponsor or counselor or something."

"Good for her, making that choice."

"It shows she has made improvements," I agreed. "I'm still not ready to trust her."

"Has she even apologized for the way she treated you?"

I shook my head. "Not yet. Though, I'm pretty sure that's part of the steps she has to take in her recovery. Since she hasn't done it, I assume she isn't ready yet, and until she is, she won't be left alone with my son."

"That is smart of you," Beth agreed before handing me the other earring I was looking for. "You look amazing. That man isn't going to know what hit him. He's only seen you looking like a bedraggled single mother lately."

"Gee, thanks for the confidence boost and love you're throwing my way. I make being a single mom look good, dark circles, bags, and all, you twat!"

"Shut your face!" She teased. "You know what I meant."

"Beth," I whispered and turned so that I could see her face as I asked the question that had been on my mind all day. "Do you think I'm doing the right thing, giving him another chance?"

"Unlike all the assholes in Marsh's life, I always knew the two of you belonged together. Now, there was a time in there when I was willing to bury his body and hide all the evidence, but I think Marsh finally got his shit together and pulled his head out of his ass."

Bethany wrapped her arms around me in one of her comforting hugs. "I'm so scared that it will all happen again," I admitted.

"Eventually, he'll prove himself. I don't think that man ever wants to take the chance of letting you go again. He saw how easily you could replace him when you refused to get back together and started to date initially."

"My one and only date was a disaster."

"No, your one and only date started out wonderfully, and his brothers went back and told him about how much fun you were having. So what if it ended badly, thanks to Joe being a double-dipper? That just showed that you could easily have a great time with someone else, and that another man would leave the woman he's with to make sure he captured you." She winked and waggled her brows at me. "Jealousy is a huge motivator for idiotic men."

That made me giggle. Beth's motto was that all men were idiots, you just had to discover the level of idiocy you could tolerate. She hadn't found her level yet.

There was a knock on the door, and Beth went to answer it while I finished putting my earring in and gave my lips a quick swipe of gloss. I hadn't even left the bathroom yet, when I heard my best friend threaten Marsh.

"If I find out you hurt her again in any way, I will make sure your body is never found. Are we clear?"

"Crystal," He answered. "And thank you for looking out for Opal. I'm glad she's always had you in her corner."

"Don't try to flatter me," She snipped at him, which made me laugh as I walked out to greet them both.

"Wow!" Marsh sputtered. "You look amazing, Opal." His hand flew over his heart, as if he was having trouble keeping the organ in place.

"Thanks, you look great too," I returned the compliment. "Was everything okay with Austin before you left?"

My anxiety had spiked earlier, over the fact that I wouldn't get to say goodnight to my boy. It was different from the nights when Marsh would have him because this was the first time that our new nanny was spending time alone with our son.

"I promise you he's fine," He pulled out his phone, tapped some things, and then turned to show me our son sleeping soundly in his crib before he turned on the audio capability. Mrs. Gliden was still reading out loud. To my complete surprise, she was reading the Percy Jackson novels, and that made me giggle.

"At least she has great taste in bedtime stories."

Marsh's whole face lit up as he smiled in agreement. I touched his cheek without even thinking and his arms wrapped around my waist in response. We were probably a hair's breadth away from kissing when a throat cleared.

I turned to see that Bethany was wearing a huge, knowing grin. "You better get on out of here before you don't make it to your first date. Thank God I was here to protect your virtue!" She teased.

"So, what do you have planned for our first date?" I asked.

"You're going to have to wait and see."

Twenty minutes later, Marsh pulled up outside a little hole in the wall bar on the outskirts of town. It wasn't one we had ever been to before, and for the briefest moment, I wondered if he had found this place on one of his other dates. Then, I let that thought go, because I couldn't handle the possibility of the answer being yes.

It was then that I knew forgiving and getting over our past experience, was not going to be as easy as simply dating again and taking things slowly. Doubt festered in my mind where Marsh was concerned, and that was something I never had to deal with before.

"Wait there," Marsh directed, as he hopped out of the truck. He reached into the back and grabbed something out, then came around to get me from the passenger side. It wasn't as though I was pregnant and needed the help, but I think it was supposed to be a gentlemanly gesture on his part.

"What in the hell are you doing with my guitar?" I questioned the minute I got out of the truck and finally realized what was slung over his shoulder.

"Have a little faith, Opal," He suggested as he took my hand and guided me into the bar. Immediately, I tuned into the fact that there was a woman already on stage, crooning to the enraptured crowd about the love of her life. She ended the song with a round of applause and immense laughter as she revealed that the love of her life was an old Chevy pickup truck that never failed to start.

"It's open mic night. I thought you might want to give it a try, and I'd love to hear you perform again. It's been a long time."

"I don't have anything prepared."

"How about you just go up there and sing from the heart? No matter what comes out, you can't go wrong."

"Thanks for the vote of confidence," I told him as nervous laughter bubbled up from somewhere inside me.

"Next up is Opal Morgan." The man announced while glancing into the crowd, until he spotted Marsh who raised his hand and pointed down at me. "Come on up here, Opal! Everyone make a path for the little lady."

With great trepidation, I took my guitar from Marsh and cursed him under my breath as I made my way to the stage. I would kill him, after I finished embarrassing myself. Sadly, there was no pit available for me to throw myself into. Too bad, because I'd almost rather be swallowed by a hole in the ground than go sing in front of a crowd when I was completely unprepared.

"Thank you," I said as the man offered me a stool to sit on and helped me adjust the microphones to the appropriate height. I looked out at the audience, without really seeing anyone, and then I sighed into the microphone before banging my head against it, much to the amusement of everyone in attendance.

"I was supposed to be out on a first date tonight," I said into the microphone. People hooted and hollered at that. "He's known me for a long time, and I guess he thought it would be memorable to throw me to the wolves as a surprise."

"Aw! We'll be gentle!" Someone yelled.

"Thanks! I'll need you to keep that promise!" I chuckled into the microphone. "I haven't played in nearly six months." There were shocked gasps in the crowd, and one that I recognized. My eyes tracked to him and immediately noticed that Marsh was not sitting alone. All of his brothers, his parents, Bethany, and her mom were all there.

I shook my head. "No pressure or anything," I grumbled as I finished tuning my guitar. "I wrote this song at the lowest point in my life. That also happened to be just before I stopped playing and singing. Hopefully, someone else out there might need to hear it too."

"*I fell*," the words squeaked out of me rather than sounding like a song, so I started over.

I FELL *for the boy next door*
 my future, my everything
 Until he didn't want me anymore

MY MEMORIES WERE STOLEN,
 The boy didn't exist
 Our life together
 Was nothing but mist.
 Hard to hold onto
 Harder still to get back
 My heart incomplete
 Nothing left intact

WE USED *to be happy*
 So much more than just friends
 Sadness and questions
 The only thing left in the end

I FELL *for the boy next door*
 That boy doesn't exist anymore
 My heart is in tatters
 My trust in love shattered
 Promises broken
 And left with a token
 A tiny heartbeat

A love so sweet
But he was gone
And it all seemed wrong.

I FELL *in love with the boy next door*
He broke my heart
He broke my trust
All in a stupid search for lust

HE WANTED *excitement*
He wanted to pretend
He wanted me still
To be there in the end

HE BETRAYED *our love*
Shattered my trust
And all for what?
Unslaked lust

I FELL *for the boy next door*
But the girl he left behind
Doesn't exist anymore

I STRUMMED a few more chords before glancing up through glassy eyes at the audience, who were so quiet that I wasn't sure what to expect until the entire room exploded in applause. I didn't want to look, but curiosity got the better of me.

Jimmy and Marsh were no longer at the table where I'd seen them before I started. The rest of the family appeared somber and defeated. I'm not sure what they expected when Marsh put me on the spot. The early part of my pregnancy was spent writing and singing either heartbreakingly sad, or maddeningly angry songs about lost love. I didn't have any upbeat, happy material to pull from.

"Wow! I'm here to tell you, these ladies are killing it and playing with our emotions tonight!" The announcer stated as I slipped my guitar back into its case.

Ryker was the one to greet me as I exited the stage. He immediately pulled me to the side and gave me a hug, then whispered in my ear that Jimmy had to get Marsh out of sight because he lost it emotionally.

"Well, I guess my date is over, do you think you can give me a ride home?"

"I'm not so sure my brother would agree with that. How about we go find Marsh first?"

I shook my head, though there was a battle being waged in my heart about what exactly I wanted to happen. Did I want to see him again while emotions were so raw? Part of me did, because I needed to see his emotions play out too. The other part of me was scared to do that and just wanted to go home and hide.

"This was an awful idea and I just want to go home," I finally expressed to Ryker.

"I think maybe you should stay, or at the very least, find my son since that song of yours just destroyed him." It was Kathy, and her declaration did not make me happy.

"Kathy, that'll be enough. Marsh deserved to hear the pain he put her through. You never let me forget what I did to slight our relationship and what he did was far worse."

"How dare you!" Kathy spun on her husband. "How dare you!" She whispered.

Ed turned to me and ignored his wife. "Opal, I just wanted to say that I am so terribly sorry for my part in all the hurt you've had to face, in the troubles that have come between you and my son. You will always have a place in our family, as Austin's mother, and I respect you immensely for dealing with everything you've been through in a healthy way. Don't ever stop pouring your heart out into your songs. I'm sure it has been very therapeutic for you."

He then took Kathy by the arm, and guided her out of the bar, before she could get a word in edgewise.

"I always thought she liked me, but now I wonder if that was ever true," I mumbled more to myself than anyone else.

"Don't take it personally, she's been a handful. We all thought she was doing better post rehab, but I don't think the drinking was her only problem. She's still drowning in her bitterness." I was surprised that it was Brixton who spoke of his mom like that and even more surprised to find that both Bastion and Ryker nodded in agreement.

"Come on, we'll take you home if Ryker won't," Bastion offered. I followed the boys outside to the parking lot only to find Marsh there with Jimmy trying to calm down a rather heated argument between Ed and Kathy.

"Kathy, I warned you that I was at the end of my rope. I won't continue to play the whipping boy for something we supposedly already worked through. If you can't handle what happened, and it is still eating at you this much, then it's time to go our separate ways."

Kathy's jaw dropped, as did her sons'. I stood there, not wanting to watch this happen because it wasn't my business and I felt like it was something that should be done in private, not in the middle of a parking lot to be a spectacle for anyone passing by.

"You can't just leave me."

"I can, and I will, if you don't agree to get the help you need."

"I went to rehab!" She shouted at him.

"The drinking was a symptom, but you still haven't addressed the problem. Either you can get over what happened between us, or you can't, but I will not sit back and let you keep using me as a punching bag and harming yourself and everyone else while you're at it. That poor girl in there used to be like a daughter to you. She has done absolutely nothing wrong to deserve your bullshit, and yet you treat her like she did something awful to our son."

"She won't even allow me around my grandson!" Kathy screamed at him.

"And you honestly wonder why? You treat her like some garbage you stepped on in the street, act irrationally, and have a drinking problem you are supposedly working steps for, but I guarantee you haven't asked for her forgiveness yet, have you?"

Kathy looked taken aback. "What the hell does she have to forgive me for?"

"And that right there is why this isn't going to work. You won't even acknowledge how awful you've been to everyone, especially the way you've treated Opal, for some reason. I'm not sure why you made that girl your target, but I won't allow you to keep doing it. I don't want you coming back to our house. You have plenty of money to find somewhere else to stay. We'll see if we need to get lawyers involved from there, or if a couple nights away will help you to remember who you used to be."

Mr. Kennedy didn't wait around after that. He simply called back over his shoulder, "One of you boys needs to give your mother a lift to collect her things."

"I can do it," Bastion offered before turning to me. "Sorry, Opal. Ryker can take you, okay? I have to…"

I waved off his worried concern. "Go take care of your mom."

That was the first time Marsh and Jimmy realized I was standing there too. "What was that about?" Marsh asked as he moved to stand beside me. "Why would Bastion, or Ryker for that matter, need to take you home?"

"Look, this was probably a really bad idea. Our date didn't work out, but at least we can say that we tried," I explained. "I'm tired and feeling a little ambushed by everyone tonight, so I just want to go home."

"Ambushed?" He asked at the same time that Beth made her way outside. I forgot she had been there for the start of my song.

"Opal? Are you doing okay?" She called out to me from closer to the door of the bar.

"I'm fine, Beth. Go enjoy your night."

"Are you sure?"

"Positive," I agreed. Beth did an awkward, hesitant shuffle before tipping her head at me and heading back inside.

"I'll take you home, Opal. I'm the one who brought you here. I'm sorry it turned into another family disaster. That was the furthest from my intention. I wanted to prove to you that Mom was better and that my brothers were here to support you too." He shook his head defeatedly.

"Marsh," I sighed, because I honestly didn't know where to begin or what to say. "I'm sorry, it was just a bad night."

"Yeah," Marsh grumbled. "Let's go." He gently pulled me toward his truck, and I allowed it because he would feel responsible for getting me home.

When we were on our way, he tapped my thigh to get my attention. "I had to leave so that my sobbing wouldn't take away from your performance, but I made Ryker record every bit of it for me."

"I'm sorry, but you put me on the spot, and it was the only song that came to mind when I was up there."

"Don't apologize for the song. It's a piece of your heart now, and while I hate that something sad stains you inside that way, it's because of what I did. Besides, you heard my dad.

You've coped with far worse from me by putting your heart-break into music, poetry, and lyrics. You threw yourself into planning for our son. You didn't drown in your sorrow, the bottom of a bottle, nor did you give up on life. You pushed forward in a healthy way and dealt with your emotions, Opal. I couldn't ask for more than that."

"I'm sorry about your parents. Your mom has been awful to me these past few months, but she was wonderful to me for years. I don't wish her any ill will, Marsh. I need you to under-stand that. She's going through a tough time and needs help. Keeping Austin from her when there's no one to supervise, isn't about punishing her. It's about keeping him safe."

"I know that. We all thought she was doing better, but tonight proved that once again, you were right and the rest of us missed the important things that she wasn't doing. Mom's been faking it, and that's not healthy in this situation."

"No, it's not."

"I want to ask you something, and I hope you'll think about it before saying 'no' immediately." I sat quietly waiting for his question. "I would like for you to spend the night. No funny business, I swear. I just would like to have you close after your song and my family's issues. If you want to sleep in the guest room, that's fine. I want you to be comfortable, but also close." He glanced my way quickly, to assess my reaction, before putting his eyes back on the road. "I don't think I can handle dropping you off and going home alone."

"Okay." The truth was, I didn't want to be far from my son for the night either, and it was technically Marsh's weekend to have him. Not that I didn't also want the chance to talk to Marsh when he wasn't driving, but being alone after the night I just had wouldn't feel too great.

Chapter 32

OPAL

WHEN WE PULLED UP, MARSH HISSED AT THE SITE OF THE other car in the driveway. At first, I panicked, thinking it might be another woman. Then, he turned his attention to me and explained his outburst.

"Mrs. Gliden arranged to stay in the spare room overnight, because I wasn't sure how late we would be out, and she doesn't like to drive late at night."

My erratic heartbeat settled just a little. "You scared me," I admitted.

"Scared you?" He asked.

"I thought maybe there was someone here you didn't want me to see," I told him, figuring the honest approach would be best.

"I would never do that to you, Opal. I know that I blew your faith in me out of the water with the shit I pulled, and I don't blame you for thinking that. It's going to take time to earn that trust back. That said, I promise you right here and now that there will never be another woman here who is not related to me or here on business to take care of our son. You will also always know who that is, ahead of time, because we'll choose that person together."

"Thank you, I appreciate that."

"Now, let's go check on Austin and figure out arrangements for the night."

My stomach did a little flip-flop, like that fluttery feeling when you crest the top of a hill on a roller coaster and suddenly the bottom drops out from underneath you.

After checking on Austin, who was sound asleep, we went back to the living room to settle on the couch before Marsh realized I was still wearing a dress and heels. He took my hand and escorted me to his bedroom.

"On second thought, we're going to get you comfortable before we settle in for the night." He grinned back at me over his shoulder. "While you are stunning in that dress, I can't imagine it's comfortable to lounge around in."

Marsh dug through his dresser and pulled out an old t-shirt that I used to love to wear to bed and a pair of his boxers. He shrugged his shoulders. "Best I can do on short notice," He admitted.

"It's fine." I took the offered clothing and moved into his ensuite bathroom to change and wash the makeup off my face. Once I was done, I came back out to an empty bedroom, but it was clear that Marsh had changed into something more comfortable too, since the clothes he'd been wearing were draped across the chair on the opposite side of the room. I chuckled as memories assaulted me of our first time living together.

"You can't just leave your dirty laundry lying wherever you take it off," I chastised.

"Sure, I can because this is our place and neither of us has a mom living here, who is going to come check to make sure our bedroom isn't messy."

"Maybe not, but I don't want to be the one tripping over your clothes either. Your mom had a point about keeping your room clean."

Marsh rolled his eyes at me, but immediately moved to pick his clothes up off the floor. Unfortunately, he didn't bother to go find the hamper to put them in, and instead draped them over the small, second-hand chair we'd picked up from a yard sale. The damn thing hadn't really matched well in the living room, so we hid it in the bedroom instead. I supposed the clothes on the ugly chair was better than being underfoot. It was our first compromise.

"Now, come here so I can take your clothes off and put them some-where that won't be on the floor." He had grinned at me so adorably, that there was no way I could refuse.

The memory was a sweet one of us learning to cohabitate. Truthfully, there wasn't much of a learning curve necessary because we had always been effortless around one another.

"You okay?" He asked from the doorway.

I turned and smiled at him. "Just got lost in memories."

He glanced at the chair with his clothes piled on top and grinned. "Some things never change."

"They did that day," I argued, teasingly.

"Well, I was semi-trainable. Probably as good as it gets really, considering I don't actually own a hamper right now."

"For shame! Wherever are you supposed to hide your dirty laundry when your chair can no longer accept the burden?"

Marsh laughed as he came to stand beside me. "Maybe, one day, a good woman – named Opal – will move in and set me straight all over again. Second time's the charm, right?"

"I thought the saying was, 'third time'."

"Nah, we don't need more than the one mistake."

Marsh tugged gently on my hand to get me to follow him back to the living room. "I made some hot chocolate for you," He stated as he leaned down and kissed the top of my head. "Well, for us. Marshmallows for you, none for me though."

I grinned. Marsh had always hated Marshmallows. He had

once argued with me that they were weird globs of dust people put in their hot chocolate. That was after he saw that I loved the packets that came loaded with marshmallows already.

"Why do you have the marshmallow kind in your house when you hate them?"

"They're a symbol of hope, Opal." My heart did that weird squeeze thing while butterflies performed Olympic-level gymnastic feats in my belly. "I mean it." We both sat on the couch, so close that our legs touched. "Things have been crazy, and I started us off on bad footing with my insecurities and failure to communicate with you. I don't want to keep going like that, babe."

I didn't bother to correct his use of an endearment. If I were being honest with myself, it was because it felt natural coming from Marsh, especially now that I'd let go of a lot of the hurt and resentment I felt for my ex. I hated the way he handled things before, even as I understood his reasoning and the pressure he'd been under.

"So, what do you want to do about that?"

"Talk," He suggested. "About tonight, for instance."

"What about tonight?"

"First, I feel like I should apologize."

"What do you have to apologize for?"

"For blindsiding you, yet again." He huffed out a breath before turning so that he was facing me, so I did the same. Marsh took hold of my hands in his as he continued. "I invited my family and your friend to watch you perform without even checking if it was something you wanted to do. I didn't realize you hadn't played in months. That's just one more thing I feel like I need to atone for too. It really hit home that everything that has happened stole your music from you too."

I shook my head, disagreeing with him. "That song was proof that it didn't. Life just stole time from me, that's all."

"Come on, Opal, it's all the same. The things I put into motion are the reason you no longer had time."

"Things happen, Marsh. You can't keep blaming yourself or how the one decision cascading into all the others that we might have made along the way. Did it contribute? Sure, but I could have chosen a different pair of shoes tonight, broken my ankle, and had to live with the consequences that came from it. Should I beat myself up for wearing the shoes, or the manufacturer for making them and causing my distress?"

"Thanks for trying to let me off the hook, but that doesn't change the fact that I should have asked if you'd be okay with it."

"Marsh, you can't second guess every surprise you try to put together for people. Sometimes, they work out, others don't, and then there are the murky in-between moments. I think tonight was the latter. There were parts of the night where I was shocked, frightened, and saddened. There were also parts, like when I connected with my music again, where I was elated and felt like a missing piece of myself had been put back into the puzzle."

"Okay, we'll pretend the surprise part wasn't an issue then," He chuckled while reluctantly agreeing. "There's still the issue of my mother. I tried to convince you that she was better, when we first talked about hiring a nanny or looking into daycares. I was wrong. You were right. She wasn't ready. I don't know if she ever will be at this point. Maybe my father taking the steps he did tonight will push her to really work on things."

"It must be awful for Kathy. She went from feeling like a victim for what your dad put her through to being seen as the villain in the scenario. That has to rankle a bit. I think she needs time to understand how that one wrong affected her, and how the choices she made were all her responsibility afterward. I knew, when she hadn't reached out to apologize to me yet, that she wasn't following the steps in recovery. At the very least, she wasn't acknowledging that she had things to apologize for."

"That's something I should have realized too," Marsh admitted. "My father did."

"He's a wise man." Marsh gave me a knowing look that said he couldn't truly be wise considering the fallout from his misstep.

"Even wise men make mistakes, Marsh."

He blew out a breath and nodded his head in agreement. "You got me there."

I shifted in my seat, so that I was angled away from Marsh a little more than before, then I scooted until my back leaned into his side. Hesitantly, he wrapped his arms around me and held me there next to his body.

"I've missed you so much," Marsh muttered against my hair.

"I never stopped missing you, even when I was angry."

"I don't deserve that."

"There are a lot of things we might not deserve in life, but some of them, we get anyway." I elbowed him gently in the stomach as I said it.

We sat quietly in one another's arms on the couch for a bit. "Marsh?" I finally asked.

"Yeah?"

"I don't want to pretend like we don't have a history. We share a son. The memories I have of us, from before you left, they are things that I cherish. I don't want to pretend to have another first date, first kiss, or whatever else. That isn't our truth, and I don't think that's how we should do this."

"I thought you would want a fresh start," He argued.

"Yes, but we can have a fresh start while still acknowledging that we also have a past. Parts of it were wonderful, some mundane, and others heartbreaking. To forget or pretend away any of that will take away from who we have become and I don't think that's wise. I think, maybe that's where your parents went wrong. They tried to pretend their issue away and sweep it under the rug instead of dealing with it in a healthy way and moving on to a different future."

"How did you become so wise?"

"I've always been wise, you just didn't want to acknowledge that because it would mean you'd have to figure out how to use a hamper for dirty laundry."

He reached down to my sides and tickled me. "I see what you did there," He teased as he continued his torture while I giggled and squirmed on his lap.

In the middle of giggling over the tickles, a yawn managed to escape me, and Marsh stopped what he was doing, stood, picked me up in his arms, and carried me back to his bedroom.

"Come on, I think we need to sleep on everything and start fresh, without hiding the past, in the morning."

"That sounds like a great plan," I agreed.

Chapter 33

MARSH

I woke to the sounds of Austin's whimpering coming through the baby monitor that was on the nightstand by my bed. To my surprise, Opal was still there, snuggled up against me. The sigh of relief I breathed was one I would never take for granted again. It also made me realize that I couldn't go back to a world where she wasn't in my arms at night.

"Sleep, baby." I whispered as she turned at the sound of the noises our son was making. I quietly got out of bed and made my way to the nursery where my boy was bright-eyed, and a little red faced. He was just on the brink of shouting out his demands when he noticed me and quietly whimpered his displeasure instead.

"I got you, little man. No one likes to wake up with shit caked to their balls," I told him. I'd swear that he grinned at me, but considering the state of his diaper, it was probably just residual gas. "You have to help me convince Mommy that it would be best for all of us if she stayed here."

My son cooed and giggled, as if he not only understood, but agreed. If only it was that easy. "Maybe it is that easy," I mumbled out loud in the same quiet voice I used for Austin in the middle of the night.

Once I got Austin back down, I went out to the living room and picked up my phone to dial Dave Brewer, my attorney. Normally, I'd feel bad about calling in the middle of the night, but Dave was a self-proclaimed night owl.

"Brewer here. What can I do for you?"

"Hey Dave, it's Marshall Kennedy."

"Marsh, good to hear from you. This isn't a jailhouse call is it?" He asked.

I chuckled into the line. "Not at all. If you have a minute, I'd like to discuss a contract I want set up. If at all possible, I'd love to have it in hand first thing in the morning."

"Tell me about it, and I'll see what I can do."

"GOOD MORNING," I said when Opal finally appeared in the kitchen just before ten in the morning.

"Oh my God, I can't believe I slept that long. Why didn't you wake me?"

"Seemed like you needed the rest."

"I did," She huffed as she plopped down into one of the kitchen chairs. "I haven't slept for a full night since before Austin was born."

That took me aback. "What about the nights when I have him here?"

Her sheepish look was equally endearing and frustrating, because suddenly I feared what she might have to say about why she wasn't getting any sleep when she didn't have a baby at her apartment to keep her awake.

"I can't sleep when he's away from me." She laughed then and the sounds felt like music on the air. It was slightly deeper, rougher-edged than her normal laughter, since her voice was still thick with sleep. "When he's there, he wakes me at least once or twice a night. When he's gone, I sleep so restlessly. It's not that I don't trust you with him. He's just not with me, and I keep expecting to hear him wake in the middle of the night. When he doesn't I get nervous and then can't get back to sleep."

"I wish you had told me this sooner."

"And what? You end up giving up your nights with your son, so that I can get slightly less crappy sleep?" She joked.

"Actually, no. I have another solution that I think would be good for all of us. I tried to do this before, but went about it the wrong way." I pulled out the folder the lawyer had left with the paperwork I requested and handed it to her.

"What's this?"

"Open it, and I'll tell you about it as you look it over." She nodded and turned her eyes down to begin scanning over the pages.

"I've always trusted you implicitly," I started to say as she glanced back up at me. "The thing is, I ruined *your* trust in *me*. That was something that took me a while to come to terms with, to understand even. I get it now. Maybe one day, in the future, I will rebuild that trust with you, but until then, you need some assurances that you are protected. From me," I tacked on at the end while swallowing my pride to do so.

"So, I'm offering you those assurances. I want you to move in here with me." I held her off with a gesture, so that I could finish explaining. "I know we're just starting over, but it's not that cut and dry with us. Like you said last night, we share a baby who we both love and adore, and neither of us wants to miss any time with him. If I'm being honest, I don't want to miss out on any more time with you either, even if you don't feel the same. I want us to try living together. If things don't work out, at any time, you are free to kick me out. The house is yours."

Her gasp made me pause. "Well, it's not yet, because turning over property actually takes a minute to get done. In the meantime though, I had my lawyer draw up the paperwork to state that the house is yours. I cannot force you out for any reason. You, however, have the power to force me out. So, if you want to live here and banish me to your apartment, then so be it. We'll swap. I'd really like to give us, living here together, a try first."

"This is a lot, Marsh." Opal said as her eyes drifted back down to the paperwork in her hands. "Are you sure you want to do this?"

"I'm sure. I believe in us. I can't fathom ever being able to give you up again, especially after getting to hold you while we slept last night. I don't want to give that up. I want us to be able to see what it's like to be a real family. I know I don't deserve a real second chance with you, but I hope like hell you're willing to give me one, anyway."

"Okay," She agreed so quietly, that at first, I thought my imagination had played an awful trick on me and she'd start laughing and explain what an idiot I was.

"Did you just say, 'Okay'?"

"Yes, I did. I happen to agree with you on everything. Lucky for you. Plus, it will put me a whole lot closer to work, so if something happens during the day with Austin, I can be here in just a few short minutes."

"Is your decision only about Austin?"

"No, Marsh, it's not. I've been angry with you, hurt by you, and in all that time I never stopped loving you, even when I wished I could."

"Well, thank God for that," I mumbled.

"Yeah, I suppose so."

Chapter 34

OPAL

"WELL, HOW HAVE THINGS BEEN GOING?"

I stared at my best friend, not really knowing how to answer that. The truth was, it had been going fine, great even, but it also felt surreal. Like we somehow skipped steps and became more adult people than we used to be overnight. We were ourselves, but wiser somehow.

"Things are great. Slightly different than before."

"That has to be a good thing," She admitted.

"It is. There's just this unrealness to it all. And before you say anything, I'm aware I probably made up a word there, but I can't think of anything else that compares."

"I think you just keep waiting for the bottom to drop out again," My bestie suggested.

"That's probably it."

"Well, then maybe it's high time you started embracing your new reality a bit more."

"What's that supposed to mean?"

"You have paperwork stating that the house is now yours. It can't be taken away from you. Acknowledge that, so you can get comfortable and turn it into the home you always wanted, not something Marsh's mom designed."

"Beth, he used my ideas when he got his mother's help. Things we had talked about before, they were all there in that house."

"Sure, but Marsh was basing the house off of ideas you had before he left you. You both need to realize, and come to grips with the fact, that you aren't necessarily the same people anymore. You're a little bit darker now than you ever were. That's bound to reflect in the choices you would make now, versus the ones you made then."

"You're right. The house seems a little too light and airy for me," I finally admitted. "I've been thinking about getting some darker colored throw pillows to add a bit more color and tone down the overwhelming brightness."

"You should do that and stop holding back."

"I think I need to take your advice for more than the house. That is just a replaceable thing. Marsh is not. I think that's what has felt so off to me. I've been holding back a bit where he's concerned. It's scary to think that it might all happen again, so it feels like I've been walking on eggshells around him."

"Okay, well, stop imaging those scenarios!" Bethany insisted with a wide grin on her face. "You know that you have some stability in your life, and security that the house can't be taken from you, it's paid for too. That has to count for something, right? I think we need to get you drunk after work tonight. Let go of those inhibitions, and just dive in headfirst with Marsh."

"I never thought you would be okay with us getting back together."

She shrugged. "I was never okay with you separating to begin with. I've always known the two of you were meant to be. Marsh just had too many people in his head, for far too long, and got confused. Besides, I think you also needed to see that you could survive without him."

"Well, shit."

"Well, shit, indeed!" She chuckled and then pulled out a flier that had been ripped off some telephone pole or bulletin board. "What do you say about another open mic night?"

I rolled my eyes. "The last one didn't exactly go well."

"Actually, I think the last one went exactly how it was supposed to go. You might even say it was life changing," Bethany teased. "Look at where you're living now, and you're happier, even if things seem unreal for a little while. You have your son at home every night and the love of your life to fall into bed with. Bonus, because you both have a deeper understanding of exactly what you have, and I don't think either of you will do anything to purposely jeopardize that again in the future."

"That's probably true. Fine! Open mic night it is."

LATER, under the heated lights of the stage, I sang my heart out about love, loss, and redemption. Once again, I was met with a standing ovation and a very emotional boyfriend, who opted to watch and wait from the side stage where the curtain could hide most of what he was feeling from the audience.

"That was beautiful, Opal. Fucking stunning and right from the heart," Marsh gushed to me when I wound up in his arms immediately after leaving the stage.

"Thank you. I'm sorry some of it hurts still," I told him.

"Nah, don't apologize. It's part of what we went through, and a reminder to never take any of it for granted again."

"A wise woman just told me something similar," I teased.

"Ms. Morgan?" Someone called out from just behind where we stood. I turned to see a gorgeous man, a little taller than Marsh, and maybe five or so years older than us, standing in a distinguished suit that did all the right things for him. Bethany showed up at that exact moment and threw her arms around me, nearly bowling me over into the well-dressed stranger.

"Ms. Morgan?" He attempted again. Marsh pulled me back away from the man and into his embrace, which made the stranger smirk.

"Relax, I'm not here to steal your girl," He said in a calm tone. "I'm here to talk to her about using some of her lyrics for one of my clients."

"One of your clients?" I asked skeptically.

"Misty Ramirez." He offered a card along with the very familiar name. Misty Ramirez might be new on the pop charts, but she was absolutely a princess in the making. It didn't hurt that she sang to an older generation, about things like love, loss, and redemption. Exactly the type of song I'd played on stage only moments ago.

"If you're interested in having a sit down to discuss the use of your lyrics, or possible songwriting collaborations, give me a call and I'll arrange a meeting."

"May I ask how your client would possibly be familiar with my lyrics?"

"She thought you might ask." He grinned widely, showing off two deep dimples in his cheeks as he did. Bethany clung to my arm tightly, nearly pushing Marsh out of the way. There was no denying my best friend had developed a quick and brutal crush on the stranger in the suit."

"Misty has been following your videos for quite some time. Her niece was in your class last year, and spoke very highly of her music teacher."

I thought about which student it might have been, but couldn't pinpoint anyone off the top of my head. The man looked down and checked his phone. "Now that she's safely away, I can also say that Ms. Ramirez caught your show tonight. She wanted to congratulate you in person, but unfortunately fame has caught up with her a little quicker than we anticipated. Some of the women in the back of the audience recognized her and security had to work fast to get her out of there."

"I understand. May I ask your name?"

He nodded to my hand. "It's there on the card, in case you forget, but my name is Austin Beckworth."

"Now, if that isn't some strange set of coincidences," Bethany mumbled.

"Pardon?" The man questioned.

It was my turn to flash a grin to the man. "Our son," I indicated to myself and Marsh, "is named Austin as well. It almost feels like a sign."

"I'm betting Misty would agree with you. Give me a call, I'll get the two of you in touch. She'll be nearby visiting family for a few days. So, if you get in touch quickly, we can make sure you are able to meet face-to-face and maybe get some work done."

"That would be a dream," I said without thinking. That was why I didn't play poker. There had never been an easy way to hide my excitement about something.

"Perfect." The man shook each of our hands, and lingered slightly longer when he got to Bethany. "Sorry, I didn't catch your name."

"I didn't throw it," She sassed him. I could have sworn I heard the man growl, but Bethany took it easy on him and offered her name anyway. "I'm Bethany."

"I hope we have the pleasure of meeting again, Bethany."

"You and me both," She insisted, much to Austin's delight. Those dimples were out in full-force once again as he finished his goodbyes and took off.

"Girl! When you go to a meeting, because I know you will,

I am so there with you. I'd like to have that man with my morning coffee, if you get my drift."

I couldn't help but laugh as Marsh's chest rumbled behind me. "At least I don't have to worry about the suit with your best friend around."

"You never had to worry about him, anyway. No one has ever compared to you," I explained.

"Nor you," He added before kissing me on my nose.

"Okay, you saps, time for drinks."

"Actually, I think I just want to get home and check on Austin," I told her.

"Damn, and here I thought we were going to ply you with alcohol, make a scene, and maybe get arrested for old time's sake," Bethany grumbled as she rolled her eyes.

"We have never been arrested, so there's no old time's sake to be had where that's concerned," I argued.

"I know. What I meant to say was that I knew you'd dip out quickly to get home to your family. I love that about you, though. So, go with my blessings and remember our talk from earlier. Just let go and be in the moment!"

Chapter 35

MARSH

"I can't believe that one of my songs, maybe more, is going to be used by Misty Ramirez."

"Not sure why that seems unbelievable to you. I've been telling you for years that you could make some serious money off your songs, even if you didn't want to be the one to sing them publicly."

"Well, I won't mind the money, but there's no way I could deal with all the hassles fame has brought Misty in her short time on the pop charts."

"So, did you finish up?"

She grinned at me. "Yeah, we finished and got the split sheets filled out and notarized, plus all the stuff I needed to get paid my share of royalties. Austin was there and suggested that the record company might want me to sign an Exclusive Songwriter's Agreement with me."

"Do you think that's wise?"

"I don't know. I have to look into it some more. Misty actually encouraged me not to, because then anything I create can be plundered, unless I have a really good attorney go over the fine print and make sure that what's mine is mine, and what I do for them is all that they have access to. The other problem is, then the only people who can gain access to my songs are the ones that work with that recording company."

"If I stay independent, and only do individual contracts like with Misty, it would be a safer bet. The problem there is that I might not ever get enough exposure or another prospect at writing for anyone. It's a tough choice, and one I need to really consider."

"I could talk to my lawyer and see if he has someone he can recommend to look over things for you."

Opal hefted out a deep breath and then wrapped her arms around me. "Thanks for being here through the craziness of the past few days. It helps to just be able to have a normal person to talk to."

"Are you saying Misty and Austin aren't normal?"

"That's exactly what I'm saying." We both laughed. "Not that they weren't normal at one point, but they live in an entirely different world than we do."

"So, Miss. Big Shot Songwriter, do you have any idea what you want for dinner?"

"Yeah, I want you."

"For dinner?"

She moaned and patted the kitchen table. "You should sit right there," Opal suggested. There was honestly no part of me that wanted to argue, so I did what my woman asked, and sat my butt on our dining room table. She moved to the fridge and grabbed a can of whipped cream and chocolate sauce.

"Oh shit!" I hissed as she came back over and sat in the kitchen chair in front of me. She put the chocolate sauce beside my right thigh, the whipped cream beside my left, and then she reached for my zipper.

"All right lovelies, I am off for the night, unless you need..." I glanced up to see Mrs. Gliden standing there with a curious look on her face. Then a slow smile spread into a giant grin before she finished her statement. "Well, it looks like you have everything you need for a good night," She winked. "I'll just see myself out and lock up, shall I?" She tottered off in her clunky, utilitarian loafers and called out over her shoulder. "Austin is out for the count. You should have at least two hours before something wakes him. Use your time wisely."

Then the door shut and both Opal and I finally made eye contact again before we burst out laughing. Her cheeks and the tips of her ears were as red as mine felt.

"Oh my God! Did we just get busted, with me about to make a Sunday out of your dick, by the nanny?"

"Yeah, pretty sure that just happened."

"I am so mortified," Opal sighed as she rested her head on my thigh to hide her face.

"Do you know what would make you feel better?" I asked.

She glanced up. "I'm afraid to ask."

"A Sunday," I deadpanned, as I pointed to my lap.

Opal threw her head back in laughter before she opened the can of whipped cream and hosed my face down with it. "How's that for a Sunday?" She asked in the sassiest way possible.

"I don't know," I told her as I swiped a hunk of cream from the bridge of my nose. "How do you think chocolate will taste when drizzled on your skin?" Then I popped the top on the chocolate sauce and started to squirt it from the bottle into Opal's exposed cleavage. "I should really clean that for you before it drips and ruins your shirt."

"I have the best dinner ideas," Opal suggested as I dipped down to lick the chocolate from her breasts.

It wasn't the first time we'd made love since our reconciliation, but it was the first time we dove into something we hadn't experienced or experimented with in our previous seven years together. It suddenly became clear, that part of the frustration I was feeling before was because we never did things like this in our last year or so before our separation. We both just took one another for granted and allowed the status quo to build and build until it it felt like we were drowning in the sameness of every day stuff. The assholes who added to that sentiment didn't help. Whether Opal wanted to admit it or not, I think it bothered her too, she was simply too content to rock the boat. While I hated the way I went about things, it felt like our separation gave us both more perspective about the work we needed to put into our relationship.

Epilogue
MARSH - TWO MONTHS LATER

"Everything has to be perfect today," I explained to Ryker as he rolled his eyes at me for what was possibly the hundredth time.

"She won't care."

"What do you mean?" I asked as panic started to rise again and my heart felt as though it was going to crash through my ribs at any moment.

"I mean that she won't care about the little stuff. The only thing that will matter to her is what you have to say and how sincere you are. I don't even think she'll care about the ring."

"Well, the ring part is true. Opal doesn't really do jewelry, but I can't see not getting her something."

"I'd say maybe you should ask Mom for a family ring, but all things considered, Opal might see that as a bad omen."

I laughed ruefully. "You think?" Mom still hadn't come back fully from the deep end she chose to dive off. Instead, she was doing intensive therapy at a facility out of state, where she wasn't making much progress. She just couldn't manage to take any responsibility for her own actions after my father's revelations about his interest in his secretary.

"I'm just saying, Opal's a simple woman who only wants to be happy."

"You're right, but I thought having our son involved would appeal to her too."

"It will."

"Have I ever thanked you for always looking out for them?"

Ryker chuckled, "Just about every day since you found out I was doing it."

"Well, I'll probably keep thanking you until we're old and gray, just so you know."

"Dude, I would hope that if one day, I fucked shit up with my future girl as badly as you did, that you would beat my ass and be there for her if she needed someone."

"Thanks for the reminder, and you best believe I have your back and that of your future imaginary partner too. Should I bring pool float patches and keep them on hand, just in case?"

"What the fuck?" My brother asked, completely confused by the seeming change of subject.

"You know, in case your blow up girlfriend springs a leak. That way, I can have her back in the best shape possible, so the two of you can hang out again when you're no longer feeling abusive."

Ryker punched me as I laughed loudly at his expense.

"I should have married your girl instead."

That just made me laugh even harder. "Yeah, because her marrying my underage brother back then would have gone over really well for her career in education."

"Whatever. We could have waited until I was eighteen."

"Waited until you were eighteen to do what?" Opal asked as she came around the corner carrying our son.

"Oh shit!" Ryker yelped, and at the same time, I panicked and tried to hide the ring behind my back. It was not a wise move because then we both looked really guilty.

Opal stared at me and dared me with her eyes to try to

hide whatever it was I had behind my back. It made my heart dip down into my stomach because my girl used to love surprises. She didn't really do well with them anymore and I knew that was all on me.

"Can you hand Austin to Ryker and then come here?" I asked. "We were in the middle of planning a surprise, but fuck it! I can't really wait any longer to do this."

She handed our son off to his uncle, who wisely took a couple steps back from the scene. As soon as Opal was within touching distance, I grabbed hold of her left hand and dropped to my knees. Both of them. Not just one, as tradition dictated, because I was begging for her forgiveness and her future.

"Opal, we once had a timeline, like the silly, young people we were. That timeline felt crushing at points because it wouldn't hurry up and get there, and then when it did, it felt crushing for other reasons. I think our attempt at planning worked against us."

"Marsh, I don't understand. Are you?" She shivered, but it didn't look like excitement, so I ignored her half-asked question, and the sheen of fear I saw in her eyes, and powered on.

"The thing is, I know we were supposed to take things slowly, and I blew that out of the water by basically forcing your hand to move in with me. One might say I nearly kidnapped you, and wouldn't take no for an answer," I teased.

She chuckled. "No, you definitely didn't force me."

"Stop interrupting," I continued to pester her in the middle of my stupid proposal because I became socially inept when I was worried she might tell me, 'No'. "I'm trying to put my heart out on the line, here."

Her hand drifted to mid chest, as if to stop her heart from beating away from her, and then she winked at me. "Please, continue before this scene becomes gruesome."

"I'm not even going to rethink this, even though you're all

smart ass and sass today," I teased, much to my little brother's amusement. And since he laughed, so did my son, as if on cue. Opal and I both looked back at him and grinned.

"The thing is, I should have done this long before Austin came along because you, Opal, have always been the love of my life. Yes, even during that brief time when I couldn't see the forest for the trees. You are the one person on this planet that I love, respect, and want to spend the rest of my life cherishing." I mumbled the end of that sentence. "Now that I've pulled my head out of my ass."

"Is this going somewhere?" Opal asked as she attempted to stifle a fake yawn.

I rolled my eyes and pulled the ring out from where I still had it hidden behind my back. "Would you please, do me the great honor of becoming Opal Jane Kennedy?"

"Oh!" She hopped up and down excitedly. "A name change ceremony, so that we all match! I love it!" I could see the hint of amusement in her eyes as she continued to give me shit during what was meant to be a romantic proposal.

I clutched the ring box to my chest, fell over backwards onto the lawn, and laid there as if her words had just stolen my last breath. They hadn't, but she was damn close to stealing my patience. I waited until she leaned down to mock check my pulse and then I grabbed her and whisper-yelled into her ear, "Just say yes, that you'll marry me, already!"

Honestly, I was ecstatic that we were to a point where laughing together had become the norm again instead of the overwhelming sadness, guilt, and regret that had swamped our relationship in the beginning – the second beginning.

"I love you, babe. With all my heart, I swear it to you."

"That's good, because I love you too. Now, get up off the ground and put that ring on my finger already."

There was zero hesitation in doing just as my girlfriend –

now fiancée – ordered. I stood, helped the love of my life to her feet too, and then slipped the ring on her finger while thanking my lucky stars that she was willing to give me a second chance.

What to Read Next:

The Forgotten Wife
A Robeson Family Novel

I didn't expect a perfect marriage.
I didn't even believe they existed.
What I didn't expect was to say, "I do" and then be completely
forgotten.

...

At least, that was how it started out.
It just got more complicated from there, until it wasn't.
Happiness was just around the corner, and maybe even, in
time, the perfect marriage too.

This is an arranged marriage, enemies to lovers, second chance romance.

READER CONTENT WARNING:
Arranged Marriage, Cheating (not after couple agrees to a "real"
relationship, but definitely after they already said, "I do".), Murder,
Betrayal, Bullying, Sexual Assault (not by main character), and maybe
some others.

Also by Christine Michelle

<u>Loved for the Holidays</u>

Cupid Broke My Heart

Ghosted by Texas

Resolving Rumors

<u>Cheating Hearts Series</u>

The Homewrecker's Fate

The Regrettable Mistake

Playlist

Three Days Grace – Lifetime
Dorothy - Flawless
Shinedown – Daylight
Allan Rayman – Completely
Post Malone, Swae Lee - Sunflower
Justin Bieber – Love Yourself
Smith & Myers – BAD AT LOVE
Cage the Elephant – Trouble
The Lumineers – Ophelia
The Weekend – Die For You
Lost Frequencies, Calum Scott – Where Are You Now
Post Malone – Wrapped Around Your Finger
Regard, Troye Sivan, Tate McRae – You
Billie Eilish – Therefore I am
Julia Michaels – Issues
Justin Timberlake, Chris Stapleton – Say Something
Maren Morris, Hozier – The Bones
Chris Cornell – Patience
Justin Bieber – Lifetime

Acknowledgments

Thanks to that desperation burrito from Taco Bell that got me through the last chapter. It was left over from my Cravings Box from the day before because I'm not a fan, but when you're down to the wire, and don't have time to cook, the desperation burrito starts looking good!

Thanks to Stacey for staying on top of things and kicking me in the butt whenever I slowed down. I'm so happy to have you back in the game!

Thanks to John for reminding me that sometimes, you have to go against popular opinion and just do what you want.

About the Author

Christine Michelle also write's under the name Anne Storm.
Anne Storm's books:
Dark romance/subjects with major triggers
Christine Michelle's books:
(mild) MC Romance, Rock Star Romance, and other
Contemporary Romance
Paranormal Fantasy & Romance

If you want to learn more about Christine, her books, or her crazy adventures into the wilderness, you can find out more through the following links:
Website:
christineandanne.com
Newsletter Signup:
https://christineandanne.myflodesk.com/newsletter
Signing up for the newsletter also gets you first option at future Beta reading and ARC (advanced reader copy) giveaway opportunities!
Universal links to everything
(social media, book links, and more)
https://linktr.ee/christinemichelle

facebook.com/M00nlitDreams

instagram.com/christinemichelle_annestorm

bsky.app/profile/annestorm.bsky.social

bookbub.com/authors/christine-michelle

tiktok.com/@christine.michelle.books